The Dragon Hunt

The Dragon Hunt

Jonathan Schlosser

The Dragon Hunt

Jonathan Schlosser

For Fitz and Fin
and all the adventures to come

The Dragon Hunt

Chapter One

I

In the half light darkly the horse twisted and called into the night and the fireflame some shriek unknown to him or to any other, but perhaps at the heart of that call raged the feeling of torment and horror combined and no one needed to understand it to know it for what it was. Brack stood watching in the doorframe and smelling all about the rising smoke and seeing the men running in to grab those reins and finally one getting them and bringing the horse down and speaking to him and pulling him from the burning yard.

All about the smoke and darkness as one and a living thing within it, the fire and embers like tendrils of some evil tearing the fabric of the world and unleashing that hell upon the living.

His expression in that flickering light that cast all as orange and dusk did not change. He stood stark and silent and his chest just moving as he breathed. Heavy about him the leather and the breastplate of darkened steel and his hand raised above his shoulder and resting on the hilt of a blade he did not draw. Feeling the power within it just from that touch and knowing all else was futile and past. He wore beneath the plate his fur which had been for warmth in this blistering winter and was now too much as the world turned to fire, but he did not remove it or wipe the sweat glistening on his face. For this was nothing to pay.

He heard her come and did not turn to her. "Kayhi."

"They say it's gone."

"They know or they think?"

"A farmer says he saw it. Going east and very high."

"In this light."

"Brack."

He lowered his hand and turned at last and smiled at her, but it was a grim smile with those weathered lines and in it neither humor nor grace. Something else there and turning in those eyes as the horse had twisted in the yard. "Does it matter, Kayhi? We've lost it all."

She looked to the floor, this small girl in a thin gown showing below the heavy fur of her coat. Her hair dark and hanging to her slender shoulders and in her face. Many years his junior and still a girl, he thought, a girl who had until this night known what he was and not known what he was. A child growing while he was gone and only in the last year learning to treat him as her brother, some lost vagabond who was hardly a brother at all. The dirt of the world embedded in his skin.

He reached out and raised her chin with his fingers. "They're riding?"

"They're forming at the gate. Grunel's leading them out. Two of them said you were killed."

The traces of the smile faded and he nodded. "Go with them. Tell Grunel I'm alive and that they should go through the gap at Taron. Down to the plains where there are real cities. Cabele and Darish-Noth. Either one is the same."

"What about you?"

"I'll meet you at Taron if I can. If not, I'll ask about where you went and go down into the plains. You'll all be safe there." He pulled her forward and kissed the top of her head and her hair smelled of smoke. "Go."

He watched as she left, running in her boots down the long stone walkway and looking back only once. He could hear down below the shouts and the horses and the creak of the wagons and the gate rising. All this far too late. He listened to it for a moment and then went through the door and to the stone stairs beyond. These both rising and falling, one to the left and the other to the right. He touched the sword at his shoulder again quickly and then went left and up and felt with each step the weight of all that stone and scowled for it had done no good at all.

Above, a second doorway. The same timber frame now blackened and smoke drifting upward like something inside was devouring it and then the rungs of the iron ladder in the wall. This the last stand against invading armies, incursions of men. Before an ancient destroyer fell upon them, for which iron ladders and trap doors meant nothing. He climbed it quickly and felt the burning in his arms and pushed up on the iron door at the top and went through.

This one building of stone in all of the small town, this tower the last retreat and fallback position. Round and as wide as two men lying down and with arrow slits in the wall. In the afternoon, light falling through like beams of molten gold; in this night, just the flickering of a bed afire, the thick and acrid smell of the smoke and something deeper as well.

Flesh burnt to bone.

The bodies were huddled against the far wall and he stood looking at them and there was nothing left to tell who they had been. Their clothes gone, the flesh blackened and cracked, the skin lost or curling like birch bark in the hearth. The hair burned and each eyeless head smoking softly. Lips pulled back from charred teeth and burned away. Each pressed against one another and fused where the fire had raged hottest and the white of bone beneath it all.

Brack stood looking and blinked and wet his lips against the heat. It filled this room as if it were a furnace recently extinguished. He took one step toward the bodies and then stopped and cursed and blinked again and went back to the trap door. He could move them if he wanted, but what good was there in it now?

As with those fleeing through the gate and for the mountain pass, it was all too late.

He'd run for them when it came, but it had been perched and hulking on the tower before he even got to the keep. Breathing that fire down through the arrow slits and flames exploding out of the others as they filled the pinnacle until it burned like a fallen star. He'd stopped on the wall with his cloak black and wrapping around him this unnatural hide and it had looked at him and raised its head and shrieked. The sound enough to drive him to his knees. Then it had lifted silently into the air and its black skin was lost to the night and he'd stood on the upper balcony looking out into the yard and fighting with himself to climb the iron ladder.

He stood now in the darkened room a moment more and then turned back to the ladder. Feeling for it and unable to see. The air outside cold as ice on his skin. Descending until his feet found the walkway again and then leaning on it and heaving and holding himself there for time untold. Perhaps days or just the space of a breath. For it was one thing to know and another to see. Raising himself up at last and passing through an interior door to the other side of the tower, this thin and decimated defense, where he could see the snowwashed foothills.

The landscape all about flat and barren as the wind tore across it, the snow covering all but the dark crags of stone where they stood in violence and refused that coating. Appearing small from his vantage but some outcroppings taller than the tower itself, rising until a man at their feet was simply a spec against the wasteland. In the far distance the mountains rising and already on their tops the flashing sunlight of the next day. That light blasting them in radiance and still hours from touching the midnight in the valley.

Below, the caravan made its way forward in the snow. Smaller and more desperate than he had hoped. These men and women and children and wagons pulled by weary oxen already frail. Perhaps half would make the gap and perhaps half again would descend into the rich green plains beyond.

Those plains where cities slumbered in peaceful bounty. Walls of whitewashed stone rising and clusters of villages in the fields beyond and gardens of stunning beauty with stone bridges and clear brooks. Nothing like this place of hewn wood walls and one stone tower now cracked and shattered.

If she was with them when they reached those cities, she may live. It was only a chance, but everything was only a chance.

He watched them for a long time. As light came down the mountains and worked its way over, chasing shadows from the valley. Their progress impossibly slow. Taking only what they could carry in fear and flight and leaving the dead behind to inhabit forevermore this place on the edge of the world. Where the bodies and walls alike would slowly freeze and then be covered over in snow and ice. He watched them until they were too small to see and swallowed by the snow and he could look out at the crags as if he were alone in the world and no one to hear him scream.

II

He walked in that snow-draped land, a man forsaken and desolate. The horses taken with carts and riders for the mountain pass the day before. He in his heavy boots walking endlessly, a thing he'd grown accustomed to in a former life of marches and miles and blood. Keeping always those mountains to his right and knowing the path well, though the road had blown under the crystals and ice and he slipped at times on the hidden sheets where water had briefly run and then frozen.

Only once did he stop to look back in that stinging air, his neck taut with a scream that ripped his flesh but soundless in his fury. The keep nothing but a black spot on the horizon, smoke rising and hanging still in the air like a dark rope between this world and some other. Perhaps a heaven but more likely one of greater death and decay than this. He'd returned to the tower and taken down the bodies and buried them, along with the others abandoned where they fell, but he could not see the line of grave markers. As if they'd been drawn out of existence.

As the town would be, in time. A town of decades erased in a night of fire and sulfur and the beating of wings.

And so on he walked and as the night fell again he found a cave in which to shelter. He thought of walking all night and knew that if he did so he would not wake in the morning and his body would be found years later as a corpse encased in ice and perhaps perfectly preserved and so he went into the cave and started a small fire in its center. A hole in the ceiling allowing the smoke to channel. Not much for warmth, but enough to char the dried meat on a stick and he ate in those shadows with his hands and then lay back.

It was in that night that she returned to him. He saw her as he last had and her eyes were closed and upon her face the sun as he had never seen it since. The sound of a rippling water he could not see and all about the green of the garden and life and beauty. Thrust upon him in greater intensity by the dead and frozen world in which he now toiled. He looked upon her and then she was gone and the world slowly receded until he woke in the cave and it was very dark.

Above him, he could hear the wings.

The fire had gone out and he was glad of it and lay in the

dark very still. Wanting within himself to take up his sword and cast aside helm and armor and scabbard and stalk out into the night and scream to it. Draw it to himself and then slay it there in a swath of red blood, pouring like pitch and fire over that white snow. He could see himself hacking out its throat and cutting those wings off to the bone and mutilating that which haunted him in a vengeful wrath.

But he did not, for he knew what it was and what it would do to him. Here in the open and the night that it owned. How short that stand would truly be.

One moment of heat in the heart of winter. And then nothing. Or perhaps the rushing of those wings increasing in a flurry as it fell and swept low over the ice fields and then took him up in its claws, the talons of some monstrous bird, rending his armor and flesh. Carrying him higher than the mountains with below him his blood falling and scattered by the wind.

To drop him from heights a man should not know to fall spinning toward the earth for time eternal until the ice again consumed him.

How short and how wasted.

So he lay as still as he could and breathed slowly. It was said they could hear a heartbeat but he did not believe it. But it could hear all else and he made no sounds and finally the wings were gone, moving into that black void above. He knew if he looked there would be no stars and so he did not look.

At last he slept and he did not know when or for how long but he saw her again in that garden and this time he felt he could smell some fragrance on the air, of the garden flowers or her perfume or the two together and then when he woke again there was light at the front of the cave. A light cold and thin, but outside harsh and blinding on the snow.

He gathered what little he had and again he set out and the snow beneath his boots was brittle like bone powdered and cast upon the world by the gods in that heaven of the dead above.

III

It was two nights after he came to a ridge and when he topped it the town lay in the valley before him. Still a league off but a town all the same. The light already nearly lost and the lanterns and fires of that town glowing warmly in the dark. He felt he could hear the crackle of those fires but he knew he could not, and he flexed frozen hands. No more than two dozen buildings, set together about a square. The far edge of the town against a small mountain of solid ice. He could hear a long way off a dog barking.

He went down the ridge slowly, picking his way through the drifting snow. Below pitfalls and crevasses covered in blown snow where a wrong step would cause all to give way and he would be falling in the dark with the ice high around him and snow falling about as he plunged toward the cold and dark heart of the world. But in his care he felt for them and made his way around and down to the flat plain before the town. That which in a place with summer may have been field or water, but in this place was always ice.

They saw him before he reached the town. He heard a man call out and could not see the man and then there was another dog barking and the light of a lantern bouncing as it was carried down a frozen street. He walked on. The lantern was gone and then returned and another with it and the two men came out to meet him at the town's edge. A third behind without a lantern.

They were hard men and thickly bearded against the winter and wrapped as he was in furs and leather. The tallest standing in front with a spear in hand and the point afire in the lantern light and his pulse quickened at that image and he looked away. The other with heavy arms crossed and a handax in his belt and the third behind with skin as dark as that falling night itself. No weapon on him visible, though Brack knew it to be there all the same.

The spearman held up a hand to stop him. "You have a name?"

"I could ask you the same thing."

"I could run you through to the ice and leave you for the wolves." There was little malice in the way he said it. Just two men here exchanging facts in the bitter wind of that which they could do if they so chose. In this world those things less of an affront than perhaps they were in Cabele or the Island Kingdoms. The details of lives as hard as the iron the men who lived those lives carried.

Brack nodded, though, and put his hand forward. "Therros. From the Ringed City."

The man stared at his hand and didn't reach for it and then looked up to meet his eyes. "Ironhelm?"

"If you have to."

Reaching, the spearman took his hand and grasped it firmly for a moment and then released it and stepped back. His posture changed and loose. One of the dogs still barking somewhere behind him in the dark and faces pressed to the lit glass of the windows. "You walked from the keep?"

"The keep's gone. Burned."

"Is anyone still alive?"

"Everyone who lived is gone. I walked here myself. Told the rest to run for the gap."

"Burned. You said it burned."

At this the man without a lantern stepped forward and reached and took Brack's hand. A gentle touch, almost, but something in those eyes. A merriment, perhaps, as he smiled, but something else as well. As if that merriment were driven by a dark and terrible knowledge.

"Of course it burned. Haven't you heard the wings?"

Brack regarded him for a moment without speaking. He

was tall and slender; even his furs could not hide that build. His head shaved on the sides and the hair thick and a knuckle long in the center. The lanternlight on his face shining like fire on water in the dark of a starless night.

"You know, then," Brack said at last.

"We feared. We didn't know. You never know until it's too late and knowing or not knowing is the same."

Brack nodded once at that. "It's been here?"

"Not yet. But passing over. I've heard it half a month now. When did it come to the keep?"

"Four days ago. Fell on the tower and killed them. Lit the town. We saved what we could and ran. I stayed until they were gone and left myself. Buried the dead as if we'd be back, but the keep is lost."

"Flown?"

"I don't see what you mean."

"Was it flown?" the man asked. Looking at the sky now and that lanternlight also in his eyes.

"No," Brack said.

"Ah."

The spearman stepped forward again. His boots heavy in the snow. The smaller man beside him did not speak nor did he look as if he wished to. But his eyes were on the mountains and the sky equally, darting in something that was beyond simple fear.

"Why'd you come here?" the spearman asked.

"I'm looking for a man. My grandfather."

"Your grandfather lives here?"

"If he's still alive, he does. This was the last place I left him."

"Seems like we'd know if someone from the Ringed City lived here. You sure you have the right town?"

"I'm sure."

"Well, how about you come on in and we get you a beer

and a fire and we see what we can find."

"I'd be grateful."

"And then you tell us where it came from so that we can go out and kill it."

Brack was silent. Thinking over this man and what he would do if faced with such a creature as that. Standing now tall and proud with the spear in hand and perhaps the only man in the village who would make that boast. Perhaps never bested by all who tried. As with men the world over, that bred confidence and confidence bred stupidity. Something that would come true in a rushing sort of way when the pieces fell into place, but which the man could neither know nor accept until the reality was forced upon him in all of its true horror and he could not deny it as his body turned to flame.

But none of that mattered as the world spun madly and so Brack nodded once and followed them into the village and the man with the half-shaved head looked at him in a way both unsettling and showing that they shared in this small corner of the world a secret only the two of them knew, but neither would speak for some secrets were best left in their graves with the bodies that covered them.

The Dragon Hunt

Chapter Two

I

In this pitted world of perpetual darkness she stood in her chains and looked above to where the light filtered in through the window and fell across to the distant wall and the shadows of the bars embedded in that light. It was a far off thing as if drowning and looking at the light that was the surface. She looked at it each day and it was always just as far.

All about her the stone of this old room and an ever-hanging dampness. The air itself heavy and the rock walls slick and growing from the gaps between the stones a thick and rotting moss. Vines with veins of red streaked through them as if blood beat in some massive and unseen heart. The droppings of bats and men upon the floor, and the smell of it.

The things she had grown accustomed to in her five years thus enslaved.

She could hear the sounds in the road above of horses on the stones and men talking and they were all filtered with the distance and faint. She had at first called to them and screamed and they had not responded. Perhaps unable to hear or perhaps simply more willing to ignore. To be on with that business which they had. Now she did not scream but just looked and listened and both sight and sound were the same.

And she waited. For what, she knew not. But she waited.

The chains bound her to the wall with iron rings, but there was enough play in those cold bonds to move slightly about the room. It was a deep and cavernous thing, the far end faded so entirely into black that she could not see what was there. At times she would hear sounds from that side as of someone breathing and then the sounds of eating and once, just once, a weeping sort of call. But her movements were just for a few yards from the wall and a few down the length of it, and she assumed that whoever was so ensnared across from her also had such limited confines.

She had once called out to them, as she had to the others. Never had there been a response. Not so much as an acknowledgment of the call.

Against her own wall there lay a thin cot of little more width than a blanket, a chamber pot of tin and a small wooden stool with uneven legs. Beneath that stool a single book that she could read for just an hour a day when there was enough light. She had read it so far six times and was reading it again.

Now in the dark she could sometimes read it, the pages recalled in her mind. But she waited for the light all the same.

She heard the key in the lock as she always did and turned to face the door. There was just one, at the western wall, set equally between her and whoever occupied this world with her. They always came from there and walked down a long stone path over a deeper pit, the bottom of which she had never seen, and stepped out onto the stone floor near her. As happened now, her attendant striding in a flowing white gown with gold trim and a slender gold band about one wrist.

The girl stopped in front of her. Looking down at the stone. "They're asking for you."

"Let them ask."

"Please give me your hands."

She held out her hands obediently and the girl fit a key

into one shackle and then the next, pulling them each apart and letting them swing back to strike loudly against the wall.

"Come with me."

The first time this happened, she had tried to run. Not in the room, but as soon as she had gotten through the door. It was years ago and she could still remember the cry as she'd pushed the ageless girl aside and turned and run for the end of the hall and the beating of her heart and pounding of her breath on the stairs. The twisting and turning in endless and mazelike passages above, hearing feet all about her closing in, and unable to find the way out. Wanting in her panic to scream and claw at her own eyes and face but just running and running and then at last stepping out into the room where he waited for her. Seated as he was on that golden throne and grinning with the dagger in his hand.

She had not run since and she did not run now. Instead she walked with this girl and they crossed the stone walkway and she glanced down into the bottomless dark and stayed in the center of the stones. Waited at the door while the girl unlocked and opened it. Stepped through and into that hall and followed as she was supposed to follow and waited.

Always waited.

II

They bathed her and she lay naked in the warm water and closed her eyes and not for the first time wondered if she held her head below the surface if she could drown herself. Their hands now so gentle upon her with the soap and rags trying in desperation to pull her from the water, raking at her flesh and skin, but unable to draw her out. How long would it take until the world came rushing into blackness and was no more?

She did not know and she did not try. But she thought it always.

Standing afterward the girl dried her with a towel and they crossed the room to where a dress hung over a wooden chair. Green, this one, like emeralds pressed into fabric. The same gold that the girl wore as trim. A long and flowing thing of silk and beauty. She stepped forward and allowed the girl to pull it over her head and down and then to begin tying the laces in the back.

"What is it this time?" she asked.

"I don't know," the girl said.

"You don't know."

"No."

"Or you won't tell me."

The girl was silent. She continued tying the laces with careful hands. When she finished she went to bring the shoes from next to the door. These a gold that matched the trim. She set them down and stepped back. Folding her hands in front of her.

The woman sighed and stepped forward and into the shoes. She had not worn shoes in weeks and they felt tight and confining but she stood in them all the same. Looking at the stone wall where a tapestry hung down and on it a symbol of a scorpion in red and all about a weaving of colors. The light in the room nearly blinding to her as it came in the windows and the smell somewhere of incense.

"Do they fit?" the girl asked.

"I'll worry about whether or not they fit."

The girl didn't answer but instead went to the door and opened it. A heavy door of mahogany. Swinging on hinges oiled to silence. Outside a wide hall with more tapestries like the one in the room and down the hall the sound of music and people talking. Two men stood there and both had spears and one was looking down the hall toward the sound, but he turned back when the door opened.

"She's ready," the girl said.

The men nodded and the one who had been looking down the hall grinned. The other motioned her forward with a hand young and strong. Leather bracers on his arms and a vest of the same. The scorpion there inscribed with crimson thread upon the center of his chest.

She went to them and the door closed and one went ahead of her while the other stepped behind. The one behind touched the small of her back and pushed just slightly and she walked. Along both sides the same stone and sconces on the walls with burning torches and the stones scorched black above them. A thin smoke against the ceiling and running along like an airborne river darkly moving toward the vents. The sound of her shoes and the guards' boots loud on the stones.

They walked and she thought of the person still imprisoned across from her and the sickly sound they made when eating, as if tearing the meat from bones and sucking up that skin through cracked lips. A sound that carried even in a room so large. The snap once as a bone broke and no one ever coming to take that faceless prisoner from the tomb they shared. And then for a moment she felt weak and she leaned to the side against the wall and the guard in back pushed her again and she straightened and walked on.

As they came into the room at the end of the hall the noise swelled. She blinked in the light of windows in the ceiling and torches on nearly every bare place on the wall and looked about. A group of men standing in bright robes before a raised dais and laughing as a jester in the middle of the room rolled. The jester's face a horror of scars and grinning merrily all the same as if his mind were broken and lightly coming up out of the roll to do three dance steps and bow and all the men laughing. Across from them a group of women sitting on pillows and a servant in leather and canvas handing down a bottle of wine to one of the women.

They all looked when they saw her, save for the broken

jester who rolled again and laughed, a high and shrill sound. The din of the room falling away and just that terrible laughter remaining and rising to the vaulted stone ceiling and wood beams and coming back from them to double upon itself.

The young man at the heart of the group stepped forward. His hair long and perfectly kept and so bright in this light that it was almost blinding to her and she looked at her own hair for a moment and touched it and then put her hand down. He was holding a wineglass the color of smoke and half filled and he raised it to her. "You've come." His voice light and careless like upon him there was no weight from things in this world or in any other.

She nodded and stood on the edge of the room and felt the guards step back from her. He crossed alone and the others' eyes on him. He did not look back at them but dismissed them as only he, of all their group, could do. The women watching and the jester dancing some jig with a leg stiff and half lame. That river of smoke moving in the center of the ceiling and just beyond her vision, but still felt there like some omniscient beast itself with its lifeblood everywhere in this place.

He stopped in front of her and did not touch her and took a drink of his wine. "Took long enough for you to get here."

"I just do what they tell me."

"Is that how it is?"

"Yes."

"Well I'm glad you're here now. Do you like the dress?"

"Do I like it?"

"Do you like it."

She nodded just so. Touched the fabric with a fingertip. It was a game as everything was a game and she knew that as well as anyone in this room and perhaps better and so she said: "Yes, I like it."

"That's the one you told me you liked, you know."

"I remember it."

"Well then, come. Let's eat. Or did you eat before you came?"

She just looked at him and her face did not change and in that shared gaze was all of it, the core of it, though he smiled still. In that stretching moment he dared her and she fought it and did not rise up to it and finally said: "I could eat."

"That you could."

So they went across the room and the voices about them were picking up again now but were hushed and he led her to a small table that had been set at the foot of the dais. A thing of metal and wood with three legs and on it a small bowl of fruit and a loaf of some type of bread. Not warm but not that far from it. He took one of the chairs out and held it for her and she sat and he sat opposite her and picked up one of the pieces of fruit and took a bite.

"Who are they?" she asked.

"They're no one. Or just as close as you can get."

"But they think they're someone. All of them."

"The next time someone comes in here and doesn't think he's someone will be the first." He grinned. "I let them think it. What's the harm?"

"Nothing yet."

"Nothing ever. They're scum like all the rest and if they ever start thinking they're not scum I can kill them and they know it and I know it. And as long as we all know it, we get along. Don't you think?"

"I suppose you do."

He leaned back and she watched him and his thin frame. He did not wear a sword but he sat like someone who had his already drawn and with a lazy confidence. She wondered how hard he worked to put it on, for it wasn't in his face. He watched everything, always, and yet still put out one leg like there was nothing to bother him and it was not for her, for she knew him, but it was for them. Each bite was for them and they watched and would not come over until they were told and not a moment sooner and if they died in the court before that moment came then so be it.

"Aren't you going to eat?"

"I'm not hungry."

"I thought you said you were hungry."

"Maybe I lied."

"I don't have any place for liars in here."

"Then why do you have a whole room of them just over there?"

He stopped chewing and looked at her a moment. Weighing something in his mind and feeling the heft of it and then setting it back down. Turning it perhaps to see all of the sides. The scorpion on his own robes moving with both heartbeat and breath. And then he tipped his head back and laughed and it was a golden laughter and behind him the tormented jester cackled and roared and threw himself on the ground with a shriek, rolling over and over and then scrambling to his feet to laugh once more.

When it died down, he took up the bread and tore it in half with his hands and set one half in front of her. Inside there was still steam and it rose gently. He nodded at it.

"Eat it."

"I said I'm not hungry."

"I know what you said."

She took the bread up and took a bite and longed to eat every bite there was and his also. Her stomach clenching at this lost and forgotten gift. In her world this something no longer in existence, as stripped from the earth as any one thing could be, and yet here in plenty and just sitting on a plate within a room full of people, none of whom would take it. The jester too feeble and the rest unneeding. But she fought that too and took a small bite and put it down again.

"They're here to meet you," he said.

"I gathered that."

"You see the fat one? He's from Plarenth and he wants to trade me some of his skins for some damn thing. He's not got enough for what he wants but he's got some. And the tall one is from Grayston and he's here about a debt my father owed and wants to know can we find the record. And the other three, they're from Mraok and they want to talk about archers and dragons."

She had been reaching for the bread again and she stopped halfway and looked at him. "What have they said?"

"Damn fools think they saw a dragon." He shrugged. "They've got a lot of gold for archers."

"What did you tell them?"

"Told them they needed the archers." The grin again. "Did I mention the gold?"

"But you don't believe them."

"About the dragon? Of course I don't. But that's not what matters. What matters is that they believe it and they'll pay for some men to go sit on the walls or some such thing. Staring at the sky for a few months until no one sees anything. Then they'll send them back but I'll still have the gold and we'll all be good friends."

"I told you they're liars."

"Not this time they're not. They do think they saw it."

She took the bread up again and turned it and looked at it and took a bite. "Let me talk to them."

"You don't trust me?"

"I just want to hear it."

"Don't we all want to hear it." He turned and beckoned to them. The fat one was watching endlessly and stumbled as he started coming over, the others trailing behind him.

And she looked then at the windows of this room and her mind in another time and place and she could hear everything as if it were happening again. The ring of metal on metal and someone shouting and another man crying as he tried to hold his entrails in with his hand and crawled across a scorched forest floor covered in ash and bone. The very air seeming to move as if alive itself. Snowblind in the memory as she'd been in life and the whole world just pain and that blurred wash of darkness and light but screaming still and her hands clawing endlessly for her sword. The sound of bowstrings and then a great rushing sound like a whirlwind coming down on them and everyone calling out and then the memory faded back and became nothing.

She felt her skin pucker and clasped her hands and at last was truly finished with the bread. On the far side of the room the jester was clapping his hands to a beat no one could hear and it was no beat at all. Just the random and sporadic sound of his palms slapping one against the other and he too stupid and ruined to know it and grinning the whole while as if this song where the song of some angelic beings with wings like the sun and voices too beautiful to ever be heard twice.

The men came over and stood opposite the table and none of them spoke and the fat one was breathing very hard and the others swallowing and all of their eyes very wide, their faces bright with the wine. Clutching in their hands accounts of what they should say on rolled papers.

He stood to join them and waved easily one arm in her direction, sweeping it toward her in a way so formal and lost to her that at first she did not know what he was doing. He bowed his head slightly to her and addressed the men as one, liars or tellers of the truth that they may be:

"My mother," he said. "The queen."

Chapter Three

I

In silence he sat with before him the glassware mug of ale and all about the sounds of men talking and in the corner a blind man playing some instrument for which he did not know the name. The sounds of it jaunty and bright and in contrast to this place with its dark clientele. The town for mining and mining alone and these men heavily muscled from years of such and with a blackness in their hair and beards and upon their skin. Two women in the corner and one sitting in some thin lace upon a man's lap and laughing and the other scouring the room.

Across from him, the man with the half-shaved head sat with his chair leaned back against the wall and the front legs up. His ale untouched before him and a warm brown in the lantern light. All the windows like black oil with the night. A great wagon wheel as a chandelier in this vaulted room with above it a balcony and doors opening off that into parts unknown. Rooms perhaps for those such as him.

"Why didn't you take a horse?" the man asked at last.

Brack looked at him and took a drink. The ale very heavy and cold and good. "You going to tell me your name or are we waiting on something?"

"What would we wait on?"

"I don't know."

"Then I guess we can't."

"I guess not."

The man did not extend a hand, but he did grin. His face slender and his eyes bright, the irises an amber color Brack had never before seen. His dark skin smooth and flawless. When he smiled he appeared childish and when he did not he appeared aged so that Brack could not figure out his true age and it seemed in this duality to move based on mood or perhaps desire. The impression in the world he chose to carve out for himself. Shifting that carving as fit his needs.

"You can't pronounce my name," he said. "But they call me Juoth."

"That's it?"

"That's it."

"And where are you from?"

Juoth finally let his chair tip forward and come down hard. One of the women looked over and then looked away. He grinned again. "Seems to me I asked a question first."

"They needed them."

"What?"

"The horses. They needed them. Those I sent to the gap."

"So you're gallant."

"If that's what it means I'd ask about your judgment."

"Travii. I'm from the island of Travii."

Brack looked at him carefully and swirled his ale in the glass and looked at it and drank. Letting it run cold down his throat and then warm him. He drank it half down and stood. "I'll see you around."

Juoth canted his head to the side and looked at him. "Something wrong with Travii?"

"Who do you take me for?"

"I'm not sure I follow."

"Travii was destroyed fifty years ago. There's nothing left but stones. Shattered buildings. No one's from Travii."

Juoth shrugged. "Be that as it is. I am."

"You're a liar."

"Some of the best men are liars."

"And some of the worst."

"And there we have it," he said. "All men are liars. So why don't you drink with this one and so will I."

Brack looked around the room. In the corner the blind man was playing a new song and the sound of it swelling and the man with the woman on his lap had gone out with her and the other woman was sitting up at the long bar and down from her the spearman and the other were talking closely and looking around with before them many mugs. They had all four come in together and those two had taken their leave and Brack had watched them at first and now knew what would come of it but could not stop it. He turned back.

"It's true?"

"About where I'm from?"

"Yes."

"Truest thing I've told you."

"Only thing you've told me."

"That's true as well."

Brack sat again and finished his ale and set it down. "How did you get all the way up here? This is a long way from the islands."

"Everything's a long way from the islands." Juoth pushed his own glass aside and took from his pocket a small metal coin and flipped it and caught it with one and the same hand and then set it upon the face of the table. That side showing a ring. On the other Brack knew there to be an impression of a helmet in relief with down the side a winding crack as if split with an ax but still holding. He looked at it for a long moment and then reached over and turned it in his hand to show the helmet and set it back down.

"Money."

"Why does any man go where he goes?"

"You can stop with that."

"With what?"

"You tell me something, you just tell it to me."

"All right. Tarek was in the mines and he'll be here. He always comes here. I didn't know who you were but I've seen him and now I've seen you and so I know."

Walking into the town he had asked again about the old man and the spearman had said they'd ask around and the islander had said this was the place to ask and they'd all laughed for there were no other places in a town like this and in they'd come. Brack had thought then of demanding more and had not done so for he had been gauging in these men different things which he still did not know, and when thus concerned he had found many times that caution was best. Especially with a man who came to a place for gold alone and little else for there was much a man could do for gold.

"Thank you," Brack said. "I haven't heard anyone call him Tarek in a long time. I'll never forget the first time I did."

Juoth turned and raised a hand and the barkeep scowled and made to come across with two ales and then he turned back and said:

"So tell me about this dragon before they've told everyone."

II

He came up the stairs and the sound of it was everywhere and the horses were screaming. About him in the low streets the women and children running and a man just standing and looking aloft with in his hand an ax and holding his other hand before his face and all the fingers gone and only blackness in their wake like curled meat fallen in the fire and when he turned the whole of his face a ruin and lost and then he fell to the side and the sound his body made when it struck the stones was like it weighed as much as all the earth together.

He ran past the burned man and the wings were beating and his sword was heavy and so he drew it to run and knew it would do nothing, for you did not kill something like this with a sword alone. He looked up also and could not see it for the smoke and it was like running beneath a sky of flowing coal and everywhere. The smell of hair burning perhaps the worst of it and the sounds from within that smoke. People unseen and in an agony he could feel to the bone.

Reaching the wall he mounted the steps and at the top were the bodies of two men and then he saw it was just one man and he had been bitten in half and both halves left here with blood between them and connected as they were by his entrails. The legs were still but the mouth moving and blood on his chin and the man trying to say something as Brack went past and up onto the wall.

There a wide path of blackness burned into the stones and he could see the direction in which it went and he ran then and he was shouting for it to come to him, to come to him. This far in there were no more guards and all scattered. The pounding of those stones under his feet as he ran. Knowing it and not wanting to know it and calling for it to come to him.

When he reached the yard where the horses were screaming he looked above and it was curled on the tower with its great claws buried in the stone itself and the tail wrapped below it and the wings unfurled and raised. Its scales black and red as if its molten blood flowed to the surface and up its back a ridge like jagged mountains thrust with violence through the crust. The tongue a lick of flame rising and curling and the heavy jaws wide and the muscles bulging as that jaw worked. The ring about its neck flexing as it looked at him.

The eyes red and burning and full of an ancient knowledge and also some great and horrible laughter. Something wrong with its face but he couldn't place it as in its fury the flames flowed from those eyes and licked up the scales but something very deeply wrong.

Then it lowered those jaws once more to the smoking arrow slits of this tall and smoldering furnace.

III

"And it flew," the islander said.

"And it flew."

"Then tell me this, Ironhelm." He leaned forward on the table and his ale gone and tapped his fingers and said: "A dragon is a beast. Reacting as all beasts do. When a wolf comes he has prey and he eats but a dragon is not a wolf. Not like this. A dragon also eats but he does not eat man. He kills. A predator and little else where it concerns men. Not even a predator. Just a killer."

"You've seen others?"

"I mean this one. The one you told me."

"All right."

"Then if a dragon kills and does not eat he kills for some reason other. Call it sport or spite or what it is. He kills men and he knows he can and then he leaves. When does he choose to leave?"

"He leaves and kills as he wants."

"But how does he decide what he wants?"

Brack looked at the man a long moment and turned and thought of it. Thought of that laughter in its eye. For a dragon was not a beast as a beast usually was. Perhaps more man than beast. Perhaps what a man wished he could be or aspired to. How many men, if given the choice, would elect to be that winged creature with a heart of fire instead of a weak and landbound man with a heart of blood? Thousands, surely. For in all ways but that they were already the same.

"You think he came after them."

"I think he did," said the islander.

"Not any men. Them."

"Yes."

"And that's why he looked at me and left when he did."

"The hunt was over. What do you do at the end of a hunt?"

"I take my game."

"But the dragon doesn't hunt to eat. For him the game is done."

At long last Brack smiled but it felt heavy on his face and he reached up and rubbed his eyes and could not remember the last place he slept. Or the length of that slumber. "So you do know dragons."

"No. I know how to think."

"Then why are you in this town?"

"Why are you?"

"Not for gold."

"And that we have in common."

The blind man had stopped playing and he was doing something to the instrument. Cleaning it, perhaps, or adjusting some part to change the sound of it. Across from him the other girl was gone and two of the men and the barkeep was running a cloth over the top of the bar. Bringing down the glasses. The spearman and the other still talking and with new mugs now set before them and always closer to what they were going to do. Lifting those glasses and drinking the dregs and turning to that which was fresh.

"I want you to ask him," Brack said. "Tell him what you told me."

"Your grandfather."

"When he gets here."

Juoth considered this and took from his pocket a pipe and neither filled nor lit it and put the end into his mouth and chewed it. A thing of wood and paper. Then he took it out and he held it in one hand and said:

"Your grandfather already thinks everything I've said. He agreed when I told him." Tapping the pipe against his own cheekbone. "Perhaps not in these specifics but we've thought it of dragons for a long time now."

Brack lifted his own mug and drank and then placed it on the table. "He sent you."

The man nodded.

"Where is he?"

"He'll be here."

"When?"

"I see you have his patience."

"You're about to find out just how thin it is."

Behind the islander a door opened. The barkeep did not look up but the blind singer turned toward the sound. The spearman also though he was now little better than blind himself.

The man who stepped through the door could have been Brack in an older life. Tall and thick in the shoulders and arms, but with his hair and beard stark white instead of the rich brown shot through with red that it had once been. Standing straight and wearing the dark leather and fur of this place. He came forward and Brack stood and went to him and embraced him and stepped back and the man did not release his shoulders.

"I'm sorry about what happened to them."

Brack nodded. His face tight. Thinking of it and stopping himself and thinking instead of the old man listening through the door. Standing there in that fallen night. The same as he'd always been.

"We sent a man. To tell you what we'd seen."

"You saw it before?"

36

"Only once. More often traces of it. Fires in the forest and bones and dark shapes in the night sky. Enough to send a man."

"He never came."

"It was only days ago."

"Sit with us," Brack said. "It's good at least to see you."

They sat and the old man leaned forward with his arms on the table and bent at the elbows and the barkeep came over with mugs for all of them and grunted and left. The blind man took up his song again and it was an older tune that had many words that changed depending on where you were when you sang it and here he sang about the mountains and the snow but elsewhere Brack had heard it sung of sun and sand and birds on the wing and forests thick with trees and endless plains.

"I sent him out to make sure you stayed," he said. Nodding to the islander. "I had to get something to show you."

Brack closed his eyes for just a moment. In all the times he had heard something like that the thing he'd been shown had never made his life any easier. He felt he could still see the firelight in the darkness and he opened his eyes again. The spots still dancing.

His grandfather reached into his cloak and took out what appeared to be a small black stone. The light bright off the slick surface. Too perfectly shaped and thin to be a stone and the surface itself moving like pooled ink. He raised it and handed it across and already Brack new what it was and he took it.

It was heavier than it should have been. Something ancient and unnatural in that weight. Still warm from the heat that would perhaps never fade. He turned it in his hands and there was no blood on it at all. Shed the way a snake sheds its skin. Death and decay and rebirth. Under it all moving a wretched sickness.

Holding the scale against his palm. Feeling in it a great many things and below it all his own wrath and sorrow and that scorching heat. Pressing his fingers into it as if to snap it in half and feeling it bend just so.

"You're going after it," his grandfather said. "That's why you're here."

"Yes."

"Juoth."

"Of course." The man stood and went to the bar and sat and the barkeep looked at him for a moment and then handed him another ale.

"You don't trust him?"

"I trust him with my life. But you don't. Not yet."

"Who is he?"

"He works with me. I'm not as young as I was."

"You thought this was coming."

"Didn't you?"

Brack turned, looking to the window. Everything outside was dark but for the snow that blew against the glass and stood in stark whiteness and piled along the outer sill. All else lost. But somewhere out in that swirling cold the beast curling with its eyes alight and the snow about it melted in a wide circle to withered grass.

"You'd have fought it. With him. If it came here first."

"Someone has to."

"It would have killed you."

"I know."

"Does he?"

The old man smiled. "You talked to him."

"How much? Of us."

"Nothing. I mean, he knows what everyone else knows of you. I haven't told him anything else."

"All right."

"So why do you need me? I'm just an old man. You could have gone to the gap with the rest of them."

Brack shook his head. Tapped the scale on the table and then handed it back across. "I needed to see if you knew anything. Patterns. Movements. I didn't know it was here until we heard the wings coming up the slope and there was no mistaking it and everything was destroyed before I could get there. I don't know how I missed it. Got careless."

"Or it got careful." Putting the scale away into his cloak, this thing of fire and hatred and age. "Knew you were there and hid and struck when you were gone. That's what I'd do."

"So you haven't seen it?"

"Just what I told you. We knew one was around and saw little signs but nothing you can track. I don't think it's been here long. I don't know when it got here or if it's nested or where."

Brack leaned back in the chair. "Then I'll just hunt it the old way."

"You want an old man's advice?"

"Of course."

"Don't hunt it at all."

Neither spoke for a moment. All about them the room now fuller than it had been and the door behind opening and closing as more came in to escape the cold. The fire raging in the hearth in the far wall and the blind man playing on and on and the barkeep passing the glass mugs down the length of the bar and someone laughing and one of the women now back from above and that man leaving as others entered. Brack listened to it, this life and fullness and then said:

"I have to."

"I know that. As I have to tell you not to." His eyes bright as he tapped the table with a finger. "There have always been dragons in this world and men have always hunted them and they're still here. If you think you can change that, then you're a fool."

"I don't," Brack said. "All I can do is balance it."

This man, so long lost but bound always by blood and something deep in that like an intangible knowledge, looked at him a long moment. Nodding in the way that they both shared.

Then he took up his mug and drank it all and set it back down again. Wiped his beard with the back of his hand and smiled, his eyes still bright. "If I were really your grandfather," he said. "Then maybe you'd listen to me."

Brack grinned at that and stood. "Maybe I would."

And it was in that moment that the spearman finally did what he had been meaning to do and stood and climbed unsteadily atop his chair and raised his mug above those below and yelled to them. The voices in the room fell to nothing and the blind man alone kept on playing and the spearman yelled about dragons in the mountains and the keep burned and all dead. These lies but he had not asked for the truth and gave this version of it.

Protests at first from those below, and then laughter, and then nothing. A sort of horrible and wrenching silence as they saw he was more than a man drunk and they turned as he pointed to where Brack stood. Eyes full of fear and realization. But Brack and the other two had already gone to the door and they went out into the night and could hear still the spearman yelling about what would come to them. This doom and destruction called down from the heavens or up from the pits of the earth where the dragon was born in fire. As they walked through the snow toward the cabin Brack was for just one moment again in the burning yard and watching the horse screaming and twisting in the fireflame, and he knew everything the spearman had said was true and had merely yet to come to pass.

Chapter Four

I

She stood on the wall overlooking the wide grounds where a young boy spun furiously upon an unbroken horse. All about him a ring of men laughing and yelling him on and the boy clinging as if death itself waited and perhaps it did. The dust rising slowly from the spot and so far below that she could cover them all with her finger if she so desired. Out beyond the green hills rising in the soft and warm light of evening and the orchards and vineyards there in the foothills and the women and men in loose-fitting clothes moving between them.

He leaned on the edge of the wall beside her and took out his knife and spun it between his fingers in an absent way and she thought twice that it would fall but it did not and it seemed to move without effort in the hands of this boy of hers. The light in the fringes of his hair and turning it to gold and his body slender and well and never sick. A child nearly a man now and taking for granted this life of ease and luxury that others had bought for him with blood as they held in their entrails on battlefields of mud and screamed curses beneath a churning sky.

Below them, the men were moving out as one and behind them the company of archers and the wagons well provisioned and commands called to the cattle and horses and rising thinly to them atop the wall. She watched the column move and he did not for to him they were nothing but men he had sent away and there were many others and if pressed he would not be able to give the names of those he'd sent.

"You still don't believe them," she said at last.

He looked up from the knife and even then it did not stop moving in his hands. "No."

"There are many things in this world."

"Save your stories for the fools." He smiled and put the knife in his belt. That oiled leather. "Dragons are nothing. An invention of the ancients for what they didn't understand. A scare tactic used by priests to keep us chained to the gods."

"Then all the stories are myth."

"When there are stories of dragons and no dragons, what else could they be?"

"Histories."

"Histories written by people both stupid and deceived. Someone saw a shadow or couldn't explain a fire in a barn and said the word and it moved from mouth to mouth and eventually it came around and grew and there were more who'd seen it than the one who started it."

"Just lies from the peasants."

"Happens all the time."

"Some say the same thing about the Whispermen."

"And they should."

"The Whispermen are real. Ask anyone in Erihon."

He leaned back on the wall and crossed his arms and looked at her. His back to this kingdom he ruled and these people his own. "Of course they're real. But that doesn't mean they're what everyone says they are. Probably nothing at all. Deranged hermits in the damned forest. A dead people. Once they were something and now we don't even really know what and the stories grow."

"Do you believe in anything?"

"I believe in what there is. Give me nothing else."

She looked away from him. The column leaving had reached the bridge over the moat and they were halfway across on those timbers with the men on either side standing with chains in their hands. Some dogs called out and then one answered somewhere else. She couldn't hear the sound of the hooves on the wood but she knew it deep and hollow and below the shallow water waiting for foes who had not besieged this land in generations.

Perhaps somewhere a withered old man who knew of the death and destruction those wars wrought. Who had once been young and holding an ax or a sword and striking down those on the field and calling to rally other men to him and charging into their hearts.

But more likely not. For those men were dead men and they were no more. If there was a withered old man with the scars of battle those scars were on his back and he would not talk of the fight and looked endlessly at the fields as if forever seeing there something unseen to all others.

"Trading gold for fever dreams," he said. "We can't lose."

"You can always lose."

He laughed. "I think you've had enough fresh air for the day."

She did not look at him and the guards came up the stone walkway side by side between the walls and took her arms and she did not protest and they led her back down and to the stairs. Hands rough on the tops of her arms. She looked back at him as she got to the stairs and he was still leaning with his back to the land and once again spinning the knife and then she was around the corner and going down the wide stone steps and she could see him no longer.

When they reached the cell the door was closed and one man let her go and took the keys off his belt and unlocked it.

She had at first looked around when they took her out for a means of escape but she did not now. The one held the door and the other stepped with her into the room and they closed the door again.

"Come on," the man said.

She closed her eyes and took off the dress and the jewelry and the shoes and all. Standing naked in the cold and the floor slick beneath her feet with mud and everything else. A thin layer over the cold stone and moving up already between her toes. She opened her eyes and they were just looking at her and one grinning but this time they did not touch her and then at last the one handed her the rags she'd worn before. Watched her again as she pulled those rags up over her head and slid them on. The feeling against her skin of canvas, the heaviness of the dead and decayed.

The one nodded at her and she went over that thin dark bridge to the wall and stood with her arms at her sides and he put the cuffs on her wrists. The chain rattling in the dark. Above the light faint now and failing. The metal so cold. He tugged on the chains to see that she had enough to lie down on the straw mat and he grunted and looked her up and then down once more despite the rags and grinned and then they turned and went out. The bolt fell in the door.

And the queen stood for a moment with her eyes closed and then sat and looked into the darkness and it was all silence and yet she knew in it the other watched her and she it.

II

She dreamt that night and it was a dream of some great worm coming from the depths of the earth. Eyes so far across she would need both arms to span them and a mouth of small teeth that ground the stones and dirt as it came up, that dirt showering off, the body pirouetting in the tunnel, thrusting its huge bulk upward and upward and the tail trailing behind until finally it was free of the earth and fell with a sound heavy and wet into the moat. The bridge snapping and breaking as it fell, the thing pulsing with the beat of every heart within.

For worms had their sections and within each a heart and if torn in two one would live and in this beat hearts like horses and it could not die.

She woke sweating and lying up against the cold wall and the chains about her and she opened her eyes and shook and lay for a time just looking at that wall. The marks on the stones of tools older than the castle above. This the ancient world, for when men built a city the first thing they built was a place to put other men and they put them in the ground with stones and water and bars and chains. And then built above them the thing both had perhaps wanted to see. The other held below as if in death until that itself came for his escape.

Turning then with the rattling chains she sat against the wall. The only light from the door and the lanterns without burning and that light falling through the bars. In this world the dark was ever present and the eyes accounted for it but even so she could not see it out there in that dark. And yet she knew it was there.

"Talk to me," she said. "Talk to me."

III

She moved down the wall and knew not what time it was and sat next to the body. This also in chains, though the life had long fled it and all that remained were skin and bones. The chains loose about those ankles and wrists and running up the wall to the bolts driven into that stone with their eyehooks and they were perhaps never to be undone. This body bound forever in the dark and underground. More fitting in that way for the dead than for her, and yet she still felt the anger rise in her heart at seeing his condition.

The old rags just as hers. Nothing on the feet but leathered skin. Here in the damp the smell of it so thick. The chains holding them just out of each other's reach, though his life had fled him there at the end of his chains and she could now sit as closely as hers allowed, two bodies stretching for one another. As they had in time gone by and in life and now would do eternally.

She did not cry and had not in longer than she knew. She'd heard it said that a person could grow used to anything if they were given enough time and she now knew that was true. For he was a fixture of this place as much as chain and stone and dark, and that which had at first horrified her now brought a sick type of comfort.

The sameness of it, the consistency.

She sat and spoke to him. First of their son and the way he had stood with his back to the kingdom and the men going out below him. Also of the court and the way he held himself and the way others saw him for it. Some of these mannerisms of a king and others not. The actions of a boy learning to be a king on his own and with no one to teach him and that incredible power to wield.

Standing and working as she spoke. She was six stones up now and three removed. Every other, with those between remaining. Crude steps or a crude ladder, climbing just the height of her body. Working over her head and in the faint light of that barred window above.

Pushing the spoon into the mortar, the heavy handle first, feeling that mortar break and shatter. Older than the city, this crypt. Old and fragile in that age, as were the bones of the dead. Mortar had once been made from the ground bones of slaves and she did not doubt that this had been some of the same. Each flake just adding to his body there below and someday all mingled together, slave and ruler alike, all arriving at that same fate in this same place.

A cruel irony in that.

She pushed the spoon and felt the mortar break again and brought it back toward herself and removed a section the size and depth of her fingernail. Almost nothing at all. Brought the spoon back and repeated the motion. And again. An endless chipping and scratching in the dark. The mortar flaking and coating her fingers, the feeling of them dry against one another making her skin crawl. She almost laughed at that, the involuntary shudder over that grating dryness when all about her lay death and solitude, but she did not. She didn't know who was listening.

Continuing her speech as she worked, covering what faint sounds she made. Telling her dead husband of the word of dragons out of the northwest, in the stone cities. The man from Mraok with his long robes and fear in his eyes, begging for archers. Talking of burning outlands and dark shadows in the night sky and saying he'd also sent word to the Ringed City. As if the rust kings could still save them, the dead hunters rising from the ashes. Her son giving the man a small company and letting him go, stripping him of gold he never thought needed to be spent.

She asked him what he thought, working a pebble loose from the mortar. Did he think the dragons had returned, or was it just fear that had returned? Would the archers die or bring it down or stand in boredom on the ramparts until they were sent back?

Other things she could no longer say. Things she did not know. But always now deeply within her. Blinking that pain like sand in her eyes. Ground in. Blood slick on her cheekbones.

The pebble came free, fell with a clatter to roll across the stone floor. She stopped and waited for his answer and listened to it roll and he did not say anything.

Returning to her work. Feeling the stone move now, ever so slightly. The stones all about the same size but with vastly different shapes. Field stones plucked from the mud when the cells had been built, thrown together as they could be with that slave mortar. She moved it up and down with her thumb and nodded and commenced prying the mortar from the left side. It went easier there, where the water had been running and wearing it away before she had begun her work. Before she had been born.

At last, telling her husband about the place she still held. For the line ran through her and it was her blood in the boy made him what he was and he kept her alive for that blood. Were it all drained from her body and she left pale and cold in the damp, he'd have no further use for her. But as her heart beat and royalty moved in her veins, she still ruled this land. Until he was old enough to gather power and they couldn't take the throne from him.

Her husband knew. He knew but she told him and it covered the sound as the mortar fell.

She did not know how many were behind it. Were the common people in the village asked who ruled, it would have been her name on their lips and they would have spoken of her riding through the orchards on a white mare with a gold dress and apple blossoms in her hair and smiling on them with favor. An event that had not happened but which became as it passed from the lips of advisers to bards and to the people themselves.

They'd perhaps talk of the king's tragic death in the wastelands to the north, falling before a dark army even as he turned it back. Those black riders on their black mounts with armored horses and spines on their helms and swords forged in the fires of hell. How he'd been struck down fighting to save them with his white cape flowing behind him and the gold crown still on his brow and the city's name on his breath.

An absurdity, to be sure. For he'd never left on such a

campaign and would never have fought in the snowdrenched mountains in cape and crown, but the bards made it what they made it. A scene painted in poetry that people would cling to and repeat and allow to grow. For people inevitably believed what they wanted to believe and so they still believed they were ruled by the queen with the apple blossoms and her gloriously slain husband.

The stone moved again, and she stepped back to work it with both hands. Close, so very close. She could move it now to both sides and up and down but it was like pulling that last tooth that clings to the bloody root when it should fall. She stepped back up and pressed the spoon sideways into the crack.

Those people would not know that she lived here in this underground. That her husband had withered here in agony and his own filth to die upon the stones at last, in the dark and apart from his people with his throne chamber far above. Too far like the light and air to a man caught and drowning. That his own son had at last poisoned him when starving him became too much and his death was loud and long and horrible.

That his queen sat and stretched just to wipe his brow but he could not lean close enough. That she spoke to him until the end. Her hair full not of flowers but of dirt and her dress not gold but these rough canvas rags.

She pushed upward on the spoon and the stone twisted and ground in its housing and then she felt it come loose. She pushed harder and it slid forward and she reached up quickly with the other chained hand to keep it from falling and grabbed the edge and carefully put the spoon down at her feet. Straightened again and took the stone with both hands and gently played it back and forth with the mortar raining down and scattering toward the bones and then it was in her hands. She drug it from the wall and held it and looked at it and closed her eyes and opened them and looked at it again.

Turning, she set her teeth and listened and when she

thought no one was there she threw it lightly. The stone spinning in the air and everything so quiet and then clattering off into the dark. Into the deep shadows behind the bones.

She looked up, then, at the others she must remove. She had counted their number once and now did not for counting them was too much and made the task seem larger than her and she contented herself to look only at the next stone. This one rounded on the bottom and flat on the top. High enough that she'd have to reach over her head with the chains swinging from her wrists to work on it.

Another step, another notch.

The queen took up the spoon again and thought of that woman on the horse with the flowers in her hair and the blood in her veins and how she had been married when she was fifteen to the steward of this city so that he would become a king and an alliance would be built. Two city states upon the corpse of the dead empire, trying to forge out something more. A peace built by their fathers' fathers after the Second War of the Splintering. Perhaps riding into the town that day with eyes wide and palms covered in sweat she had last felt like that girl she had never truly been.

But now, in the dark and the bones, she worked back toward that lie again. The girl she'd been now dead twenty years and replaced by a woman who knew far more of the world and who had truly found just what her blood would buy her.

She stepped up to the wall and worked the spoon into the crack and brought it toward her along the wall and felt the mortar drift down as dust in her hair, in her eyes.

Chapter Five

I

Outside the men standing in the dark and swirling snow and more of them now under the cracking sky than there had been all night and some with torches and all talking to each other and moving in a fashion both aimless and menacing. Brack watched them and drank the dark tea Tarek had brewed and felt it move through him and watched them still. These who would not come closer but would wait until he stepped out.

Not to fall upon him in anger, but to plead. For their very lives, they felt. He knew it as he had seen it before and would again and the way men looked when they felt only another man could keep them from death and whatever hell waited was something he could not shake.

"What do they think I am?" he asked. Raising the tea and drinking again and still unable to determine the type but knowing full well what it did to the blood in his veins.

"Exactly what you are," the old man said.

"They think I'm more than I am."

"I don't see it that way."

Brack turned slowly and looked at him and did not blink. "You know what happened last time? You know how many men died? Screaming and clawing at the air and some burned the way a pig looks on a spit with their flesh blackened and eyes gone and still running. Not dying. For how long? Seconds, minutes, it's all the same." He pointed back toward the window. "All of them looked like those men before it. Only a handful looked like it after, and even they weren't the same. One of them doesn't speak anymore and another, when he does, nothing he says makes any damn sense."

The old man crossed to the window and stood with him. The other sitting on the far side of the room with his eyes closed and smoking his pipe in this early morning.

"And what happened in the end?" Tarek said.

"You know what happened."

"Tell me anyway."

Brack was silent for a moment. Chewing it and turning as they both thought of it and what he would say. Then he said: "I killed it."

"You killed it."

"But they think I can save them. I damn well can't do that. I never have."

Tarek took out his own pipe and lit it with slow and careful hands and raised it lightly smoking to his lips. The scent of that within rich and yet fresh at once. Filling the room and adding to the scent of the tea in a way that intertwined the two and made one scent new and all its own. Brack waited in silence while he did it and the sun rose.

"They think they'll die without you."

"They'll die with me."

"Then what difference does it make?" He smoked. "Are you here to kill it?"

"Don't question me."

"That's not an answer."

"You know I'm here to kill it."

"That's what they know, as well. The spearman told everyone who you are and they know why you came from the keep. You can't be what you are and also expect no one to think it means something."

He drank his tea and the mug was cooling in his hands and he went over to the fire and filled it from the kettle and came back. Wiping his hand on his pants where he had spilled the tea and not feeling it but knowing it was at least hotter than it had been. The fire burning down now toward the core of the logs and no one adding more to those flames. Perhaps for the reality of true fire lurking out in that hinterland.

"If they know I was at the keep, then they should look at the keep," Brack said. "All there burned and dead. A handful fled for the gap. Will they join them?"

"Still, they know. You came to kill it and now they want you to kill it."

Brack stood silent for a moment and then he closed his eyes and opened them again. "That's not what they want."

"Then what do they want?"

"They want to live. All men just want to live."

"Is that why you're here?"

"No. I'm here to kill it."

"There's no way that can be the same?"

"It never is."

Juoth stood and came over at last. His pipe left on the arm of his chair but the smell of it still in his breath, hair, clothes. He too looked out at the roving crowd and slowly licked his lips and did not look at Brack or the old man as he spoke. "Let's go out to them."

"And tell them what?"

"Tell them to go home."

Brack laughed, the sound harsh and clipped. Took another drink of the new tea already cooling. "Go tell them."

"You have to."

"And they'll go."

"They won't. But when they die, you'll have told them to

go." The man shrugged and his face did not change. "These men will die. All men die, but these ones. These ones die today. Tomorrow. Next week. It doesn't matter. If it comes here, they die here. Might as well have it on their own heads."

At long last Brack smiled and shook his head, then tipped it back and looked at the ceiling. There the wooden beams hewn from trees in these very mountains and the roof pitched hard against the piling snow and the chimney rising in stone and shadow, the firelight flickering at its edges, to go through mortar and wood to that open air. Somewhere above the howling of the wind over the opening of that chimney.

"So I shouldn't care?"

"Men do what they do. They die how they die. You can't save them all and you know it and they're fools if they don't know it. So go tell them they're fools and let them be fools. You're not going to kill it if you're thinking about anything else. Wash your hands of them."

"I could send them to the gap."

The islander snorted. "You can't send everyone running for the gap."

"I can't?"

"Then they die in the snow or they die in the mountains or they cheat the gods and they go down to the plains and they die in the fields and the cities."

"This meant to make me feel better?"

"Not at all."

They watched again. One of the men left and a short time later came back and he was carrying an ax and he stood leaning on it as if waiting for someone to see it. Then another man walked up and he was wearing a sword and he nodded to the man with the ax. A third with a bow, then another with a sword. Two young men with their picks from the mines, one wearing a dagger the length of a finger.

Brack stared at them and thought of the things he'd seen

the last time and a true knight of the Springlands clad head to toe in plate and holding aloft a shield with the crest of a tiger painted in brilliant detail and in his other hand a broadsword the likes of which these men would never see in their lives and that man cooking and boiling in his armor as he struggled with fingerless hands to tear the helmet from his own head.

II

After a time they left the window and went to sit beside the fire and the old man brewed more tea from the leaves in the kitchen and they three sat watching the water boil and finally Brack again asked Tarek what he had come to ask for you could never ask such things enough times to be ready and then he sat back with the mug hot in his hands and listened.

He had been seeing it now for weeks. The first time trapping in the mountains and walking with the metal and rope traps rattling in his hand through snow as deep as his calf and each step adding to the pounding of his heart. His fingers cold about the traps and lashes and yet his back dripping sweat and his hair soaked under his hat. Carrying with him a handax and nothing else and the bodies of two raccoons he had taken. He had bent to set a trap at the base of a cedar and as his hands had been working it down into the snow the shadow had passed over him.

He'd seen nothing more that day, nor had he heard it. Drifting and silent perhaps on some updraft, wings unfurled and scales hot in the sun and those burning eyes casting about earth and air. But the shadow had been as large as a boat's sail even at that height and he'd shivered the entire way returning as his sweat turned to ice and his eyes always on the sky.

Two weeks later, great tracks in the snow. Three steps. Filled partially with new-fallen snow and so the edges softened, but unmistakable for what they were in that high mountain field. He'd stood at the edge of the trees for a long time just looking at them and then gone out to the field and walked about them in slow circles and stopped in front to clear some of the snow. Six inches down a long swath of blood, all ice now and hard and crimson and dark. Just blood and no animal to be seen, no parts left behind.

Lying there melting the snow around it, the lone scale. Fallen and lost and horrible.

It had come down, he guessed, dropping without a sound in that sky, its prey unaware below. Sensing it perhaps at the last moment, screeching in a horror that suddenly ate the entire world to the bone, to the heart. The animal had run and so the dragon had struck the earth behind it in three light-footed steps and grabbed it on the last and taken back to the air as the hot blood poured and hissed in the snow.

Another time: Standing on the edge of the town and looking off toward the keep at sunset and on a far peak something dark moving. Smaller at the distance than his little finger and so at first ignored. Then he realized the distance and how enormous it must be to be seen at all. Perched and watching something with the tail twitching from side to side and the head still as if cast from iron or carved from stone. Once it unfurled its wings and then brought them in again. He watched it until darkness fell and then the next morning it was gone.

That the only time he'd seen the beast itself. Ten days ago, no more.

But there had been reports. A miner sent back early who had never returned to town and when they looked for him the tracks vanished and most assumed he'd fallen and been buried in some crevasse now covered and then one of his boots was found. The foot inside it still and the cut through the bone cleaner than any sword.

Two horses found run into the trees and the hair on one

scorched and blackened in a long streak along its back. Just below, the flesh blistered and bleeding. Both animals cowering and afraid and unwilling ever to leave the forest and the trees.

The third horse never found. Neither in track nor body.

"I should have told you sooner. Sent someone up to the keep before I did. But I wanted to be sure. No one's seen one this close to the cities in twenty years. They've never seen one here. You know how it is." Tarek smiled. "I'm an old man."

"I wouldn't have doubted you."

"I know." Leaning forward just slightly. "When's the last time you saw one?"

"If they're not near the cities, I'm doing what I'm meant to do."

"But when?"

Looking through those blackened windows. The wild beyond. A vast and cursed world with in it a rampant darkness and here this fragile empire of a thousand years. Beyond, the things he'd seen that men living here could not fathom nor believe.

"Always," he said. "I see them everywhere."

The old man looking at him in the firelight. Heartbeats and swirling snow. That darkness twisting and growing and encroaching on this world of men as it always sought, a living thing and a dead thing all the same.

Brack had finished his tea and so he set the mug aside and settled into the chair. Looking at nothing and the whole world and the dragon out there in it. The way it had looked as it breathed fire into the tower through the arrow slits and they roasted alive above the iron door. Then he said:

"What do you think we do?"

"To kill it?" Tarek shrugged, then swirled his own tea in his mug. "Way I see it, we have two options. Maybe three."

"Start with the worst."

"We track it. Hunt it down."

"And the better?"

"We wait for it. When you hunt you either draw the game in or you go to it. When you go to it, it always knows before you get there. When you bring it in, lure it to you, that's when you get the kill. You only need a moment of surprise."

"Don't think we'll even have that."

"Probably not."

"And if we bring it here, they'll die." He nodded toward the window and the men waiting outside and Juoth looked but the old man did not. Brack thought of the dragon standing in the center of this town and the snow melting and running beneath it and the carnage such a trapping would bring. He may kill it, but how many others would he kill at the same time? Most of them, surely. Those who lived would be as the men who'd lived before, voiceless and witless if luck was on their side.

"Then the third," Tarek said. "We do both."

Brack nodded. "It's the only chance."

"Where?"

"That's why I came to you."

Tarek nodded slowly and then stood and went to a shelf and when he came back he was holding a rolled map of the mountains. He unrolled it and lay it on the table before him and set his mug to hold down one corner. Brack set his also on another and held the other side down with his hand.

"Here," Tarek said. Touching the map lightly with one finger. "There's a field before this pass. It's where I saw the tracks before. He knows it."

"How far?"

"Four hours if you're going to walk. Less on horses."

"I'll take a horse."

"And we'll walk back."

Brack shook his head. "I will walk back."

"Brack."

"Don't."

Juoth had been quiet and only now spoke, his brow furrowed. Looking from one to the other and settling on Brack. "You're going to try to kill it yourself."

"I am."

"You can't do it." He held up a hand. "I mean no offense. But it's not possible. You'll need all of us and some of them if there's going to be any hope."

"I'll go alone."

Silence fell in the small room and Juoth looked at Tarek and the old man looked back for a long moment and then nodded once and Juoth's eyes grew larger and he sat back and shook his head and looked at the far wall. What he saw there invisible to the other two.

Tarek touched the map again. Something almost reverent in it. "You think it will be enough?"

"I'll bring gold," Brack said. "He'll come to a horse and gold."

"He'll know you're there."

"He already knows I'm here."

"How will you take him?"

Brack thought for a moment and looked back at the map and traced along it with his finger. Tapped a place when he found it. "A crossbow from here. One shot. An eye if I can. Then the sword."

"And if the bow misses?"

"Then the sword."

"Look," Juoth said, leaning forward. "What you're saying is going to get you killed. Is this some sort of joke?"

"Not at all," Brack said.

The old man smiled softly and stood, looking at Juoth. "It's not what you think it is. He can do this."

"The one he killed at the city was different."

Brack stood as well. "You know dragons," he said. "So

you know there's no easy way to kill them. Yet I've done it. I'll do it again."

"In land you don't know, with a crossbow and a sword."

Bending, Brack picked up the mugs and the map curled into itself and rolled to the edge of the table. He watched it roll and thought of what he'd seen and how far it was and how the blood had been under the new snow and then he said: "Think maybe I should leave the crossbow. Just so it's a fair fight."

III

He woke the next day at early light and they were gone from before the cabin, but they had left a man. Clad in fur and canvas, holding himself against the cold. As Brack stepped from the doorway the man looked up and his eyes widened and he turned and ran and shouted something as he ran that was lost and taken by the wind.

Brack watched him go for a moment and shook his head and turned to where the old man was bringing the horse up from the small stable behind the cabin. A big black pack horse, the type used to bring the wagons through the country. Nothing like the lean and powerful horses he'd ridden on the field in front of the Ringed City when the red dragon had stood roaring in a sea of mailed men burning and dying as they ran with pikes and swords, the arrows so thick on the beast's back until he raked his wings and tore them free or sheered them off and then the rolling wave of fire as he bent and killed whole companies at once.

But a horse nonetheless, one that would get him where he needed to go and serve its purpose well enough. This not a dragon he would fight with long charges and a lance and then the sword.

In his other hand Tarek held the crossbow, made of wood and leather and the string fresh and new. Three bolts in the quiver. Brack looked at them and thought how if he had time for even the second something had gone quite differently than he'd planned and very wrong but it was all the same. Better to have the bolts and never fire them than to find time to loose them and run out. He reached out and took the bow and patted the horse's flank while it eyed him and began to attach the bow to the rough saddle.

"You remember where it is?" Leaning closer to Brack. Urgent and calm and fire all together. Juoth stood back by the cabin watching and when Brack looked at him he looked away.

"I do," Brack said.

The old man reached and put a hand on his shoulder and looked at him for a moment. "I didn't get to see you kill the one at the Ringed City. I wish I could see you do it now."

Brack smiled. "I'll show you it when it's done."

"That's not the same."

"I know."

"You're sure I can't come?"

"It's better this way. Try to slow them down if you can."

"I'll tell them you went toward the river."

"Even better."

Brack stepped forward and embraced the old man and felt his strength through fur and leather and armor and then released him and turned and put his foot in the stirrup and pulled himself onto the horse. The iron helmet hanging on the far side of the saddle, opposite the crossbow. His other armor already on and heavy but not too heavy for this horse. He looked out at the path before him and then back.

"Listen," he said. "Anything else happens, you leave here. All right? Don't try to come kill it."

"Nothing else will happen."

"If it does."

"If it does I will."

"Take as many as you can. They'll want to stay but you

have to tell them. Get down to the plains."

"You know what a city is for a dragon."

A feeding ground, Brack thought, but he said: "Walls are better than none. If it kills me, it's going to track me back here. There won't be anything left when it leaves. You need to be gone before that. Ignore the cities if you want, but get to the plains."

"I will."

"And tell Kayhi."

"I won't have to."

Brack nodded, then looked up and raised a hand toward Juoth. The islander raised his hand briefly and then turned and went into the cabin.

He turned the horse and rode out. The spine of the ridge tall and dark before him, the top blown free of snow and just black rock jutting in jagged relief. As if bathed in fire and smoke and now burnt all to the core. The trees stunted and dead. He rode and the horse struggled in the deep snow here in the valley and then found the path and when he turned back the town had been consumed by the wilderness and snow as if it did not exist and it was just he and the horse and the dragon, alone and all three being drawn together by the movements of fate or the world and when those paths came to the same point two would die and one would live and all moved to that intersection to see which those would be.

Chapter Six

I

He brought the horse to a halt on the edge of the plain and stood looking out at it. All about a ring of dark stones rising. This ancient caldera. On the far side and to the north that stone ridge falling lower, perhaps twice his height, but rising to three times that on his left, the crags and outcroppings free of snow as the wind tore it from those surfaces and sent it swirling away down the side of the sloping mountains, running toward the true mountains where they towered like behemoths on the horizon. There the land too wild and untamed for a man to live and all raw as if in the world's forming.

The field itself perhaps four hundred yards in each direction, a rough circle with the stones jutting in at points and retreating at others. Flat as the calm sea of a dead morning. Drifted in heavy snow. The horse breaking through it, but hard enough that he could stand on it were he to dismount. It looked like the mouth of a volcano where the molten heart was frozen solid and the burning rivers plunging away were made of ice. He looked back along the ridge to the lower plain and the forest that stood between him and the town.

A good place to kill a dragon, here in this frozen world.

He got off the horse and tested his weight on the snow

and nodded and held up a hand for the wind, though he knew where it came from. Turned slowly in that spot to look all about and determine his hunt. For a hunter must know his place better than the game for that one slim moment in which the game's life is in his hands and he can make no mistake or that life will slip swiftly off and be lost to him.

And when seeking the game that he sought, the roles of hunter and prey would quickly be reversed and the kill would be made.

It would have to be an open place along the cragged ridge. There in those heavy stones he could wait for as long as he needed without getting soaked to the bone and he could hide himself in his dark plate armor. The dragon wouldn't smell him over the bait. He could take the shot and then come down the side as the beast reeled in its blindness and finish it with the sword.

And for that, he knew, he would have to take the lower ridge. Some place where he could come down the slope swiftly and without fear of falling. No more than six feet high. The taller cliffs would be better for the shot, but he would lose too much time advancing. You did not kill a beast like this slowly, but swiftly and all at once.

When the bards sang of dragon slayers, they sang long about the fight, allowing it to ebb and flow like the tide. First the knight with the advantage, then the dragon pushing back. They sang as normal men who had seen a normal battle and knew how it went on the field, drenched in blood. The way a siege could last for hours or days or weeks. The shifts in strength.

But they did not sing as those who had fought dragons. For if you fought a dragon for long, it would always win. Without fail. It was a beast more powerful than any man and the songs lied. If the battles were fought that way, dragons would rule the earth and men would be no more.

He went to the cliff and found a thin path where he could climb and pulled himself up. The horse still in the field watching him. Its eyes like dark pools of oil. He topped the cliff and stood there in thin snow and the wind howling about him and bent and checked that wind again to be sure it was at his face and not his back and then knelt and looked out. Here with stones before him upon which he could rest the crossbow and which would break up his shape, but the path close and easy.

If he ran hard, he could be down and across the field in less than half a minute. Still longer than he wanted, but it was what he had and it was good enough. He'd have to note the eye the arrow struck and stay to that side of the beast and buy himself what time he could.

The horse was bending and licking the snow and he went down to it again and led it to the center of the field. Eyed the cliff to be sure he'd have a clear shot and moved the horse slightly north and nodded and then went to the saddlebag and took out the gold. A small pouch with the string drawn in the top and the coins heavy and rattling within.

He bent and emptied the bag in a meager pile. The gold glittering in the sun. He pushed it with his foot, spreading it out, knowing it didn't matter if it went below the snow crust or not. The dragon would smell it either way. There were two dozen coins and he spread them until they were a rough circle a meter across and then he reached to his shoulder and drew his sword and brought it back and drove it through the horse's neck.

The animal screamed and reared and the sword tore free in a great gout of blood. The horse tripping back and falling and regaining first its knees and then standing and falling again. He stood watching it and could tell from the blood that he had taken it through the vein and it would not be long. This the fastest and most painless way it could die, but still those shrieks to draw the dragon.

When the horse at last lay still on the frozen snow with

the blood pooling and spreading around it, he went to it and cut off the head and dragged it back over to the gold. Setting it at the center of the coins. He took up some of the blood in his hands and spread it on the coins themselves to mingle the scent and then he went back to the horse and took off the saddle and quartered it. Bringing each piece and laying it about the outside circumference of that circle of coins. Like four winds on a compass rose. At last he pulled the body over and put it on the far side of the circle with the mountains behind it and he again spread the blood over the coins and then bent and washed his hands in the snow and stood back to look at it.

He hadn't needed this for the red dragon. That city had been full of gold and blood and it was coming down on them regardless. But here in the wild he needed to bait it precisely and this would do. He nodded once and went to pick up the saddle and the bags and the reins where he'd left them and went back to the short cliff and climbed it.

From the top, the spreading blood looked dark and ugly, the coins glimmering within it like eyes.

II

He waited a time and the dragon did not come and the sun moved slowly above him until it hung directly aloft and not a cloud to break that merciless glare. When he could crouch no more he stood and set the crossbow aside and stretched his legs. The pop of tendons, the fire of feeling spreading back to feet too long motionless in the snow. His eyes the whole time on the sky and wheeling far off two carrion crows and he closed his eyes when he saw them and then looked away.

Never had he been one for patience. For waiting. Even in this occupation in which those were the most important qualities a man could have.

When he'd ridden with the Chainmail King along the

banks of a river with a forgotten name, he'd found in him a kinship in their desire to push forward when others would wait. Falling into battle and letting everything sort itself out at the edge of a sword. They came down many times on towns that way and fought through and reveled in their triumphs and in the last town a company of archers not well hidden in the forest. But still unseen.

They'd ridden down into an empty town and a maelstrom of arrows and while the king lay gasping with a splintered bolt through his throat Brack had learned something of the value of patience. For the rebellion had died there and the world had continued to turn and he'd put those days behind him. But he had never forgotten the feeling of reining up the horse on the empty street and looking back and forth in confusion and then dawning realization and the sound of strings from the forest giving them the smallest warning of the death coming so quickly.

The way she'd looked at him when he'd returned and told her of it and all in his voice and her eyes the knowledge of what he'd done. His hands and face still coated in the king's blood. The real worth there of a king who yearned to reign and did not, the world now about them twisting in violence and in her face also the knowledge of what was to come—the endless nights on the run and in caves and forests and the pounding of hooves on a night's road as they held their breath.

And so he settled himself back and he waited, his eyes on the sky. Knowing it would come and not knowing when.

He saw it the first time far off and circling. Below it a wide field of ice and the path up to the keep. So small at that distance that this beast which had dwarfed the castle tower upon which it landed now was little more than a spinning fleck on the horizon, but he knew already it was scenting the air, and he knew also the ground it could cover. He sat forward and watched it circle and then a cloud came and when the cloud was gone, so was the dragon.

The second time it looked as large as the crows—those long departed, knowing the terror that approached—with its wings beating just once every few minutes. Gliding there in the still air, dropping from the east to the west on the current, then rising again. He felt he could hear the drumming of the wings, that heavy beating, but he did not know if he actually heard it or only remembered.

He watched it as the sun fell into evening, the crossbow in his hands. He knew his body was cold but he could not feel it, could not feel anything. There was nothing but the drifting creature, so unnatural on that wind, as it moved slowly before his vision. Ever closer. The size of a hawk, then an eagle, then surpassing them all. The great serpentine tail snapping in the air.

He did not realize that it meant to pass him by until he could make out the legs and the row of spikes along its back. It had been swinging closer and then farther, a child perhaps of indifference or a slothful arrogance, and he kept waiting for it to drop down for the gold and blood as he knew it would. The drumming of its wings now unmistakable.

But it did not. It flew on in that pendulous motion and swung past his field of stone and ice. He thought he saw the head turn in his direction and gaze at him for a moment, and then the wings beat twice, three times as it pushed for more speed and he stood and felt in his gut something like the twisting of a screw and an immense falling and he brought up the bow but it was much too far.

The tail flicking through the air as it turned. The shoulders and the long neck twisting. Lungs like a bellows forcing air into the furnace of the ancient world.

He wanted to run and did not, for there was nowhere to run.

At long last it rose slightly in the air, the talons coming up under it, the neck arching. Preparing to dive. He could not hear the voices on the ground but he had been there when the red dragon emerged from the shadows and when this one fell upon the keep, and he knew the screams and terror that must live there.

The dragon seemed to hover in the air for a moment, suspended and unmoving, and then it called out once in a horrid and primordial shriek and it fell like a stone. Wings furled as it dropped, then snapping out as it neared the ground. In Brack's vision, the ridges and hills rising to block what he could see. Just before it fell out of sight, the jaws flared and a wall of flame poured out, a torrent of living fire, the sun itself being birthed suddenly on the ground.

The fire struck the unseen earth and raged and the beast's black body was for a moment washed in the curling orange light of flame. And then it was gone, falling too low to see, descending on that town with its small ring of homes and the bar where once a blind man had played for the ears of drunks and miners.

III

He watched for a long time as he walked. All of him yearning to run but it was miles and he'd killed the horse and there was nothing to be done. So he ran at first and now walked in fevered exhaustion and felt the distance with every step. Throwing the plate aside in the snow. The crossbow on his back and the sword uselessly in his hand. Watching as the dragon rose and wheeled like some black soul cast from another world and into this one with a ferocious anger and the tail snapping behind it and the beast diving again with the lance of billowing flame before it.

Rising and falling, this bringer of fire and light and death. Dealing in that which it had dealt since the world was raw and empty and it crawled from the cracks below to test those infantile wings on this new air. Claws clicking on hardened stone, a heart of magma.

So the legends told. He had never believed that and did not now, but it was easy to understand how the stories had been crafted as that fallen archangel rose in the sky to hang floating on black wings and then dipped one and dove with a screech to kill again. For what else could a man surviving that destruction think than that he'd seen the very evil all men knew was in the world, this manifestation in scale and bone?

At long last it was done. The dragon circling twice and looking down on its killing field. Beating its wings intermittently to stay aloft, the sharp eyes always on the ground. Looking for anything alive in that fiery carnage into which it could lay its claws, its teeth. Then, satisfied that even the bones had burned, it came about a final time and hung in the air.

And looked at him.

Too far away to be sure, but Brack knew dragons and he knew it turned toward him where he stumbled both hunched and beaten. The wings drumming softly to hold it there, the smoke rising all around and behind in a backdrop of the dead. That smoke still mixed with orange flame and sparks flying aloft, but already the fires burning out.

When cabins burned down to the snow, there was nothing else for the flames to devour.

He did not feel time pass and he did not turn away. The bow and sword very heavy. Then the dragon turned, the head and neck going first and pulling the body around and the wings increasing their beat and he watched as it grew smaller, soaring over those snowswept mountains like an arrow itself, and once it called out long and high and full of rage and then it was gone.

Only then did Brack stop and stand still, lingering now at the top of an embankment. He tried a step and stumbled and dropped to one knee and stood again. A feeling inside him deep and wrenching. Falling again and again rising.

Then he turned at the top of the bank and he walked in his own washed out bootprints back the way he'd come. Traversing it all a third time to the field in the ring of stone. Walking forward to that caldera's heart and beginning to pick the gold out of the blood and meat and putting it back in the bag. His fingers were numb and he kept dropping the gold and then finally he had it all and he stood and began walking back toward the town, the towering pillar of smoke to guide him, fading slowly into black as night claimed the land.

In that darkness drawn on by the distant glow of the burning world.

IV

He went through a tall and thin walkway between two immense stones, the walls rising and so close his shoulders touched each side as he walked and on the walls of those stones some robust lichen growing thick in this hidden place where the wind could not touch and when he came out the far side Juoth was there and sitting his horse in the middle of the path.

Brack stopped and looked at him. His clothing was blackened on one side and his hair burned. The flesh along the edge boiled and smeared with blood, but only just below the hairline. His eyes still alert. He wore one glove and kept the other hand in his coat and he was wearing both sword and bow.

"Is he dead?" Brack said.

"You saw."

In that the world entire.

Juoth folded and unfolded his hand. Looking up at the sky and something in his face like a deep pain and he did not touch his head at all and closed his eyes. "It's all gone. Down to the foundations by now. The fire eats everything."

"Is he dead." It was no longer a question.

"Ironhelm."

"Tell me."

"Yes."

Brack was silent. He had known but it was different to know than to be told and now he had both. He bowed his head and put a hand back on the rock behind him and then he could stand on his own again. But he felt deep in his gut something breaking off and moving through his body, something with a life of its own and the same darkness as the dragon's form wheeling in the sky and he knew that if it worked its way through his veins and heart and to his mouth he would scream until there was nothing left of his voice and it was ragged and tattered and broken. And so he closed his mouth and he guided it and he did not let it escape and after a time he did not feel it anymore and he could look up again.

"How'd you get out?"

"Ran during the first dive. Everyone runs at first and if you run later there's no reason. So I ran and it couldn't chase us all and I got to the horses and I got out." He paused. "He told me to run."

"I know he did."

"Brack."

He waved a hand. "Don't. I don't blame you."

"Do you want to go back?"

"To the town?"

"Yes."

Brack nodded. For just a moment that thing was loose in his blood again and he had to force it back down and then he thought he might be sick but he wasn't. He nodded again. "I have to."

"It didn't come for you at all?"

"No." Brack looked up and his eyes were flint and steel and he walked toward the horse. "But he saw me."

"Then why?"

"Because that's what he is." He grabbed the saddle and Juoth reached down and clasped his forearm and pulled him up onto the horse. They were heavy but the horse did not flinch. "He's just playing with me. He's toying. He wanted me to see it."

They rode then in a long silence over the snow and ice. The way back infinitely longer than the way there and riding under stars like chips and shards of broken glass strewn about the sky. Clear and brittle and endless. The sound only of the horse's hooves crunching in the snow and their own breathing, their breath and the horse's rising in clouds in that stark air. He touched his beard and it was full of snow and each hair turned white with frost as if he were carved whole from this landscape and would melt with the coming sun.

Once they stopped and he went to the side of the trail and he was sick and then he got back on the horse and they rode on.

When they at last came to the town it was not a town anymore but just blackened beams and stones on dirt dry and crumbling. The snow and ice here burned away in a terrible patch around the town. Not a building standing and all of the rubble reduced to near nothing and a little smoke still rising faintly.

The dead were little better. A scorched skeleton lying in the path with nothing human left, just bones and some of those melted on the ends and smooth as glass. Two more behind it. A skull leaning against a pile of stones near what had been the inn. Riding past he could smell it even in the cold air. A tangled dress and two legs and on the other side nothing but blood and the top of the girl gone.

The blind man lying in the middle of what had been the bar, the instrument clutched in his hands. Perhaps having played to the end. His body burst and split.

He got down off the horse and he walked through this carnage and he did not want to look and he did anyway. In it the only blessing that it had been a small town and so the number of the dead wasn't what it could have been and that a small blessing indeed. He went on down the street and past piles that had been homes, barns, sheds, and then he came to a place he knew and he stopped and closed his eyes and then turned slowly to look at it as the horse stood behind him.

It was only bones and it could have been anyone's bones and they were charred black from the flame with the white showing through. Those old teeth. The eyeless sockets. Arthritic fingers now twisted one last time. All about the body the house gone and all in it a choking pile of ash swirling in the mountain wind.

The tea kettle alone and lying on its side and cracked like the helmet on those gold coins and just as empty.

He knelt on the warm stones and felt the dark thing inside of him bloom and surge and for just a moment, he let it.

Chapter Seven

I

She paused at the ends of her chains, clutching the gaps between the bricks, her bare toes dug in below her. Breathing in that dust and mortar and blood with every gasp. The window still high above as she scaled the wall and the ground of this prison more than her own height below her feet.

Here, as far as she could continue her climb. For the chains held her fast and all of this climbing for that infernal sun meant nothing as she had known it would when she started. The nights and days and weeks wasted. Briefly she lowered her head against the wall and cursed herself and then began to climb back to the floor below.

That floor of cold and damp. How much more of that she could take before something in her mind snapped with a soft click and she was no longer herself, she did not know. Not as much as she hoped, surely. She stepped down onto it and shivered and listened to the chains clink down around her feet and leaned back against the stone wall. Fingers and toes throbbing.

The carved stone ladder could reach to heaven itself and she could not climb it as long as she was chained in hell.

She sat and looked at the chains around her hands. They

had been also about her feet when she arrived here and since the guards had stopped. Perhaps too lazy to hook them up over and over, perhaps content after all this time that she would not and could not escape. Either way, only her hands remained bound and she closed her fingers like folding a glove and pulled the manacle up toward her wrist and felt it cut into the skin.

Her hand small and withered with the lack of food, the time. But not small enough. She closed her eyes and pulled and felt her skin slide over the slick bones and still it was not enough. Released the chains and sat back, a thin line of blood running down from the base of her hand, hot and dripping.

They weren't chains she could take off without the key. In that it was simple.

A shuffling sound from the far darkness. In those early days she had risen and stood her ground, ready to fight for her life or call out or do anything at all. Now she barely turned her head toward the sound of her unseen companion. Lost there in these dank shadows.

"Talk to me," she said.

It did not respond and never had. The sound of bare feet on the stones. The silence again.

"Talk to me."

Then, from deep off in the darkness, a soft voice. More a whisper than anything truly spoken, but enough in this silent hole in the silent ground. A hissing voice coming through broken teeth. "Talk to me."

She sat looking and did not move. All this time pleading and yet getting what she asked for was somehow more terrifying than the persistent quiet and shuffling feet. The slurping sound as it fed. She could feel her heart in her chest and she wiped the palms of her hands on her rough clothes. Feeling a slight shake there.

"Who are you?"

Again, that voice coming back, soft and broken: "Who are

you?"

For a moment she had the horrifying thought that there was nothing in here with her at all and there never had been and it was her own mind, just her mind bending and breaking and splintering. Splitting up as he wanted it to. Breaking free of that grounded reality and leaving her here in the dark, talking to herself and answering herself and shadows moving behind her eyes alone. Sanity a slithering thing slipping away through her fingers.

And then he came out of the shadows. Standing far across the room with his back hunched and a hand to his face. The edges of him still fading into the blackness so she could not fully tell his size. His hair knotted and thick on his head and in his face, the hair of one down here for many years without it ever being cut. The canvas clothes the same as hers, though older and spotted and worn and covered in grime.

He stood for a long moment facing her in this silence and darkness. He was not chained but the manacles hung from his wrists and feet. Links trailing away and the ends twisted. This the sound as he moved. He looked once at the door and then back at her.

Finally, she found her voice: "Who are you?"

He did not answer, but just cocked his head to the side and looked. Then tipped it back to crack his neck, then looked again. His hand still covering his face.

"Come forward."

"Come forward," he said. Appearing to think it over, to consider. At last stepping forward just one step, then two. Pausing there and looking long at her. Stepping again.

She let him come and she did not speak. Afraid that if she said anything he would turn and flee back into the dark and it would be months or years before she saw him again or this would be the end of it entirely. The way she watched a deer in the field as it ate an apple and looked around from the base of the tree and saw her standing there in the tall grass, thinking if it should run or eat, tail twitching, and then carefully ate again.

So he came until he stood not ten feet from her and would come no more.

She could see now that his face was scarred. Two long puckered scars, so white against his dirty skin, running from scalp to chin. A third on his forehead near the hairline. Two others disappearing beneath his hand, their true impact unknown. Perhaps more in that ragged beard, though it was wild and full enough to cover them. Age spots along his arms and his fingernails grown yellow and long. He blinked at her and stood with his back still hunched but also looking as if he may flee.

"Lady Arisine," he said.

II

She sat looking at him a long moment before speaking, feeling that voice move through her, that name she hadn't used since she truly sat the throne above. Here there were no names for this was a place in the world in which they weren't needed. Names were a thing born of necessity and they died when that was stripped from them and she had expected him to say anything but that.

"You know me?"

He nodded his head and it was the smallest movement, just a twitch. The hair flicking and the eyes blinking twice. "The queen."

"Who are you?"

He lowered his hand, slow and careful. She had expected the scars below to cross his face and twist or torment his features, his lips split and rolled back from his teeth, his nose gone. But it was not so. The scars faded to nothing and his face below was wrinkled with age but whole. The lips and nose thin and slender, the skin pale.

"What do you need from me?" he said.

"What?"

"You've been trying to talk to me. What do you need?"

She just looked at him. It had to be something said in jest, she thought, but there was no humor in his eyes. A soft kindness perhaps, and something else as savage and untamed as a wildfire, but no humor. It was a question to which he actually wanted an answer.

And that frightened her in a way she could not explain.

"How did you break your chains?"

"Ah, you want freedom."

"Of course."

"Not all want it. Only some."

She shook her head. "You do." Waving a hand toward those hanging chains at ankle and wrist.

"Do I?"

"Do you not?"

He sat then, slowly, on the stone floor. The dim light falling from above. He glanced once at the door as he did it and listened and she listened also, but all was quiet. He sat with his legs crossed and looked back at her and ran one of the broken chains through his fingers. "I don't know," he said at last.

"Why are you here?"

"Crimes against the crown." He grinned. "As are you. But that's your son up there."

She nodded and did not speak. Suddenly her throat tight and her eyes on fire, but she fought it down. He watched her do it and she felt from the way he looked at her that he could see her doing it. Inside. The way it ripped through her body and the tearing of tissue. Clenching every muscle in some desperation to bring the world back under her own control. That little she still possessed.

"I can help you with those chains," he said. "If that's what you want."

"How?"

The old man reached into his dirty robes and from them drew a thin metal file. The edges worn down and beaten. Slightly rusted about the wooden handle. He held it up to the light and the light would not catch that worn metal. But he nodded and tossed it lightly and it landed at her feet. Bouncing on the stones.

"It took me three days," he said. "And your hands will feel like fire. But you can cut through the chains."

"Do they know?"

"The jailers?"

"Yes."

He shook his head. "They don't bring me out. When they bring my food, I sit against the wall with the chains and I don't speak and they don't ask." He nodded toward her. "You can't, though. They take you out. They'll know if you cut them."

Elation had been growing in her, and she felt it evaporate like water and blow away with the wind. But still she said: "I'll be faster."

"Perhaps."

"I'll have to."

He looked up then at the ladder above her, where the stones had been removed. That climbing series of rough steps in the darkness, barely visible in the gloom unless you knew to look for them. The high window and bars above. Then he shook his head. "No," he said.

And she looked also and did not want to but knew he was right. For she had to cut them off, then climb and remove more stones, then find a way to remove the bars at the top. It was a thing that could not be done. With time, it could, but not in a night. Not between meals, between being called up and paraded in front of her subjects as if she were still the ruler and not the boy at her side.

"I can help you," he said then.

"How?"

"I'll do it is how. But you must wait. I'll climb it, I'll dig them out. I'll get rid of the bars. Then we'll try to cut you free and you can run. But you can't do it yourself."

"You'd do that for me?"

"No," he said.

She wanted to ask him what he meant but she was at once sick of his dancing around the points and yearning for his help and so she said nothing. Just looked at him. He was not looking at her now but was instead wrapping and unwrapping the links of the chain around his wrist. Rolling it first one way and then the other. Looking at it and nodding and rolling it again.

"Talk to me," she said.

"Talk to me." He looked at her and grinned and again she saw moving in his eyes those elements in such contrast, the kindness and the wildfire. Something loose and wrong and ravaging. But also rooted there something else, something she no longer saw in her son's eyes.

"Please."

"I'll do it," he said. "For myself."

III

He worked the next three nights above her in the dark. When the guards left he came over in his chains and robes and took from her the spoon and put it between his teeth and smiled with his lips only and then climbed barefoot the tall steps, his chains rattling against the wall. She moved aside as he dug so the dust would not fall on her and when he got a stone free he called out softly and dropped it down out of the darkness and she caught it and carried it back to the bones and put it down with the others.

Then returned and waited again until there was another.

This over and over, his form rising in the darkness to twice and then three times the height of her chains. Until at last he reached the bars above and dropped the final stone, one she could barely catch to prevent the noise as it struck the floor, and then he stood with his feet in the mortar and his hands wrapped around the bars and for the first time since she'd been cast down here—that dark and horrific first night—something moved across the light.

A shadow passing. His face pressed to the bars.

He looked out for a time and said something but she did not know what. And then he began to work, pushing the spoon again into the mortar. By now that lone instrument bent and battered, mangled by this hard labor. But still the mortar and stone drifting down.

It took two more nights before he had the first bar free. He did not drop it to her but put it in his robe and tied it and climbed down with the spoon in his mouth and handed it to her. It had been set into the mortar when it was poured and it was of black iron and the ends brighter where the stone had ground at them. Just as long as her arm from the elbow to the tips of her fingers.

"It will be close," he said. Holding the bar sideways against her body and nodding and sliding it up and down. "But you'll fit."

Then he climbed again and set to work on the second one.

She'd asked him his name many times and he would not give it. Would not speak to her about anything regarding himself. He went through periods where all he would do was repeat what she said and others where he spoke on his own. There did not seem to be anything else different about him at those times, save for what he said, but still she was afraid. She did not know if he saw it, but she felt it clutching her heart and hoped he'd work faster.

It was the night after with the dust falling down about her

face and shoulders and the second bar halfway free that the door opened. He froze and she turned frantically toward it and the light that had seemed so dim and worthless before now seemed to be pouring in from the hall with no end, the shadows thrown back.

The guard—of course not the girl, through the damning of fate—coming across the floor. Walking slowly with the keys in his hand and those keys swinging and him grinning to himself as he looked at her. Something predatory in his eyes that made her want to cross her arms over herself and she did but then put them down. For she could not let them win at anything which she controlled and she would not now and if he was looking at her that was all she had.

She stood and tried not to look up. A small sprinkle of dust falling from above. How much, how much. She stepped to the end of the chains and held out her hands. "Hurry," she said. "Don't keep him waiting."

The guard raised an eyebrow and then laughed. "You're telling me what to do?"

"I know he sent you."

"I bet you do."

She nodded as if that settled it and held out her hands. Heard a soft grinding from above. A bare foot twisting in powdered mortar atop a smooth stone. Losing purchase now with the first bar gone and the second loose, only one left to hold.

Don't fall, she thought. Damn you, don't fall.

"Got someone here wants to see you," the guard said.

"Take me to him."

"Just like that?" He laughed again. "Don't even want to know who it is?"

"What difference does it make?"

"Maybe makes a lot."

The grinding again. Something falling and striking her

head, perhaps a small stone. She tried not to move and didn't know if he saw it or not. Her last prayer one said as a child and long ago on her knees by a bed so large it felt as if it were a great blue sea and soft, with oil lamps around and long swaying curtains and pillows larger than her small body and all this so, so long ago and yet she found the prayer rising in her mind now. Running through those familiar words like a chant, a plea, a prayer of desperate supplication and desire.

All the time, dust moving in the light. So much more dust than had ever been in this place of mildew and water.

"He'll be angry if he has to wait." Still holding out her hands.

The guard shook his head. Leaned in and took one hand, fitting the key into the lock. Turning it, turning it. A soft click and the release as the iron dropped open. The second hand. Everything taking ages, entire lives passing in the swirling stars as he switched to the second lock. She heard the grinding sound again and it was louder and she just knew he was going to fall and he did not and she watched the guard the whole time and then they were at the end of eternity and he unlocked the second wrist and stepped back.

The prayer still repeating, rolling through her mind like the tide, the cycles of the moon. Tumbling again and again.

"Let's go," he said, taking her arm and pulling her toward the door.

Chapter Eight

I

They rode four days out from the village in this wasteland
and rough terrain with the horse carrying them both and all
about the mountains sloping down from the town which was in
turn down from the keep and the land always growing lower as
it ran to the seas. So far off it felt like a different world and
perhaps one they would never see again. They rode through a
frozen forest where the trees were all stark white and brittle and
the branches shattered when they touched them, as the horse
brushed by. Across a wide lake that was as solid as stone and as
clear as glass and looking down where the snow had blown
away they could see the rocks of the bottom and at one place a
man in armor with a blue and frozen face and his arms
outstretched and mouth and eyes open and the eyelids eaten by
fish that lived and swam in the ice itself. Through a deep valley
with boulders all scattered about as if giants had come and
rolled them and white deer in that valley running between the
boulders ahead of the horse and then climbing the shale cliffs
along the edges and standing beneath their clouding breath to
watch them pass.

    Brack had seen much and more of the world, but this was
nothing he had laid eyes on before. When he rode in front he

watched the horse's steps and guided it carefully and kept an eye on its breathing and felt its lungs move in its great chest. But when he rode in back he looked all about him and drank that country and did not know what it meant that this place could exist at all.

Looking above at times for the dragon, but never finding him.

They camped the fourth night in a cave in the shadow of a short mountain and on the peak of that mountain an old lookout of tumbled stones. Brack went and stood among those ruins and could not date them but did find a knife made of stone with a chipped blade. Picked it up and looked at it and turned it in his hand and put it back down. But went in the end to the cave and lit a fire in the doorway and sat behind it in the warm glow with his hands to the flames.

"We need another horse," Juoth said. His blistered skin bright in the firelight. Both hands sitting in his lap. The one glove still on and holding that hand very still.

"He's spent?"

"If he's not already, he will be."

There had been no villages and no men and no tracks and no horses. They had the gold and could buy one but they had to find one to buy him and they couldn't.

They watched the fire for a time. The flames moving over the wood they'd brought from the forest, scraping it free of ice and frost with their knives and a handax. Splitting it so it burned on the edges. The flames still meager but better than none, the smoke rising thinly.

"What are you doing?" Juoth said. Just looking out over the country.

Brack regarded him for a moment. Leaning forward to set another branch in the fire and watching as the flames licked over it and trying not to think of bones among the ashes. Then he said: "I'm hunting him."

"How long?"

"There's not a beginning to it."

"No?"

He shook his head and settled back. Looking at this man with whom he rode. "How much did you know about my grandfather?"

"Only what he wanted me to know."

"Then you know he watched for me."

Juoth nodded. Nothing else needed to be said.

"I knew he'd be looking and I came to him to find out what he'd seen," Brack said. "I've always been able to trust him in that. He saw everything. The things you miss. He saw them. Noted them. When it left the keep and I knew he was close, I went to him."

"Don't blame yourself."

Brack sat staring for a long moment and then bent his head and put it in his hands. Holding it and thinking of all his life was and all it had become. Not wanting to raise it again and continue on this journey but also knowing he must. As all men must do the things laid before them or perish in the doing or shirk that duty and live long and fat lives hating themselves and knowing exactly what they are.

"Who did it kill there?"

"At the keep?"

"Yes."

Brack scowled, eyes focused on nothing and everything. "My cousins. Brother and sister."

The other man looked at him and watched his eyes and said: "You think something."

Brack blinked and then nodded. Smiling in a grim fashion. As a man who has seen so much death must smile if he is to smile at all. "It's following me."

"You're not just hunting it. You think it's hunting you."

A long silence. Juoth got up and brought over more wood

and cleaned it with the handax and set it on the fire. Moved it and rolled it when it wouldn't catch. Until it did at last, with the heavy wet smoke as it dried and then the thin smoke as it burned.

"It's not hunting me," Brack said. "I said it before and it's still true. It's toying with me. Some damned game."

"How so?"

"Did my grandfather tell you about it?"

Juoth shook his head. "I knew what he was doing. In a general sense. But did he tell me about this dragon? No."

"Two hundred years ago," Brack said. "My grandfather's grandfather's father

II

came down into the grass plains and stood with the fall wheat blowing about him and the smell of it warm and dry on the wind and everywhere the smell of smoke. He stood with the long bow in one hand and the arrow in the other and the sword at his back and tasted the air. The beast nowhere to be seen but also everywhere and he knew it would come. It must. In the far distance the caravan moving out of the burning town and in the center of this field the crypt with the old man's gold and bones and all about the dead horses. Three of them with their bodies quartered and the blood splashed over the crypt and the smell of that blood as thick and heavy as the smoke.

He saw first the shadow moving over the earth, running along through the grass as a ship over the choppy sea. He turned and looked and then it was gone, darting from sight. This beast so huge and still nimble, especially when in the air that it owned. And also which owned it. He moved toward the crypt and he kept the bow up and then that shadow returned and then he saw it.

Dark and long in the air, flashing down with the wings

spread wide. Muscles gleaming and slick in places with blood not its own. The eyes like fire itself above a jaw powerful enough to snap a horse in two, clean through hide and bone. It came down toward him and shrieked and there was no other sound in the world.

This the call it had made as it drug itself from the furnaces below and stepped for the first time into the night air.

He knew he could not kill it with the bow but he did not mean to kill it that way and he brought it up and loosed an arrow. The distance far too great, but the dragon closing. The arrow falling away beneath.

Looking down and seeing the stone crypt, just steps away now. He ran forward and got behind it and the dragon went close over his head and it felt as if the air split. The way it felt when lightning struck the ground and everything ripped. The sound of one claw dragging hard across the top of the crypt.

And then he was up and climbing over and not even looking at the dragon. For he had seen dragons before and he would see them again. The stone too smooth and his hands and feet slipping. But he pulled himself up and over to the other side and stood on the ledge where he could rise and shoot or drop behind as he needed.

Both in their time.

The dragon shrieked again, furious at the miss, and wheeled in the sky. It turned like a sail into a headwind, one wing billowing as it brought its body around, legs trailing and swinging, the neck arching and curving sharply back as if it were where the dragon wanted to be and the rest of its powerful form was a hindrance.

He watched it turn. Swallowing once and tasting the dust on the back of his throat. Looking at it for the weakness and finding it.

For everything had a weakness. In chariots it was the spokes of the wheels, in horsemen their very mounts. In footsoldiers their heavy armor, also their life. In kings their greed.

In dragons it was the eyes.

The beast came back again and he loosed another arrow and watched the dark shaft fly to its peak and then begin to fall, whistling in the air, and then the dragon lashed out with its teeth and tore it from that air, snapping it in half like a twig beneath a heel. Letting the pieces fall from its jaws to spin back to the earth. Never looking away through all of this, never blinking.

He threw himself from the top of the crypt and behind the wall, and fire washed over. He could feel his shirt aflame and he rolled and pressed it to the stone and the very stone was hot. Like that of a stove. He laid down and the flames on him went out and he could feel his back naked and blistered and raw.

The dragon swept by again and he repeated the earlier escape and hauled himself up and over the crypt while it turned. The stone on the far side partially melted and blisters now also on his hands as he slid over the side. The pain barely felt. For when death was so close pain was nothing and he'd never felt much pain in his long life.

Until later. He always felt it later and the next day in the clutches of hell itself. But now there was nothing but the bow and the dragon and those eyes, and his body would do as it must until it fell.

It came back at him again and he saw it for the arrogance that it was. This repetition. It did not believe it would lose or could be killed and so it would do the same thing until all others were dead, as it had all its life. For it could not fathom an outcome other. It rose up on those black wings and drew its feet up and threw itself at him.

And again he waited just that much longer. As the range closed and he thought he could feel the dragon's heat pouring from its body as it came and he knew he couldn't but still felt that he did. The rushing wind from those wings. It opened its gaping jaws again and shrieked like a demon tearing all sound from the world and the fire swelled in those lungs and he brought the bow up and unleashed the final arrow.

At this distance, closing instantly. Just a flash of wood and metal in the firelight, too fast to follow, and then burying itself in the dragon's eye.

The beast fell and crashed to the earth and rolled in a tangle of wings and legs and claws and scales. Calling again now but in pain and shock and terror. The head rising up and burning blood spraying from the ruptured eye in a scalding torrent and running down that long serpent's neck. The jaws working open and closed and the dragon struggling to gets its legs under it and its wings above.

He leapt from behind the crypt and tore his sword free and brought it around in front of him and ran at it. Perhaps in folly or courage, and sometimes he thought they were the same. But this was the one chance and the dragon would not be so foolish and arrogant again and he could not let it rise.

Now he did feel the heat of the thing and it was like running into a parched desert and everywhere the wheat was burning. A line of ruin behind where the dragon had fallen and the rest of the field now taking up. Smoke and flame and dust in the air. The dragon's calls and the cracking of those jaws.

He came around at it and went to the side where the eye still bled. The dragon had struggled over in the torn earth and was trying to stand and it got one wing up with the other trapped and in doing so killed itself as surely as it had by taking a third pass and not circling to come from the west. The wing rose and it could not see him and he saw the open place below with the skin soft and free of scales. Just a long thin line, a crease where the flesh must move freely as the wings beat, and in this the dragon's end.

Stepping beneath that rising wing, that black sail, the

*claws on the end. Knowing what it would do if it fell and how
he would be crushed and broken before he knew anything and
running still as the dragon turned its head. Bringing that long
and slender sword up and seeing the flame glint off the edge of
the blade and the fuller and then burying it to the hilt in the
dragon's side. Feeling it slide over rib and bone and into that
beating inferno of its heart.*

III

Juoth sat looking at him in the cold and windbeaten cave,
the snow drifting against the mouth and the air howling in the
dark night, far off through the frozen forest. "You were trying to
emulate that kill."

Brack nodded. The pieces had been in place, the trap laid.
But it had not played out as in that story now centuries old.
Perhaps the dragon was wiser, or perhaps not. Maybe it had
been its intention all along to kill Tarek and he could have done
any damned thing he pleased in that field and it wouldn't have
made a difference.

"Now what do we do?" Juoth said.

"We track it."

"How do you want to do it?"

Brack stood and went to the fire and turned one of the
logs. The embers burning down now and smoking more than
producing heat and already the cave cooling. The back wall
where ice glistened wetly now freezing back to that shell of
crystal on stone. He took up two more logs and set them on the
fire crossing each other, the heart of that cross in the flame
where all of the edges could catch. The bark first smoldering
and smoking and then little flames licking at the sides and
growing as they moved toward the core. He stepped back and
sat again.

"The way you always track a dragon," he said. Raising a

hand to his jaw and feeling the beard growing there and wondering how long he would be traveling now in this world and seeing no end to it. "Not in the usual ways of lesser game. You track it by the swaths of destruction it leaves behind. You go from one burning hellhole to the next until you find it and you kill it."

Juoth smiled and it was a wicked thing on his face and all teeth and also a sheer joy in it and Brack had seen that look before and knew what it meant. "But a dragon is like a man."

"He is."

"So we can guess where he'll be."

Brack nodded, already feeling it and hating what he knew. "What is it?"

"My sister," he said. "It's my sister."

IV

They left the cave the next morning and went on down the mountain and into a valley of stone. The snow lighter here as they descended, just a thin skim on the surface of the world, in places a dusting. Melting off in the sun. All around the stones rising high above them and in one place three inexplicably stacked, one atop the next, each seven meters tall and more than that around. The hands of gods perhaps all that could have placed them in such a position.

They came after that to the remains of a town and it was there that the dragon had nested. Dismounting and walking through the ruin, but this an old ruin of age and time alone. No one having lived there in a generation. Everything fallen in and rotted, the beams of old homes and barns and a fence running long into a field with tilted fenceposts. A simple place for farming and the raising of animals and all now fled or killed or taken. He knew not which, but no bodies or bones remained.

In the center of the town a scuffle of tracks in the mud and dirt. The beast's talons as long in that soil as his arm. The great depression where it had curled its tail about itself and slept with those burning eyes horrible and open in the night. Atop the remains of a barn as if seeking the straw that had long since been blown by the four winds and rotted itself.

Perhaps the dragon felt that in a place like this it could find a home, he thought. A place of abandonment and death already. Lacking blood and fire and gold, but already little more than whispering ghosts. Where nothing lived.

In times ancient and mostly forgotten the dragons had ruled the earth and not the men and he felt the whole world must have been like this. The eternal rangings of huge creatures brawling in the setting sun to control a wasteland and a territory. Feasting perhaps on the ancestors of the men. Turning all the world to their will.

They did not speak in that dead town and got back on the horse on the far side and found a river running down toward a low valley. The floor of which they could not see, as it was shrouded in cloud. The water black and churning over the small stones, coming out of mountains and snowmelt and falling. They came to the bank and the horse drank and then raised its dripping muzzle and they went on along in moss and roots and scrub trees. Picking their way down in short steps and not pushing lest the horse fall and break its leg and leave them to walk an untold distance.

It was along this river that Juoth spoke without turning back. His voice soft and light as if saying nothing at all but a hard edge to it and all the world in his words.

"Do you know how I met your grandfather?"

"No. He didn't tell me."

"Do you want to?"

"Of course."

Juoth straightened. Looking upward as if seeing it for just a moment. His voice in that far off place when he spoke.

"We were slaves," he said. "Your grandfather a prisoner of the Goldencrown War. In the islands that means you fight. Not always, but it did for us. Thirty years ago. We'd been moving all over Carrison and fighting in the rings and pits there and once in an amphitheater. All around us people cheering. There's always money when there's blood."

Brack was silent. He knew well the link between money and blood and he felt those bloodslicked coins riding in the bag at his hip.

"He'd made a name for himself, you know. Killed a hundred men. They said it, anyway. That no one could kill him. I fought once before him and won and afterward watched him. Facing two lions and a huge man from Hydone. Eight feet tall. Arms like pillars." There was a slight grin in his voice as he spoke. "Your grandfather killed the lions and him in no less than three minutes."

It was a time Brack had known about but not something they ever spoke of. Something that took guts and hours or perhaps days and always the threat of those opened doors and where they led and neither he nor his grandfather chose to walk into that dark forest and see what it held, though they both knew everything there was to know. But there was no way around it and it was many years ago and he closed his eyes and saw those burned bones in the rubble and opened them again and touched his face, his cheek.

"I was ten," Juoth said. "Perhaps eleven. One of the youngest fighters but you do what they tell you and they were making money when I fought. And then one day I walked out into the ring and it was hot and the ring was all sand and I was thinking what it would be like for my footing and then I looked up and he was standing there and looking at me."

He paused, then, looking away. Beside them, the river still ran darkly over those stones and turned in a widening bed. As deep now in the middle as his waist and the dim shapes of fish moving in the hollows. Once a silver back breaking the surface and then descending again in a swirl of ripples quickly lost to the current.

"He didn't have a weapon," Juoth said. "He was just standing there and looking at me and I came out with the spear and knife and stood looking back at him and thought of what he'd done to the lions and I realized they wanted me to kill him. And he knew it. We both looked at each other and we both knew it and then he looked to that raised gate behind me."

"What did you do?" Brack said. Not feeling like his voice was his own.

"We ran," Juoth said. A snort of laughter. "If it were a real tale we would have fought the guards and overcome them and thrown the cages open and freed the slaves and they'd sing of us now as we sat on thrones. But it's never like that. No, he just ran toward me and past me and I let him go and turned and followed. They tried to get the gate down but they couldn't do it fast enough and we ran out into the streets. I dropped the spear at some point and they chased us but we ran until we found some trash to hide in and we hid and that night we snuck out with a group of lepers and we left the islands forever."

Brack shook his head and could see Tarek doing it, doing all of it, and then he said: "Why are you telling me this?"

"So you'll know," Juoth said. "So you'll know why I'm here."

They rode the river down to a plateau and stood at the edge of the trees. There was no snow but just thin grass lightly frosted. Gray stones standing up out of the soil at places, low and flat. A type of tall weed moving in the wind like wheat but the color all wrong. The river swelling out and slowing. Five hundred yards away the descent continuing into that mist-covered valley, the water resuming its speed and the river there heavy and loud and powerful.

They let the horse free to roam that grass and built in the

center of the field a small fire. Lay out their bedrolls one on each side. Scavenging the wood they needed and keeping it small so the rising sparks would not be seen. The frost making the grass brittle and everything on the edge of frozen, but both of them sweating in their furs and leather and armor. The sun had fallen and a heavy gray dusk lay on the place and after they had eaten they both stretched out and looked up at that starstrewn sky for the black shape of the dragon moving in the night, but it did not come.

After a time of silence, Juoth turned and looked at him in the glimmering light and his brow was creased and his eyes distant as if again turning about all the words spoken and looking in them for new meanings or perhaps old ones there confined. "Tell me something," he said. "You told me of your great grandfather's kill. The one you tried to emulate. But what did that story have to do with this dragon?"

"He killed it," Brack said.

Juoth just looked at him for a long moment. The way he had, with his eyes dark and full of thought. Again turning over everything that was said. Then: "He killed that other dragon?"

Brack was quiet for a moment. "No," he said at last. "He killed this one."

The Dragon Hunt

Chapter Nine

I

She went in and stood while the guard chained her to the wall and went out and already she knew something was wrong and stood longer waiting to see just how bad it was. The door closing heavily behind her and the thick smell of this place. Bones and mildew and age. And then she saw him sitting in the halfdark against the far wall and he was grinning and holding his arms back against the wall behind him, over his head.

"Worlds turn and mountains fall," he said. Eyes wide and staring and bloodshot. Hands not moving as if themselves made of stone. "But still he comes."

She did not answer and just looked back at him. This old man with his rotten teeth and long hair. His skin nearly gray from this place. And she thought then that maybe they knew he'd cut his chains but they did not care and perhaps this the reason. A dead and lost man still chained in other ways, if not with iron.

For an invalid was not one to attempt a bid for his own freedom.

"Still he comes," he said. Then licked his lips. His tongue darting out quickly, almost as if it were afraid of this dank air. Wetting those already glistening lips and then disappearing between the crooked rows of teeth. "Still."

"Are you all right?" she said.

"Mountains fall and worlds turn. Which way is the wind coming from, and which way is it going?"

"Listen to me."

"And still he comes. Mountains turn and worlds fall."

She opened her mouth and went to speak again, but did not. For it was something deeper, something ingrained. He was looking at her almost eagerly, as if waiting there for some response. For him, this was a conversation with two participants, not the incoherent rambling of one and the confusion of the other. Both on equal footing.

Once she had known a woman who was perhaps her aunt. Some relative distant and yet usually at court. She could not remember now. Long ago, this had been, long before everything had come apart at the seams and the world had fallen into its current form. Her world, at least, trapped here in this dungeon and only shuffled out to pretend to rule a people she had once dreamed of ruling.

The woman had suffered an affliction. They knew not what at the time and still did not. She had been standing in court and watching on a long afternoon while others talked and then suddenly she had been stepping and turning and falling. Not making a sound, her wrinkled mouth clenched tight and her gray hair descending ever so rapidly. The man next to her turning as well and catching her as she fell and calling out even as he did so for others. But the woman never making a sound.

She never spoke again. Arisine had seen her at times. The skin on one side of her mouth turned down, her legs not broken but stricken with near paralysis. Unable to walk on her own or even to stand without help. The left side of the body much worse than the right.

They'd brought her many potions. Chanted the dread spells as slaves gave their minds and filled the rooms with smoke or steam or sunlight or night air. Given her herbs and flowers to eat, or taken away others. None of it made a difference and she sat in her chambers with her blankets about her and did not speak. This silence like one who had taken a vow.

But once, sent there for some reason she could no longer remember, the girl Arisine had been climbed the stairs in the flickering light of lanterns and pushed open the tall oak door with its metalwork and window, stepping through and into the woman's rooms. Two rooms, with a wide doorway and a stone wall between. A bed on one side and a sitting area with arched windows on the other. Those windows looking out over the long fields and the orchards and the world.

It was before those windows that the old woman sat. The blanket upon her lap and one hand raised to her chin, supporting it. Gazing out at nothing and everything at once. She turned as Arisine came in and half-smiled and the girl walked across to her and sat on the sill. The drop below soaring and causing her stomach to jump, but she liked the feeling and leaned over just a bit more to look down the sheer stonework.

And it was then that the woman talked to her. But she also did not. For every time that she spoke, the sound she made was not words, but fragments. Perhaps pieces of the same few words cut up and moved and put back together into a string of nothing with no meaning or sense to it. A babbling of confusion.

But it was not as if talking to someone who did not know what she was saying. The same eager look had been in that woman's eyes. The same patterns of speech. Arisine would tell her something, of the day's chores or the war to the south. And the woman would speak, as if answering, and say nothing at all.

Between her mind and her tongue, those words lost. But Arisine could see they were there, at least to start. Forming in her mind as true words and sentences and working their way down and in the process coming apart and then being spoken as nothing. They were whole when this broken woman thought them, but gone by the time they passed her lips.

"The world turns and mountains fall, and still he comes," the man said again.

"Who comes?" she said

"The mountains."

"The mountains come?"

"The worlds turn." Nodding now as if in affirmation. "The mountains."

She did not speak again for a time and thought of the old woman whose name now escaped her and who was gone these long years, but she saw her here, in this old man and the only words he now knew. And when the hours had fled by he lay down and slept and she watched him sleep and the light from above moved through the dust as it floated in the air and then he woke and all was returned and he could speak as he once had.

When she asked him of the mountains and the world and he who was coming, he had no recollection of any of it.

II

He climbed the next morning the ladder of brick and stone and stood looking out the top for a time and she asked him what he saw and he told her it was a street. Brick and mud and across it the rising wall of some building unknown. Then he leaned forward and put his head and shoulders slowly through the hole, those shoulders grinding in the dirt and mud but this time at last the dirt and mud not of this place. Instead the mud of that road with above it open air and that air covering all the world and when he came back down he was grinning madly and his eyes very wide.

"You'll fit," he said.

"Did you see anything?"

"Nothing." Nodding emphatically and then sitting down beside her and looking at her. "It's a little street. I don't know where it goes."

She thought she did but she could not be sure. "What was on the wall?"

"On the wall?"

"Signs, letters, ivy. Anything so I can find it again."

"Ah." He closed his eyes for a long moment, then nodded once more. "Part way up there is a window. It has shutters that are brown and look like a bat's wings. Something is written above it but I haven't been able to read in years." Grinning as if that news was some enchanting thing saved until now when life was light and easy. "But it was written in white."

Bat wings and white letters. She looked up at the ladder to salvation and licked her lips and found them as always slightly coated in the dust of the room and thought she tasted in it perhaps the dust of the world and what it meant. Dust blown on that long-carrying wind from the Island Kingdoms or down from the mountains or from the long gray desert to the east where the red stones rose from that colorless expanse like spires and creatures skittering in the night moved between the stones and called to a forlorn and pale moon.

"I'll find it," she said.

"Then what'll we do? About your chains."

"We'll take them off is what we'll do." It was her turn now to grin.

"When are you going?"

"After the next time he calls me," she said. "Once I know where to go."

It was not as long waiting as it could have been.

III

She stood for the last time on the wall and looked out at the land. He was with her now but a mood had come on him like some storm and he was not speaking to her. Dressed all in black with his shirt white and an iron sword on his hip and looking like some relic here so far from battle but she did not tell him that and only looked.

They'd met with two lords who were fighting over land. One portly and rich and the other tall and poor and both claiming some vineyard and he had not listened as they spoke but had sat brooding and when they were done she had said that the deed must be produced and neither could and she'd sent someone to check but knew already that neither had a claim to it at all.

He had not spoken upon their arrival or departure and she had stood there and let them loose to tell of a queen who still ruled and the appearance intact. To talk of the small servant girl smiling and bringing her wine and cheese and bread. Squeezing her hand just so as she passed it across. To tell of this girl who loved her like the kingdom loved her and thus loved him.

Below them the buildings spread out from the castle to the south and east and in front the orchards. But it was to the city that she turned her eyes. Short buildings even near the wall for no building was allowed to stand over two stories there lest it be taken and used as a siege tower and they then grew taller as they moved away before descending once more. Toward the riverfront and the docks and the rattle of chains and the creak of rope.

She thought she knew where the dungeons sat buried in filth and perhaps knew the orientation of the wall and she looked and did not see the bat's wings nor the writing and was standing thinking through the map in her head when he finally spoke.

"We're nothing," he said.

She did not want to look at him but she knew she must,

especially now, and so she did. Him staring out across the field and not seeing her and the clouds moving in his eyes. "What do you mean?"

"You know what I mean."

"You can say that, but I don't." She regretted it as she said it, but he only scowled and didn't move to strike her.

"You know what we were. Now look at us. We're nothing."

"We're at peace," she said. "We're prosperous. What else do you want?"

"You call this prosperous?"

"It's enough."

He leaned forward off the wall then and put his hand on the hilt of the sword and for one moment she thought he meant to draw it but he did not. He stood with his hand on it. "In the Island Kingdoms there is more gold than can fit on a fleet of galleys. In Dalimar they're mining diamonds from the mountains and piling them so high in carts the horses can't pull them. On the south sea the Tungisian fleet has ranged to the end of the world and come back with stories of another land where the men are ten feet tall and the land is beyond measure. And what do we have? Fields, timber, orchards. Nothing."

"You call this nothing?"

Then he smiled and it was slow and perhaps worse than his eyes. "No," he said. "You're right, it's not nothing." Looking out over those long fields and the villages and cities in the plains and the rising mountains with towns of their own. "I have men."

"You don't want war."

He stepped toward her with hard eyes and was so close she could smell him and she did not flinch but it took all that was in her.

"Don't I?"

"You don't remember war. I do. You don't want it."

But then he was done with her and she saw what was moving in his mind and behind those eyes and it made him care not even for her insolence and she thought she could have told him he was a fool and a coward and even then he wouldn't have struck her. For he was elsewhere and had what he wanted from her and now there was more he wanted.

"Not all at once," he said. "Not all at once."

He went to the battlements and looked out and they were silent again and she thought of asking him and then thought the hell with it and walked around the wall. Tracing these steps in which guards clad in iron strode and where other men had sometimes stood screaming while archers rained upon those below a swift and terrible death. She did not look back at him and he did not say anything and one of the guards came out from a little wooden door on the inside wall and followed her and he also did not speak, a silent wraith whose only sound was that of his boots on the stone.

She walked and kept her eyes forward and even so all she could think of were his words and the war.

Waking once beside the river in the small cloth tent and looking out and thinking the sunrise on the water was red, so red, and then going down to the bank and all the little stones awash in blood and it rolling in the current.

Running another time with the smoke in her lungs and a sword in her hand, the heft and weight of it, the blade broken half a meter up and still a splintered sword better than none and behind her a sound like all the world ending. In truth the pounding of the horses as they came down on the town. She had not looked and had never seen the horses but had heard them and smelled their sweat like salt on the air.

Walking her own horse with the rope in her hand and the burns from that rope all up her palm and her feet aching and the horse just a day from its own death. Coming to a long stone bridge carved over a river by the Old Ones, an ancient thing that supported itself somehow and needed no pillars and which looked as if it could crumble and fall into the river at any moment but which had stood there in steadfast strength longer than any of the cities she'd ever seen. And all along the underside of that bridge gibbeted men and women in their hanging cages, some sitting in silence and others lying with their hands stretching between the bars and one with his head through and the skull gone and fallen a thousand feet into the crashing river below, for they were all dead and just husks of people now in their rotting clothes and parchment skin.

She had to stop then on the wall and she did and breathed in deeply and when she let it out again the world was at peace. A fragile thing, that. The blossoms in the apple trees and the ivy growing up and spinning itself around the tower and the stone shingles. The women talking beside the stream and a child naked and running in water clear and flowing. A man sitting on a fence and looking out on a field burning only with the setting sun and between his teeth chewing a long piece of dried grass and at his feet his son looking up at him and then turning to find a piece of grass of his own.

All this and no one thinking of war and feeling that this world they lived in was so firm and secure, like a thing carved from stone. Hewn into ironoak.

But in truth all of it as fragile as the ice early in the year when it was black and glass as far as could be seen and the water still moved below it and it called out, groaning long and loud as it shifted.

Smiling, she looked to the side and the buildings of the town and heard her dead father speaking to her. When did you start thinking like this, he asked. Grinning and turning in his old hands an old pipe and packing it with a thumb. Shaking his head and looking away and then looking back to grin at her again.

And then she remembered his death and the sound of it

and her smile faded. The world falling again into this new darkness.

She blinked twice before it caught her and forced herself on and around the next corner of the wall and she found it there, that window with batwing shutters and above it white words in old paint turned to dust and it was not where she'd thought it would be at all and looking at it she felt then weak and old. This a kingdom that had once been hers to rule standing on these same walls with her dress blowing behind her in a restless autumn wind and thousands at arms in formation below her and now she did not know it as she should.

She closed her eyes for a moment and when she opened them she felt almost herself again and she turned to walk back to him. Inside her, something growing and changing. A child with a great and terrible hunger. A child with teeth and eyes of fire.

Chapter Ten

I

It was in the early morning under a rising sky of clear blue so dark on the edges it neared some color unnamed that could swallow all within it that they came to the fence and the remains of the cattle. They'd found a second horse at a small cabin on the edge of the forest with only a dead man to inhabit it and they stood them both now near the treeline for a quarter of an hour and did not speak and Brack smelled the blood on the wind and looked out over the field. The hour of waking birds but not a sound from them nor the fluttering of wings. Not even the circling as there should have been of vultures and carrion birds in that open sky. At last he looked at Juoth and nodded and they rode down with the brittle grass breaking under the horses' hooves and went to a place where the fence had fallen and rode into the field.

Most of the cattle were in pieces. One halved entire, the head and chest remaining and all else gone. Torn skin, scattered entrails. Others just raked to death. One lying on its side with its glassy eyes wide and no wound upon it at all. But dead just like the others.

It was worst in the center of the field. There the bodies had been dragged and it had stopped and eaten. Sitting beside this pile of slain cattle and bending to reach with that serpent's neck and holding them down with a claw and pulling with smoking teeth until part came away and then straightening to chew, eat, consume. Then bending again to its task.

Brack got down from the horse and Juoth stayed mounted and looked always at the sky and the horizon lines. They had been riding now for weeks and they operated like this without speaking to one another but each knowing what the other would do and how it should be done.

He did not have to go up to them to know what had happened, but he did it all the same, for he was a hunter and he knew thoroughness was the heart of his craft. Many thought the bones of hunting were aggression or luck or some otherworldly ability to kill that other men lacked, but he knew it was just seeing the details and being careful and taking your time. Going over everything in this meticulous way. For all of the signs to point you to a kill were always there and the only difference on any hunt was that some men found them and others did not.

It had killed a hundred head but only eaten perhaps a dozen. A few blackened and charred but most eaten raw. The bones snapped in half; when wolves ate, they left on the bones the marks of their teeth and those could be seen still years or decades later and the kill thereby identified. When a dragon ate there were never such marks for it destroyed the bones or ate them as well. But the snapped pieces, shattered like the branches of a dead tree, were all he needed.

"How old?" Juoth asked from the horse.

"Three days, maybe. More likely two."

"We're getting closer."

"I know." He raised his head to scan the sky and there was nothing and in that also he knew they were close.

This was the fourth such slaughter they had found. One of sheep and now three of cattle. In the first the farm had also been burned and there were a man's bones in the field and the remains of three people in the house. The man had been holding a short hooked sword like the officers in the last war had carried for ceremonies and the blade had melted and twisted and then set again, as if cast into some hellish blacksmith's fire with no care to the result.

That first killing ground they had found two weeks back and it was all old and the animals still living had returned. By the second, they'd halved the distance, then made up another day by the third, losing time as they came out of the alpine fields and into the valley country when a storm swept up against the wall of mountains and pinned them for half a week.

But always they marched closer and soon they would be upon it.

The path had been predictable as he'd feared and this wasn't really hunting, not the way he'd hunted elsewhere. The beast was heading for the cities of the plain and Kayhi and it was moving slowly so that it could feed. If it wanted it could have crossed that great distance in days, flying so high that its huge bulk was nothing but a speck in the sky and its heat couldn't be felt, but it did not. For it knew that what it sought would not escape it and it preferred to move at leisure and with much rest and sustenance. An arrogance in that.

Brack stood back and looked out to see if the carnage spread and it did not. Either this had been the herd entire or the rest had run. Then in the far distance he saw a horse and rider coming down the dirt road and the dust rising up around him and he went back and got on his horse and wheeled it around to wait.

At last the man neared and drew the horse up a hundred yards from them and looked at them and then slowly came forward. He was unarmed as far as Brack could tell and wearing the rough clothes of a farmer and old boots made from leather and tough and probably worth as much as his horse. But in this work a necessity.

"These your cattle?" Brack asked.

The man nodded. His face was long and the jaw angular and his hair thin on the top of his head, though he did not look old. His skin marked with patches from the sun. Dust coating his whole being as if he were born from it.

"They were," he said.

"Did you see it?"

He nodded.

"You were wise not to fight it."

The farmer looked at him a moment and turned and spat in the road. Looked back up. "I'm as dead now as if I had fought it and been killed with the cattle. This way's just going to take longer. You may see that as a mercy, but I'm not as sure."

Brack reached to his belt and took off the leather pouch he wore and poured into his hand a fistful of gold and held it out. The man did not move but just looked at him and then turned again and spat. "Who are you?"

"That important?"

"You carrying that much gold and throwing it around, I'd say it is."

Brack nodded. Did not lower the gold. "Therros Brackson," he said. "Do you know the name?"

The farmer looked at him a long moment. Then snorted and shook his head, the flicker of what might have for him been a grin at the edges of his lips, the smallest movement. He turned his head as if he were for a third time going to spit and then thought better of it and looked back at them. "Come on," he said.

II

The house was a modest one made of mud and stone and wood and it sat on the edge of a small stream with willows hanging out over it and the sun golden in their arching

112

branches. They came to it down the dusty road and from there it did not look as if a dragon had passed and all the carnage from the field seemed a thing distant and perhaps even untrue. The sound of the water moving lightly over the stones, the breeze in the tree branches. There was a woman sitting on the porch and she stood as they came up. Dark hair and clasped hands and two children coming out to see when the farmer called out.

They got down from the horses and tied them to a tree in the front and the farmer went and got a bucket of water from the well and Brack took it before he could lift it and carried it himself over to the horses. Setting it where they could all reach and wiping briefly his wet hands on his horse's coat. His hands coming away dark with the dust. He did not know when he'd bathed last and had not thought about it on the road, but did now.

The man's wife was named Marna and she smiled as they shook hands and her eyes widened when the farmer said his name and Brack smiled and looked away and saw the two boys staring at the sword. He bent down and shook their hands each in turn and their eyes did not leave the sword the entire time.

Inside it was plank wood floors and walls and ceilings and light from the windows slanting in the dust of the air and a stone hearth in the center of the main room. Two lanterns sitting on the mantle and neither burning. Candles sitting about and rough wooden furniture and the chairs covered in hides. The whole place meager but clean and kept and dry. They nodded their thanks and took off their weapons and hung them by the door and sat and looked about the house.

The woman went into the kitchen and when she came out she had a stoneware pitcher full to the brim of clear water and she poured it into clay cups and nodded to them and they thanked her and she went back out again. The farmer calling to her about the meat they'd dried and coming also to sit before his own cup at the table.

"Don't eat all you have on our account," Brack said. "We've got some food in the saddlebags."

"It's nothing," the farmer said. "We were going to eat it anyway. Now we'll just eat it with you." He shrugged. "A man has to eat and there's never enough so why fight it?"

Brack took the bag back out and poured again the coins into his hand. A few more this time than before. Reached across and set them in front of the man, the metal rattling as they spread. The farmer opened his mouth and Brack raised a hand.

"For the meat," he said.

The farmer looked at him and then nodded and reached and slid with one hand all of the coins over the edge of the table and into his other hand. "For the meat," he said.

The boys were out in the yard playing and they could hear the crack of the sticks coming together and them yelling from time to time. Slowly the smell of the meat came into the whole house, strong in the midday air. Already dried and salted but cooked all the same to make it feel new and fresh and the smell of it was very good. The farmer leaned forward with his elbows on the table and looked from Brack to Juoth and back again.

"You're making for Cabele?"

"Or Darish-Noth."

"Cabele is closer."

"Then we'll go there first. Which is the best road?"

"The old road," the farmer said without hesitation. As a man in country he knows very well and who trusts that knowledge. "The new is fine if you're with a caravan or a company and you want to stop and trade, but it goes out of its way to hit the towns. Harihold. Stallfast. Barrion. The old road goes up through Krassmark Forest and under the Fall of Revian. Then you come down through the hill country into the plains and you can see Cabele for two days before you get to her. Unless you're riding hard."

"We'll be riding hard."

"If your horses will survive it."

"We'll buy new ones if they don't."

The man leaned back in his chair. Picked up his cup and drank and set it down again. "You really mean to catch the dragon? You saw my cattle."

"And yours aren't the first."

"I thought as much." He looked away and then licked his lips and seemed to be turning something in his mind. Rolling it and getting a feel for it and what it was. Then he said: "Is it true what they say about you? I saw the helmet."

Brack nodded. "It is."

"You killed the red dragon." He said it as if speaking of something barely believed. The trust one places in a dream. A tale that must not be true but has been passed down for generations. A feat not accomplished twice and so the first time is suspect.

"It was young and stupid," Brack said. "But yes. I killed it."

"And now you're sitting at my table."

"And we thank you."

The farmer waved it away. "I heard the stories, but you know how those things are. You took it with a lance first?"

"I didn't take it alone," Brack said. "I had three companies of queen's men from the Springlands and archers also and many of them are dead now because of it. But yes, I rode it down with a lance and buried it and came back with the sword to finish it."

"Is that the way to do it?"

"There is no way to kill a dragon," Brack said. He nodded toward the wall where his sword hung with his cloak. The crossbow outside and strapped still to the horse. "I don't have the lance now but I'll do it with what I have. Each time is different. Men who try the same thing every time are men who are killed." Thinking then of the bow and the quartered horse and the gold and the damned dragon falling on the town while he watched.

"So you don't have a plan."

"We'll make one when we see it. For now we're just trying to get to the cities."

"And you're sure it's going there?"

Brack nodded but did not say anything. Hoping the man would take it as fact if he said it and not ask why. For the explanation was not one that could be easily swallowed, no matter how he knew it to be true nor how the dragon had so far done exactly as he'd known it would.

"Where do we find the road?" Juoth asked.

Marna came out then with the meat and called to the boys in the yard and she set it down as they came running in the door and it slamming open and closed and her yelling at them to wash up and stop running. It was not as much as Brack had hoped and he was glad for the gold and nodded his thanks as she cut a piece and set it on his plate. Then Juoth, then the farmer, then the boys and at last herself.

The farmer cut his first to show them they could and put the cut piece in his mouth and looked at Juoth. "Just follow this one until the swamp where the creek holds up. Then it goes up and to the east, though the treeline. There's a ridge there and on top is the road. Take it from there and you'll be in the plains in two days and at Cabele in four. Darish-Noth is another day's ride if you want it."

They ate and the meat was very good and full of salt. The woman got up after a moment as if remembering something and the farmer waved her down and back to her food and he stood instead and went out the door and came back with another pitcher. This one of ale frothing still from the cask. He took their empty cups and poured and Brack drank deeply and felt it almost immediately in his blood and drank again.

When the food was done the farmer looked at his sons and they both stood and took away the dishes and then went out through some other door for Brack did not see them again but shortly heard them in the yard. Marna went to sit in the main room and the farmer sat back in his chair with the noon light on the top of his head and picked his teeth.

"You should stay here the night," he said. "Sleep and rest the horses. They're about beat, those ones. Then take the road in the morning." He nodded at Juoth, eyes flickering to the burned and halfhealed skin along his hairline. "Marna can give you something for that."

"Thank you," Juoth said. "But we can't."

"Afraid it'll get to Cabele before you?"

"It will anyway," Brack said. "But it's what we can do."

For in that, he knew, it was toying with him always. It could be upon Cabele in hours and by the time they arrived it could have reduced it to ash and bone, stone and cinder. So always it was far enough ahead, even as they closed the distance. But it wanted him to see Cabele and to see the fire and to hear the screams of the dying and to know Kayhi was among them.

And for that want he would kill it. For in this creature birthed of fire that could destroy the world, it was the one weakness.

But that was how you hunted, for everything had a weakness. And killing was only the art of finding it and knowing how to use it and then using it when the time came.

III

They rode out an hour later and each with a skin of ale and more of the dried meat for the trip and the farmer went with them as far as the road. Pointing to them the way and then shaking their hands, clasping each about the forearm and saying not a word of the gold but thanking them for it all the same. Brack looked back after they had gone a distance and he was still sitting his horse in the road and watching them.

It took the better part of an hour to reach the swamp. A deep and dark thing with mud all up to the road and a dense look to it that felt unnatural in this land of open fields breaking to plains. The sound of birds and other things within. The creek running to it just as the farmer had said. They turned there to the east and soon crossed another short field and went through the treeline and into a thin forest of cedars and birches with their bark peeling like pink paper and the ground below them a bed of brown needles and they rode through this for a short time. The ground beginning to swell beneath them and then rising in a ridge. The horses breathing hard with the effort, the soil full of sand. They at last came out on top of the ridge and there was the road before them, an old thing of beaten dirt and grass and sand and with boulders standing at places on either side of it, the rolled destruction of some prior land, the road snaking through them and moving down this spine of hills and out of sight.

They stopped shortly and let the horses breathe and looked out over the country. On their left a string of short mountains, an open valley between them. Barren to the dead and dried grass, not even scrub cedars in that withered expanse. The trees returning on the side of the mountains in groves, but these nothing like the mountains they'd just ridden down out of or the true mountains of the north beyond. That an endless world of stone and snow, these short mountains that could be ridden over in a few hours and put behind, hardly true to their name. Forested hills and shallow valleys.

Beyond them, on the far plains, the stone walls of Cabele.

They followed the road and the day grew hot and Brack took off his furs and packed them and then rode in his leather armor, the mail and plate strapped also to the horse's sides. If the dragon came he would be horribly exposed but it would not come. The worst things to fear now were the wolves and bears and either he could handle as he was.

They saw one of those bears off to the east and at the bottom of the ridge, standing with his great padded feet in the cool river and his head turned and looking up at them as they passed. The horses shied but did not run.

It was two hours later when Juoth spoke into the silence and the light wind. The ridge had been rising below them and turning to merge with the mountains and the drop on either side was near a thousand feet, down through boulders and grass. The slope so steep he could not stand on it and little could grow. The horses rode one behind the other but Juoth did not have to speak loudly to be heard in this deserted world.

"Your great grandfather didn't kill it," he said.

"You've been thinking about it."

"Of course I have."

"And that's what you think."

"That's what I think."

Brack nodded and looked into the mountains, still above them. The dark path of the road visible going up into the stones and trees. "I know he killed it."

"I'm sure he thought he did, but it's the only thing that fits. He wounded the dragon and it lived. It wouldn't be the first time. Dragons are great deceivers. It could have been an intentional move for survival."

"I'm telling you he killed it."

"I heard you."

Brack reined the horse up and trotted it sideways in the road, turning so they faced each other. Crossing his arms and sitting back in the saddle. Juoth stopped as well and regarded him.

"My great grandfather killed it, first with the bow and then with the sword. Through the ribs and into the heart. When it was dead, he took an ax and he cut off the beast's head. Then they buried the body in the mountains and they buried the head in a lake. Leagues apart. And then the city feasted, for the threat of a generation was gone and they no longer had to look to the sky every time they heard something on the wing or saw a shadow moving through the grass."

Juoth was silent. As if knowing he was not done.

"When I saw it, at the keep. I saw its neck. Have you ever seen a man hanged who lived? The burn of the rope on his skin, a scar bitten into him for all time. The dragon has a scar like that around its neck, a ring where the scales no longer grow. Right at the place where my great grandfather took its head off with the ax. It still carries those marks and it always will."

Juoth would not look at him. Looking instead down over the countryside and then up at the mountains and anywhere but at his eyes.

"Well?"

"You mean magic." A weight to the words.

"I do."

Juoth pulled back on the reins with the hand without the glove and brought the horse's head up and went past Brack on the side of the road. Not turning his head and his back straight. Brack watched him go and turned the horse with him but did not follow. Leaning forward and resting his arms. Then he said:

"You think I'm wrong?"

Juoth stopped and did not turn. Facing forward and only forward and his words swept back on the wind. "There is no such thing as magic."

Brack smiled. "There is and I've seen it."

"You think someone used magic to bring a dragon that was killed two hundred years ago back to life. That's what you think."

"Believe what you want. I have no other explanation for it."

Juoth wheeled then, his eyes flashing. "There are a thousand. The dragon didn't die. The story you heard is wrong.

Your great grandfather didn't kill it at all. It is a different dragon. Pick the one you like. They're all more likely than magic."

Brack did not answer then but just looked at him and they two sat in the road. Far off on the wing, a bird called, a low and sorrowful sound that carried to them over endless distance and the bird itself not even visible in the sky. But returning now to these lands in which it lived, the dragon far off and searching elsewhere for its prey. At long last Juoth turned the horse again and kept on down the road and Brack watched and then followed him and beside them the small mountains rose with their stone caverns and the secrets they kept.

The Dragon Hunt

Chapter Eleven

I

They took the road on into the evening and about them the cedars rose up to saw the sky and the stones grew to great heights so that the road went through them and it was like riding in canyons of shadow and darkness and the ground littered there with smaller stones as if at some time long ago a stonemason twice the size of any man alive in the world which they inhabited had come and crouched and there inscribed some words or shapes now lost to the wind and rain and age. These small stones the mere chippings of his work. That unfathomable giant a ghost now moving in this place.

Perhaps the shapes and names carved there of gods and dragons.

It was in one of these passes that a shadow fell over them. The two stones between which they rode had in millennia past been one, and it had split in a jagged line down the middle at some time unknown. Both sides towering twenty feet above them and four times that long. The road well worn and many travelers having taken this path. Moss and lichen covering these new faces and on the top cedars growing from the very stone itself and their thin roots moving under the moss like veins.

The horse shied and stumbled as the shadow fell and in

that heartbeat Brack knew how they'd ridden themselves into this prison on their own and there was nowhere to run. Dragonfire could fill the slender canyon like a molten tide, the flames rolling over themselves and billowing up to scorch the sky. Men and horses both turned to ash. The smoke of their bodies spinning skyward to mix with the clouds and perhaps later to return them to the fields and dirt and thus to complete the cycle that all men must make.

Juoth was off his horse faster than could be followed, sliding with barely a movement and bringing the bow up as he fell. The arrow nocked before he touched the ground and drawn as he crouched. Brack did not dismount but swung also the crossbow from the saddle with its bolt already in place and twisted upward to track the beast on the wing.

They waited and the minutes ground by and nothing came. Neither shadow nor the beast itself. He held the bow aloft on shaking arms and the horse pranced slightly and when he finally put it down he half expected the shadow to return and mock his lack of vigilance, but it did not.

Juoth turned and looked at him as he pulled himself back atop the horse. His breathing heavy. "Maybe it was just a bird."

"If it was I haven't seen one like it before."

"There are a lot of things you haven't seen."

"There are a lot I have."

Sitting then in silence and breathing the world's bones and the predestination etched in them. The time now for flight but standing in that place and waiting. For a man who believes his death is upon him must know and all else falls aside and he will find out or he will die and in doing learn that the fates have cast their lots and he has come up wanting. But he must know and he will always do what he can to know and so they waited to see what would come to them and nothing did.

For now and in this ringing silence, both of them alive. The shadow of the beast fallen and fled. They were a long time looking at the sky and then finally they put their heels into the horses and went on through that canyon and out the other side and still there was nothing in the sky to see and they rode on. But the feeling remained in his spine for a long time and he rode with the crossbow in his hands and when it got heavy he shifted it and would not put it down.

After a time the ground began to rise more below them and the road twisted in and ran along the side of a sheer stone cliff. The cracks running upward through the red and gray rock and the marks of the water coming down and at some points ledges where birds sat and looked down and called to them. Along the roadside a flashing of metal and Brack looked to it as they passed and saw an ancient breastplate in the tall grass and above it a man's skull. The lines and cracks in it like the ledges above and all the rest of him gone and Brack could imagine this man trying for reasons that would forever be his own to climb that cliff in his armor and the stone loose and dusted beneath his fingers. Eventually those fingers slipping off and the man's scream as he fell and the shower of stone around him as his body first slid and then dropped free of the wall and he fell in nothingness to his end. His broken body food for the wolves that stalked out of the timber at night with their eyes yellow and luminous.

When they came to the pass where they would move up and through the mountains and into the plain, it was tall around them and a stream ran through the center, moving swiftly with them over the smooth stones. Banks of grass and scrub trees. A dirt path where those who did not want to go in the water went up the side, but they ignored it and walked the horses into the stream and it flowed about their legs with the hair brown and dark and the water breaking cool and swirling around them.

Juoth stood his horse and turned in the saddle. Looking up at the high walls rising on either side. "You want to get out of it?"

"I don't see how."

"It's like the stone, but I can't see the end." Nodding in the direction they traveled. The canyon again pinning them on both sides, a beautiful channel for destruction and death.

"You think it's the fastest?"

He nodded.

"All right."

They went on, looking again to the sky. But Juoth more than Brack, for Juoth knew dragons and how they hunted and what they would do to prey trapped in a flowing river by stone walls, and Brack knew this dragon and what it wanted and it was leading them and drawing on strings and they were following as they were told. But it would not kill them here for if it was just the kill that it wanted, it could have had it long ago.

They'd ridden this stream on the dripping horses for just over two hours when they found the dead girl.

II

The man was kneeling in the stones at the edge of the stream with the girl's head in his lap and her hair light and soaked and flowing in the river, twisting in the current. He had his head down and he looked up as they came around the bend. His beard thin and dark on his face, his eyes wide, his hands on the girl's arms as they lay limply at her sides. The color gone from all of it. Washed from the world. Her feet in the water and already a dull gray though Brack knew she had not been dead long.

They drew the horses up and stood them and looked at the man and his jaw worked and he did not say anything. Did not raise his hand to them in greeting or to fend them off. Brack looked at him for a moment and then got down from the horse and went to them.

There was less blood than there should have been and all he could think was that the river had taken it and with her heart still and dead in her chest that was the end of it. The break jagged along her temple. The rock lying there in the short weeds. He could see the laceration and within it the ripped skin now turning white and even under that the white of her skull where it had broken. There were no other wounds on her body and it had taken her all at once.

"You do this?" Brack said. His voice quiet, the sword heavy on his back. His feet wide and his arms folded, still a distance of two strides between them.

The man shook his head and looked back at her and said something and Brack could not tell what it was. His voice was gone. A dull rasp in his throat and nothing more.

"Look," Juoth said from atop the horse. Pointing with the gloved hand.

The other man lay in the weeds up along the bank. His throat cut and the whole front of him soaked in blood and the flesh a deep and sickly red. His hands lay on his chest and were coated in blood as if he'd died trying to hold its flow within his body. He did not have on a shirt nor pants but just his underclothes and they were stained and ruined. There were two more cuts on his face but they had not mattered as his life slipped between his fingers and he fell. This also done quickly for there was not a mark on the man sitting with the woman's head in his lap.

Brack knew how it had happened and he did not ask and walked forward and knelt by the man. "Did you know him?" he said.

"No." His voice still rough but able to be heard at this distance. "Met him down in Canntal. He was selling a horse for food and asked if he could go with us through the pass. Said it was safer that way in case there were thieves. We've been traveling with him now a week, eight days. I don't know."

"A week."

The man nodded. He had not let go of the girl and he would not.

Brack looked down at her and could not tell her age. Perhaps once she had been beautiful with her slight build and long hair but now the whiteness stole her body and made her an ancient thing, a crone with two hundred years and a withered form. He looked away again.

"Your wife?"

The man shook his head. "My sister."

He had not expected that and all at once he thought of Kayhi as she came up to him on the wall, calm and strong and terrified. Telling him of the men and the progress. Kissing her forehead and sending her down to the cities and thinking even then that he shouldn't have done it but not knowing what else to do or the hell it all would become and now it was done.

"You can ride with us," he said.

The man shook his head. "I can't leave her."

Brack spoke softly. "We can bury her. If you still want to go through the pass, ride with us."

"I won't."

"It'll be weeks walking."

"I won't bury her."

"And what will you do instead?"

The man looked off down the river the way they were going. Where the land rose up and curved again into the cedars. Moving toward the higher pass where they would go through. "I have to bring her."

Brack looked up at Juoth and the other man said nothing. His face unreadable.

"We can't bring her," he said.

The man sat and looked at him. Brack did not see the knife and did not know his thoughts but knew he was thinking of meeting the other man who had been selling his horse. In whatever place that man now inhabited. That other side of life. He let him take the time he needed to run it through and then he stood.

"All right," Brack said. "All right."

The man looked back at him and his eyes were lost but in them was something moving and it was desperate and frantic and Brack did not like it but he could think of nothing but Kayhi and in things like that there was only the illusion of choice and nothing real.

III

They rode with the man behind him and the girl rolled in a blanket and lashed on the horse behind Juoth. It was the only way and they knew it and hated it and rode all the same. The young man looking over at her all the time and saying something to himself again and again and Brack trying not to listen for there were some things he did not want to know.

The river curved up and then they lost it through the rocks and the road split away and climbed toward a worn peak. Loose stone and shale beneath the horses' hooves and once they got down and walked them, all slipping in the stones, until moss and roots took hold and they could ride again. When they came out on the top of that peak it was not the summit but they could see it from there and they stood the horses for a time in the sun and looked out about them. The mountain now a long thin plain running away in rises and valleys and the river far down below and sparkling in the sun and the forest slipped away and down below a great distance.

A thin finger of black smoke rose back the way they'd come. Slightly twisted as it moved toward the clouds. Three vultures circled it on the air and hung there, those false birds of prey that were cowards and worse. Brack looked at them and thought of the farmer and his family and could not know and cursed anyway and looked away.

"It could be anything," Juoth said.

"This your first day riding with me?"

"Could be a barn burning down. A field being cleared. Any damn thing."

"Could be." He spit the words and scowled and thought even then he could smell the smoke and everything in it.

"Don't make things that aren't there. What we have is enough."

"There's a difference between making and knowing."

"I know there is."

"Well."

"Well what?"

"Well this is the difference. This right here."

"I don't think it is."

They rode down a little way into the valley and made their camp in a copse where two trees had fallen one atop the other, each as high as Brack's waist even lying down, forming a windblock and the wall of the camp. Others had been there in times past and there were the remains of three fires, each older than the last, and who knew how many built atop each other on each spot. The camp was meager and they had little and soon Juoth had one of the fires going again and he was cooking and the young man was taking his dead sister off the horse.

Brack rose and held her thin body and the man nodded at him and worked the knot loose.

"She was older than you," Brack said.

"I'm no boy."

"I didn't say you were."

"I'll be twenty in the spring. She'll be twenty-six."

Brack noted how he said it and did not say anything. The boy got the knot loose and pulled the rope through itself and cursed and licked his finger where it was shot through with rope splinters and wiped his hand on his pants and pulled the rope again. It came all the way off and he took her by the feet and Brack by the shoulders and they set her on the ground. Near the logs where nothing would come to her in the night without first passing them.

"What's your name?" Brack said.

"Varin," the boy said. Offering nothing for his sister.

They tied and watered the horses with the bags they'd filled in the river and set them to grazing on the far side of the camp and Brack looked once to see if the smoke was still rising and it was too dark to tell and this camp too low. All about the trees stretching and the sun on the far side of the mountain and everything here in shadow. In this hollow where they hid like animals from all the world offered.

Juoth had shot a rabbit with his bow and he had it on a spit over the fire and they sat and watched it while it cooked. The fat snapping as it hissed in the flames. Brack closed his eyes and opened them again. When it was done Juoth took it down and cut it into pieces and threw two to each of them and they ate and it was too hot and very good.

The darkness was complete then and Brack watched the horses. They would know if the dragon was coming and they would try to run and perhaps it would save them. Perhaps not, but they had nothing else. They sat for a long time and Juoth sang softly some song of the Island Kingdoms and the boy watched him with rapt attention and the song wound a mournful tale through the hills. When it was done the boy lay down on the flat ground near his sister and put his hands under his head and looked at the sky where the stars were breaking and the dark expanse covered in them.

It was some time later in the deep night that Brack woke and for a moment did not know where he was and then remembered and lay very still to hear that which had woken him. The fire down to nothing but red embers, the stars covered now in cloud. The boy talking in the darkness. Brack rolled slowly and looked and he was gone from where he'd slept and so was the blanket and his sister's body.

Chapter Twelve

I

He stood slowly and listened and he did not know the
words the boy was saying. Some tongue foreign or perhaps lost.
A language now dead in the world but for the few who carried it
and to what end he knew not. Juoth was lying there in the dark
with his eyes open and Brack nodded to him and he stood also
and they walked to the voice.

The boy was not far off and kneeling in a shallow stream.
The water moving slow and quiet below them over smooth
stones. Dark as pitch, the only light from the moon breaking at
times through the cloud cover. His sister's hair flowed all out
around her head like some veil or burial shroud pulled back and
she floated on the surface of the water as if her very bones and
flesh and waterlogged skin held no weight at all. The boy
kneeling beside her and both hands on her forehead and
covering her eyes. The skin of both stark white against the
darkness when the moon fell.

Juoth moved to step from the trees and toward them, but
Brack reached and put a hand on his chest.

The boy spoke into the wind and it was as if in his throat
burned the very embers of the fire. Stolen in the night and
placed between his lips as some delicacy of another world, then

swallowed and now lodged there in his throat, twisting and burning and blistering the flesh, devouring his words and giving each utterance a guttural sound. A wicked and lost language. Even with the meanings of the words unknown, filled with a hatred and depth.

They stood and watched him for time unknown. In later days Brack would remember and think it had been but a minute before the boy turned his head to them and his eyes were on fire. Other times he would think it was hours, the night somehow suspended and lashed where it was, the moon hanging in its movements and waiting for this thing to be done. He would turn both over in his mind and he could never sort one from the other or decide which to trust and eventually he stopped trying.

For all that had mattered then was the boy's sneering face, his lips drawn back over his teeth. His eyes burning orbs, no smoke or flame moving out and up his flesh, but all contained like fire raging in a globe of glass or ice. Swirling around on itself. Iris and pupil lost in the inferno. Impossible to know what he saw or if all vision was stripped from him.

Even at that distance, Brack could feel the heat coming off of him.

And then he blinked, and his eyes were black. The color of coal or soot or night itself. All light lost and suddenly a great darkness in the thin forest. A stream of tar moving under a moonless sky, the clouds sweeping back across as if protecting the heavens themselves from what this was.

Not a sound in that darkness.

Then again the boy blinked, and the darkness was gone. His eyes were normal, just white orbs with the pupils dilated. The moon back to cast his face in harsh relief. His own skin and his sister's not that different, both like poured wax. He looked at them for a moment and breathed once long and heavy and then fell forward, slowly, and splashed face down in the running water.

They went forward and pulled him out and his sister also. Both in their sodden clothing. The boy did not make a sound and when Brack rolled him on his back and laid him by the fire his eyes were back in his head and all white. They stripped him of shirt and pants and Juoth gathered wood and got the fire up again and burning hot.

A risk here in the night, a signal to the beast that could be turning silently in that dark air, but without it the boy would die. It was warmer on the road and in the lower country but not as warm as it would be in the plains, at this elevation, and the water had been very cold. They laid his clothes out next to him and Brack gathered heavier wood to keep the fire going and then they sat down and watched it burn and for a long time neither one said anything. Checking the boy at intervals to make sure he was still breathing.

Then Juoth said: "What do you think?"

"About what?"

"Should we ride?"

He looked at the horses and then the boy and the girl's body. It would not be hard to mount up and leave them here and if the boy woke and wanted to go on as he had been going, so be it. And if not then he was already dead and it made no difference.

"No," he said.

"Why?"

"You can leave if you want."

"I didn't say I was leaving. I asked you why."

"And I'm telling you you can leave."

"And I'm telling you what I asked."

Brack pursed his lips, looked away in the direction of the city. Kayhi perhaps waiting for him there if she had made it through the pass. Perhaps dead in that snow but he didn't think so and if she was then he'd already lost her and it didn't matter.

And then he looked back at the boy and tried not to think of him with his eyes on fire and he looked at the dead sister and swallowed what he felt coming and shook his head.

"I don't know," he said.

"You always make decisions you don't know why you made them?"

"I make decisions for a lot of reasons and that's one of them."

Juoth was silent and Brack thought he would stand and curse him or rise in silence and go to his own horse and leave, but he did not. He looked at him for a long moment and then tipped his head back and laughed. Sighed. Shook his own head as if mocking him and said:

"You're a hell of a lot like your grandfather, you know that? Stubborn as a damn mule."

Brack smiled and watched the fire warm the boy and wondered when he would come back and said: "People always did say we shared a lot. Especially when he was younger."

II

It was two hours later when the boy woke gasping and sat up straight and gasped again and held his knees and then looked at them with wide eyes. The sun was rising behind the mountain and neither of them had slept and when he sat up Juoth put his hand on his knife but did not draw it. Brack did not move but just watched him and especially the eyes and what was in them.

The boy blinked a few times and worked his jaw and then looked at his sister's body. Reached out and put a hand on her arm and took it back and sat staring and then turned back to them.

"What happened?" he said.

"You tell me," Brack said.

"I'm asking you."

"I know you are."

The boy half started to reach again for his sister and then did not. He was looking down at his hands and he looked like he was trying to figure something out and could not put it together but could feel it or the shadow of what it was. Turning his hands over and over. Finally he put them in the dirt and looked back up and he looked afraid.

"I don't know. I don't know."

"What do you know?"

He licked his lips and tried to stand and grimaced and sat back against that tree, the trunk old now and rotting from the inside. "I remember waking up in the night. Going down to the river. Then nothing else. Just right now." He reached out and touched the bottoms of his pants where they had not been close enough to the fire to dry and he pinched them between his fingers. "What happened to my pants?"

"You went in the river," Brack said. "We found you kneeling in it."

"Kneeling in it."

"Yes."

"Then what?"

Juoth stood up. Looked at Brack for a moment, his eyes like flint. Then he turned and walked off in the darkness in the direction of the path. They could hear him walking in the loose stones for a while and then they couldn't hear him anymore and Brack imagined him sitting there in the half dark and wondered what thoughts turned in his head like the boy's hands and did not know.

"Why'd you do it?" Brack said.

"Why'd I do what?"

"You know what you did."

"I'm telling you I don't."

"I don't care what you're telling me."

The boy looked away and then back at his sister and Brack knew and had known but wanted him to say it and to see if he was telling the truth when he said he didn't know. He couldn't imagine it worked that fast but it might and that was important. So he waited and eventually the boy met his eyes.

"It didn't even work."

"You don't know that."

"Look at her."

"I am looking at her. What is it supposed to do and where'd you learn it?"

The boy looked up the path where Juoth had gone. "Is he afraid of me?"

"I don't know. I've only known him a short time myself. But he doesn't want to believe in it."

"But he does."

"Yes."

"It's," the boy said. Then stopped. Licked his lips and turned toward the fire. Closing his eyes as if he couldn't say it to anyone else but knew he had to and so could only say it if he wasn't looking at anyone and it was just him behind his eyes and maybe the whole world gone from before him. "It's supposed to bring her back."

"To bring her back to life?"

"If it works."

Brack was quiet and went and took up another log from the stack of them and put it on the fire. Moving it carefully so that it sat across the others that were there and formed a bridge. The fire licking up greedily at the sides. The smoke rising and no fear now of the dragon for if it was coming to the fire it would have come already. He watched the log catch and put another crosswise over it and then went back and sat down again.

"You think it will work?"

The boy shrugged and his shoulders looked very small. "I

read it in a book. I don't know if I did it right. It wasn't hard."

"Magic never is. It's very, very easy. You just have to know what's asked. Follow those things, and in that order. You did it correctly."

"How do you know?"

"I saw you. If you could have seen yourself, you'd know. Did you really forget?"

"It's like a dream. You know it but it's not solid. I remember it a little."

"But less now than when you first woke."

"A bit."

It was already happening and Brack knew he could not stop it and he did not know if the boy knew what it would do to him or not, but there was no point in telling him now, for the thing was done. When a man was dying with an arrow in his heart or his throat cut out you didn't tell him he was dying and the boy was not dying but it was the same. He watched him and the boy was very stiff and Brack thought he knew and had done it anyway.

"Can I still come with you to the city?" the boy said. "Will you still take us?"

"Can I?"

"I don't know what you mean."

"I mean if I take you, am I going to wish I hadn't?"

"No."

The boy couldn't tell him that and know it but Brack looked at him and felt like it was true all the same. They were only a few days' ride out now and he did not know how much time he had but he felt it would be enough.

He held out his hand, palm up, the dark leather glove wet below the place where the fingers were cut off. He hadn't known he'd been clenching his hands but he could now feel the ache in them. "Give me your knife."

The boy took it out of his belt and handed it across. He

had not cleaned the blood and it was dried on the blade and Brack put it into his own belt. A short blade, maybe a hunter's knife. Made for gutting a whitetail in the forest and nothing more, but he'd seen the highwayman and it was enough.

"I'll take you to the city," Brack said. "And your sister. When we get there, you're on your own. I want nothing more to do with this."

"That's fine."

"Damn right it is."

The fire was burning up now and the new logs were ablaze. Tongues of flame rising from the corners of the wood and the logs blackened around them and the bed of embers below. The wind came through the tops of the oaks and shook loose a shower of leaves and they fell in a small scattering into the field and one came down and spun and flicked on the updraft and settled its battered parchment on top of the fire. The edges curling and then the glow from the inside out as the center burned and soon it was nothing but ash.

III

Juoth came back after a time and would not speak to the boy and they mounted the horses with the dead girl on behind him and rolled in the blanket and the boy with Brack and they rode out as the fire died in their wake. The trail now moving down through the meager forest of rawboned trees and the horses picking their way over rocks enshrouded in lichen. Smaller rocks pushing through the moss and needles of the trail, roots breaking the ground. It was slow going but the horses were surefooted and they went down a long way until they came to a meadow.

In the meadow were two rams and each standing and looking at the other and neither looking at the men on horseback. One pawed and they both lowered their heads and ran hard and long and came together. It was a sound like a rock splitting. The rams both stumbled and shook their heads with the heavy spiraled horns and looked at one another and without turning began to walk backward until they stood again at a slightly greater distance. Each eyeing the other. Then one pawed and they ran again.

They went up the side of the meadow where a thin waterfall came over the cliff and dismounted to drink and looked down at the rams where they still fought and then remounted and rode off and never had the rams acknowledged them, so intent were they each on the other's destruction. For a long time they could hear them striking as they went and always that same heartbeat to the sound.

IV

As the day drew to a close they rode in the falling dusk and the horses streaked with dirt and Brack felt the boy moving behind him. Shifting as if to look again at his sister. He had done this many times and Brack did not think much of it and then the boy said:

"We were coming out of the sea with golden sails. The wind was behind us and we could see the other ship sinking on the horizon and we didn't turn back."

Brack closed his eyes. Thinking of an old man in Gadilion and a cup in his hand. Meager coins rattling within. Then he opened his eyes again and the trail stretched out before them through a stand of birches. The ends of the branches were dead, perhaps beset by plague or beetle, and all about the roots of the trees lay their own branches where they'd broken and fallen in the wind. Below the leaves still green and above withered and that death moving down to the roots.

"When was it?" he said.

"What?" the boy said.

"When did you sail?"

The boy was quiet then. Brack waited for some time for him to answer and he did not and after enough time had gone by, he knew he never would. They continued on and Brack felt him move again to look at his sister and then it was getting too dark for the horses to see the trail and so they came to a place where that trail widened and pulled the horses into the clearing. No fires here but plenty of wood and a good place to see both in front and behind.

Juoth got down and they tied the horses and then he unlashed the girl and moved her limp form to the side of the clearing and laid her down. The boy watched this intently and Brack watched the boy. Juoth looked at the girl a long time and then Brack saw that he was smelling the air above her and looking at her and then he shook his head and moved away from her and began to gather wood for the fire.

Brack still watched the boy and he went and stood beside his sister. Then knelt. Putting a hand on her chest, her forehead. He sat back on his haunches next to her and he stayed there a long time and eventually Brack went to the horse and got down the crossbow and left the camp. Nodding at Juoth as he went.

It was not good forest for deer but it was for rabbit and he took one and then recovered the bolt and took another with the same one. Checked the fletching and found it still intact and put the bolt back after he cleaned it in a stream. Took the boy's knife out and cleaned it too and thought for only a moment of the highwayman's body lying beside the road with blood on his chest and fingers and then used the knife to split the rabbits and take out the entrails. The hair was thin and came off easily and he butchered them and threw aside what was left for the wolves. Far from the camp. Then walked back in with the meat in a bag at his side and found Juoth had the fire going and hot and a spit already made over it.

The boy was sitting still beside his sister and looking

down the trail and not seeing it. The glaze over his eyes of some faraway place.

Juoth stood from the fire and came over. Motioned toward the boy with his head. The line of twisted skin there where it would scar and the short hair growing back around it. "He hasn't said a damn thing. Just sat there like that."

"You talk to him?"

"I tried."

"He didn't tell you anything about a ship sinking?"

"A ship?"

"A ship going down."

"Didn't even open his mouth. Just sat there."

Brack took the rabbit meat from the bag and went over to the fire and started putting it on the spit. It was hard with the pieces and he wished he had kept the rabbits whole to roast them but he knew he'd done the right thing for the wolves and eventually he got them on and moved the spit across the fire so that the heat and smoke would reach them and the flames would not.

"What do you think?" Juoth said.

"About the boy."

"Yes. Look what he's doing."

"I know what he's doing."

"Well."

"You do too." Brack looked up. He could hear the rabbit cooking. "You know what's happening to him and you can act like you don't and that won't change it. That won't change any of it."

Juoth did not answer. After a while the rabbit was cooked and they took it off the spit and ate it with their hands. There were ten pieces and when they'd had enough Brack took the ones that were left over to the boy and held them out to him. He did not take them, but did look at Brack in the same way that he'd been looking at the trail. When he'd held them for long enough Brack took the boy's hand and put the two pieces into it and folded his fingers closed over them and then the boy held them. He went back and sat by the fire and when he looked back again a few minutes later the boy was eating the rabbit, pulling it apart with his teeth, ripping each piece off and holding it up to the moonlight and nodding and then eating it. One and then the next and then the next.

Chapter Thirteen

I

She sat in that pestilent darkness and leaned her head back against stone both cold and wet and watched him come to her in the shadows. He moved like a thing very long imprisoned, picking his way with a strict care and silence. Looking always at the door and stopping to listen and on his face endlessly the hint of a smile, as if he possessed some knowledge the rest of the world did not but which it craved at every turn. He came through that gloom and sat next to her and for a long time said nothing and then said:

"It's time."

She held a hand up, the chains rattling. Black and rusted and unbreakable. She had tried many times when she first arrived and then given up and now they were a part of her the way that the changing of the guard marked time. Her world and all that it contained.

He nodded. "You're ready to cut them?"

"I won't have a week."

"I know."

He leaned back against the wall and closed his eyes and when he closed them he looked very old and she became all at once afraid that he would die. But then he opened them again and that light was still in them and he said: "I'm a young man, you know. A—"

And then he stopped and his mouth hung open for a moment as if he had forgotten it and he blinked twice and then looked at her and turned his head to the side and closed his mouth. Looking very calm, as if expecting nothing, as if not knowing that he had just been speaking. He nodded once and looked away across the room.

"Are you all right?" she said.

"Mountains fall," he said.

She'd forgotten how it made her feel and it was as if her vertebrae were all ice. A sudden and cold feeling as it moved in spine and nerve and bone. She swallowed hard and was very aware of her own chains and that she could not run and she watched him carefully.

"Mountains fall and worlds turn," he said. "I've told you with the young goat and you've not listened. But they fall as they fall as they fall."

Now he looked at her and he was gone. There was no other word for it. In his eyes was another man or the lack of a man altogether. A great and hollow emptiness where once he had been. That light of youth in old eyes replaced by nothing and more of the same. She did not know if he saw her or not or if it was even to her that he spoke.

Then he reached over calmly and said: "Have you heard?"

She moved to the side just slightly and he did not follow. His hand extended as if wanting something. Asking perhaps for coins in the drizzling rain, a vagrant under a bridge. A child perhaps in need of food. The fingers slightly bent and white at the ends and it was then that she saw he was barely breathing. His chest moving like that of a man already looking into death's realm and seeing him there in his robes and steadying himself for that meeting.

"The mountains fall," he said. "They always fall."

146

She did not speak and he looked over at her for a long time and then finally he lowered his head to his chest and he slept. His breath still shallow but in sleep at least in constant time and growing stronger. She wanted to wake him and did not and just watched him sleep. Hearing the guards changing in the hall and not knowing what she would do were they to come in and find him there.

When he opened his eyes again, they had changed back. He blinked as he had before and looked at her.

"It's time," he said.

"What's happened to you?" she said.

He looked at her a long moment and she could see tears in his eyes. There contained and pooling, but also something else. A deep-rooted fear like someone standing on a snow bridge over a great crevasse and understanding only at some vast midpoint that it was snow and ice and not stone and suddenly feeling the distance below them in a different way as from the bottom that bridge crumbled and the burning sun rose over the mountains.

"I don't know," he said. "I don't remember." He raised a hand, touched his face. His temple. "But I know that it's time. I know it."

"Time for what?"

He motioned to the chains. "Don't wait. You have enough time but you must do it now and you must run. For what is coming is coming. I know it. You must run."

She leaned forward, curiosity pushing away the fear. This broken man, his mind splintered and cracked, within him in pieces. First one and then the other and maybe more. "What's coming?"

"I don't know," he said again. "But I know you have to do it now or it's going to be too late. You have to believe me."

She looked toward the door. The silent guards beyond. Impossible to know when they would come and when they would not. Days or hours or minutes.

He reached up and took her chin in his fingers. The flesh thin and drawn and very cold. Turned her head toward him where he was crying and his face tracked with it. Rivers in the mud of years upon his skin. "Please," he said. "Mountains fall and worlds turn."

II

She set to the chains and the file was very small and it was very slow. In the first hour just working to make a small track in the link where the file would follow. The blade moving first to one side and then the other. In the end she had to make small, slow movements, always drawing the file toward herself and watching the line carefully. Over and over on that black metal.

And then it began to bite. Slowly at first, but she could feel it catch. The resistance on both sides. The file would no longer jump the line and she could move first backward and then forward. Doubling her speed. The movement still so slow that she could not see the work, but each time the groove just a little deeper, a little closer.

He watched her work and muttered to himself. First about the worlds and mountains. Then leaning against the wall in silence. Returning to ask her how it was coming and to tell her it was time. Then walking away into the shadows and muttering again things she could not make out and coming back and sitting beside her. At times alarmed and at others unconcerned.

Her progress in that darkness like trying to dig a grave without any tools. Clawing dirt and stone with broken fingernails. Painful in its slowness.

But progress all the same.

"How do you know?" she asked him at one point. The groove now deep and clear.

"I can see it."

"What can you see?"

He did not answer. She glanced at him and could see that he was himself, but he did not want to answer. She stopped filing and he looked very quickly at her and then shook his head.

"Tell me or I'll stop."

"There are many futures," he said. "I can see them all. There is one where you don't cut them and what follows is a horror like we've never known. There is another where you cut them and you look back for me and you are found and then it returns to the first. And there is still another where you run and then I can't see you. But in this one you are gone and this is the one that must be."

She could not speak. She had known he would say something she would not believe but she had not thought it would be that. "You're a seer."

He shook again that old and frail head. "No, I am just a man. I don't know how I see it. But I saw it before they brought you here and I knew I had to wait and when you came you were the same as what I saw." Waving a hand about them. "This time, when you can cut them without being found. The ladder I was to make, the bars I had to remove. You climbing them and going up through the window and running."

"You see all of that?"

"As if it already was. I see it the way you remember yesterday. Like it happened, but I know it did not. A memory that has yet to be created."

"How?"

"I don't know," he said. "That's what I don't remember. All I remember is being here and waiting for you. Helping you." He smiled and it was sad and thin. "And now you're here and I've done what I've always known I would do."

She could find no words for that and she set back to work

and the link grew thinner. She would need to cut first one side and then the other. Unless she could bend the link open when the first side was cut, but she did not think she could. The file would have to be sharp enough. Then she could cut the other hand.

She knew if she asked him he would tell her it was sharp enough. This man who had watched her cut that link already.

"How long have you been here?" she asked.

He shrugged those thinbone shoulders and raised a hand. "My memories of before were lost. Maybe they're traded. I don't remember being anywhere else."

"Ever?"

"No."

She stopped then but not to make him talk. Just to look at him. Her own imprisonment so short compared to this man who knew nothing else and had been here in that sense all his life. She did not know if he was telling the truth about what he saw for the future but she knew he had helped her and there was little else to bet on. And looking at him there in the jail she knew he was not lying about what he remembered, or at least did not know that he was.

And that had to be enough.

She worked then and forgot the time. Everything was just the movement of the file. Back and forth endlessly and each stroke seeming to accomplish nothing, but the cut in the link growing deeper all the time. She heard the guards often and they never came in and he did not even glance toward the door when they passed, so sure was he that they would not.

III

She began to climb and she felt as if she were being born anew, the violence and struggle to emerge into air and life. Each handhold loose with grime and dust. Slipping once the first time and falling back to the ground from only the third step and all the air out of her and lying there by her husband's bones and the old man standing over her and saying nothing but blinking rapidly and waiting for her to recover.

And then she stood and climbed again. For it was the only way and the thing she must do.

Now it was not only for herself. It was for the people who still thought she led them. Her people. She could die falling from the top of this ladder or squeezing through the small gap in the bars or running down the street to find archers on the walls. But she must do it and she would risk that for at least in death no one could blame her for her failure.

And she could not blame herself.

For how many would die if her son took them to war? The men and boys would die in the fields, lying in mud made from dirt and their own blood. War was glorious when the army stood flashing in the sun and marched out in a long and invincible column, but it became its true self when men were cut down by others they hadn't seen, the battle raging. Lying in the fields and gasping for breath that would not come, staggering with a cut throat and a shower of blood no one could quell, calling out for lovers or mothers as they tried to hold their slick entrails in with a hand and could not.

The rest would die in the villages. Run under by advancing armies that took food, clothing, women. Leaving the towns stripped bare. Other villages burned as examples or because they harbored soldiers. Still others destroyed as battles swarmed over them, men and horses and a torrent of bloodshed to leave only broken buildings and shattered bodies behind.

Her people would suffer, and they would die. In greater numbers than she could count. To be written out in the next history by the victors, a forgotten and faceless multitude of the dead.

And so she climbed. For them, she climbed.

He watched her from below and did not speak. She knew somewhere within her that he would be killed and she thought he knew it also and so she'd told him of the war. He had not asked nor responded, but she wanted him to know. It made it easier to think he was risking his life for the people and not for her alone. She clung to that, not knowing if it was true or not.

Not knowing exactly who it was that needed to believe.

She'd asked him to come and he'd said nothing. Asked again into the silence. But she knew he had not seen himself in that future and so he already knew he would not come and there was little more to it for a man who remembered what he had yet to do.

Halfway up she could really start to see the light. Early morning in the city. The shadows moving in that light. People walking down the dirt road to the stores, a wagon going to the market. Men and women calling out. The city waking up, but not yet fully awake. The sun on the horizon in a bold orange as it rose.

She climbed for that light. Every step closer, every handhold. Slipping a second time and feeling it in her stomach and holding on to press herself against the stone. Breathing very hard. In a moment the feeling passed and she placed her hand carefully and surely and moved up the wall. Alive again and unwilling to look below.

And then she was at the bars. They were so far away and then came up all at once and she wrapped her fingers around those which were left, the three in the center torn away, and she held to them and felt more secure than at any time during the ascent. The metal solid and firm in the stone. She pulled her face close and leaned forward to that gap and could not tell if she would fit or not and looked out.

The alley cast in shadow. Empty and desolate now the road. She looked long down to her left and a man was walking around the far corner with something in his arms. The other way was nothing at all, the road running along below the wall, curving away and disappearing. She looked at it and could hear nothing and looked back down finally at the old man below her. He just stood in silence and did not pull his eyes from her. She steeled herself and looked back to check the empty road again and then began to pull herself through the bars.

She thought that someone would come and no one did. The bars tight on both sides of her. Once for a moment she was stuck in that metal claw and then she thought of her husband below and pushed and then she was free. Lying in the dirt of the road and gasping and the sweat running down the back of her neck and it felt like nothing else. Looking down the road and seeing no walls. The chains still hanging from her wrists shortened and shattered.

And then all at once she was terrified. For this freedom she'd dreamed of she now held and at any moment someone would call out and it would fall apart around her and be swept away. Precious and fragile and maybe more precious for that fragility. She looked back at the hole between the bars and thought about what he had said and then turned and ran in that rising sun, her bare feet in the swirling dust, running as the morning light washed out the shadow of the wall.

The Dragon Hunt

Chapter Fourteen

I

The boy woke the next morning and seemed himself and they packed what little they had on the horses and Juoth rode out first into the road with that road falling away below him into the sweeping plains and he trotted his horse sideways and stood it in the road and looked down on that world as it stretched. Brack still pulling the boy up behind him and looking at the dead girl lashed and rolled in her blanket on the other horse. Hauling his mount about by the reins and glancing once more at the camp where they'd left only ash and the grease from the rabbit dried in that ash and the dust from the road rising about them in the early morning sun as the horses pranced.

He rode up to where Juoth waited and looked ahead. It was a long fall through timber and rock and open grass into a valley deep below. The range ran out to both sides of them and a point pushing forward to the west where he could see the thick cedar forest rising up the slope and giving way in that valley to grass alone. He thought he saw a long way down a stone bridge over a gorge but there the trees were thick. Rising on the far side the last hill and much shorter and just glimpsed beyond it—a view they would lose as they rode down—the open and yawning yellow plains.

Above the sky nearly white as if all color had bled from it. An empty firmament without bird or cloud or dragon. He could see Juoth looking with his hand on the bow and as always he knew the dragon's heart and where it would be and so he only looked as he must and knew instantly that the emptiness confirmed that knowledge which he already had. It would not kill them here and yet death clung all about them and he could feel it in his clothes and hair and skin.

The dead girl lashed to the horse.

They rode down in that rising dust and the day began to warm as they went and it was as always farther in life than it had appeared. The slope not heavy but endless and the horses trotting and soon breathing hard and the sun coming up above the range to the right and baking the world. He had not worn his furs again and was glad for it and he began to sweat all the same and the boy also.

They passed halfway down the remains of a mill. This abandoned for many years. A ramshackle house with the roof fallen in and a long storage barn now little more than posts and trusses standing and in the water the old wheel still turning in the current of a small stream. Pieces of the wheel missing and it no longer driving anything but turning all the same. Spinning in revolutions without end. How long it had done so or how many revolutions it had made Brack knew not and thought that no man could know and there was something in that.

He had never seen it in another time but he could imagine what it had been. Everything along this forgotten road now abandoned where once men and horses and cattle and wagons had moved. Women and children also and calling out to one another in the warm sun. Sheep perhaps being driven, carts full of goods. This road the heartblood of some world and seeming to all who used it as if it had always existed and always would and now the lie put to that for few men knew its path and fewer used it.

That life not depleted, but elsewhere. Somewhere other roads with the sounds and life this had once borne. Those too to be abandoned and forgotten in their own time. As others had before and would after.

But here the dragon had never been and Brack saw Juoth looking at him and he did not return it for he knew the other man was no fool and knew he was not hunting but just riding.

They came at noon to the Fall of Revian. A towering stone cliff rising up before them, the rock running up in straight lines to a crest covered to the very edge of the cliff in moss and cedars. The moss running down the face of the rock. The river above entirely lost in the trees but the waterfall pouring out like the rock itself was broken and this river a living thing born from it. Cascading down in showering white and falling over the break in the stone where the road tunneled through. That stone endlessly drenched and dark and the foothills very green where the land moved away from the wall and they rode on through on the stone roadbed and the horses shying at first and then going through the spray. The air full of color and light in the mist, the sound everywhere and filling the world entire for that passage.

Coming out the far side through the gap in the rock with the fall thundering behind them they found a small pool and the ground flattened out around them and they could see little beyond this clearing for the trees. The road picking its way forward ahead of them as the river curved around. Somewhere the bridge and gorge and then the shorter rise of that last hill. Lost now and only the rise visible slightly before them and the jagged mountains at their back. How the descent moved them into this other world.

He pulled the horse up at the edge of the pool and the boy dismounted and he followed and then he led the horse over to the water and put the reins down to let him drink. Juoth doing the same and looking about at these thin trees with their paper bark and the empty sky.

Brack looked at the boy. "You feeling all right? You've been quiet."

"So have you."

"Why don't you tell me something."

The boy went to the water and knelt and drank with it cupped in his hands. Dripping through his fingers and from his chin. Beading brightly. "What is it you want to know?"

"It's you I want to know."

"What's that supposed to mean?"

"It means where'd you come from and how'd you get to be where we found you."

"I told you that." Sitting back on his haunches as if unsure if he wanted another drink or not. "We met a man selling his horse. Told him he could come with us."

"Go back farther. How'd you get there?"

"You figure now you don't trust me? We've been riding for days and just now you decide it."

"I never said I didn't trust you." Brack went also and bent and drank. Perhaps that similarity would put the boy at ease. If not the water was cool and fresh and in its own right a relief. "I just want to find out how you ended up there and where you're going."

The boy looked at him a minute. Squinting into the sun. "All right," he said at last.

II

The story the boy told was this:

He and his sister had set out from a town deep in the mountains, a place with little farming and nothing else and which had been beset with plague. Their parents dead and many others. Rotting bodies in the streets. Those still alive determined to leave and as they left the others burned to the ground every house and store and chapel and barn. The bodies of the dead dragged inside to burn also and the smoke horrible and they rode with their cloaks over their faces until they couldn't smell it anymore and still he could smell it in his cloak for days and at last threw it away and carried on without.

The next town they came to knew where they were from and drove them out in the night. Holed up as they were in a field left fallow. The men came with torches and pulled them from their tent and their bedrolls and put them outside and told them as blades glinted in that torchlight that they'd never be seen again or they would die. His sister pleading and crying. And in the end they left and they walked two weeks with nothing and were almost dead when they came to the third village and there no one knew them.

In this place they found work and it was hard but it was work. The boy a farmer's hand and rising with the sun to work the fields and turn soil and tend crops. The girl also but her duties to the animals. Milking cows and scattering feed for the chickens and when those chickens had fowled their pen moving them as a flock to a new place where they could live while the old sat in rain and sun and turned all back to dirt.

This a small farm and the flock not large and the wages as meager as all that would bring. But they had a place to sleep and food and they needed little else and lived there for some time.

Brack asked him the name of the town and he could not recall. Could say only the name of the farmers they'd lived with but it could have been anyone's name and Brack had met more men with it than he could count.

But this too had come to an end for the blight had followed them and soon the village was sick. The town began to die and the farmer's wife and then the farmer himself fell ill. Laid all day in his bed and the field rotted and the chickens died in their pen and the cattle called to be milked. The boy and his sister at first doing what they could but they could not do it all and then the farmer was dead and they left.

That town did not burn when they were there for the people did not know what was on them or what it would do. But it burned a few days later, he said. They were living then in a cave in the mountains and could look down to that valley and the scattered farms and for seven days people flooded by on that road, some sick and dying and others healthy and terrified and all going where they went. He called out but they would not stop and some looked at him with fear and others told him to run.

He woke that night and the whole valley was fire. He could smell the bodies and somewhere off a man screaming. The next morning they left the cave and the smoke was still heavy and everywhere and the fire was in the timber. Burning and rising and thick. They rode out on the stolen horse with the fire at their backs and hours later when he looked again the whole mountain was in flame and he did not know if it had ever stopped but they continued on.

The fourth town they came to their last. This one the same the boy had named before: Canntal. Here they had looked for work and not found it and already rumors had followed them. The hooded glances of strangers. Men who would not look at them nor speak to them when they asked for work. Talk of plague and fire and a faceless god of wrath or judgment. Others walking these same roads.

And so they had left, he said. Heading for the road and the other man selling his horse for food and people would not speak to him either and they three had set out and hoped perhaps in the plains and not these close mountain towns they would again be unknown and they could carve out for themselves something that was a life.

III

They stood in that depression with the fall roaring and the horses drank their fill and the boy took off his clothes and walked out into the water to wash the rest of the blood from his body. Juoth checking the ropes holding the girl in her blanket and Brack standing beside the horse and looking up the side of the far mountain where starkly silhouetted against the sky moved a line of travelers. All on foot and leading pack animals. Too far away to see anything but the black shapes of their forms where they came out of the trees and walked along the spine of the mountain and then went back into the trees again.

These vagabonds with an unknown origin, a destination the same. Perhaps wandering without end or perhaps even now approaching some place where their journey would cease. He could not hear them over the waterfall and they moved as ghosts. After a time he lost count and then he looked away and when he looked back they were gone as if they had never been.

The boy finished and dried himself with his own shirt and pulled on all but that shirt and held it out to dry in the sun and the thin air and they remounted and moved on. Forward through the stands of trees and here the ground level and easy for the first time in days. Littered always with green and brown needles, those dead and those dying. Shot through with grass. The horses walking slowly and eating as they did. The sun so close to hot now but still a deep cold when they moved through shadows of trees or clouds. The boy shivering and then putting on his shirt when it dried and all three riding in silence.

For perhaps to some others they were the vagabonds and the whole world the opposite of what Brack saw now and those other men and women with their lives and desires and dreams watching them move across the valley floor and disappear into their own trees.

All men so alike and so blinded to it.

It was a half an hour riding through that forest before they came to the edge of the gorge and the old stone bridge standing across it. The span four hundred yards and the bridge as wide as six men lying down and sweeping gently upward as it rose. The rock faces below it red and dark and jagged. Far below the sound of water rushing, but visible from the edge only that sheer face dropping away as if it descended to the center of the earth and the hell that waited there. The stones of the bridge dark with age and ivy running long and heavy along the sides.

They stood the horses in the road and looked at it and Brack looked at Juoth and the other man shrugged. In this all that needed to be said. The horses were shying from the edge and did not want to carry on but they would do it if they were forced and once they were on the bridge itself and those stones too wide to see below they loosened and walked as they should.

Every step hard and echoing and then lost. The rushing of the water now louder and in the air that faint feeling of mist. Everything in cloud and a perpetual wetness.

They passed a man at the crest of the bridge. Walking along in robes dark and heavy and his eyes downcast and nothing on his back and no animal to be seen. He did not look up as they went by and the boy tried to hail him and still he did not look. He was not armed and carried nothing. He stopped as they went by and stood at the edge of the bridge looking the way they'd come and Brack looked back twice as they rode and both times he stood in the same place.

A man now carved of stone. The world and its weight all about him. Perhaps only with that drop below him that weight negated or somehow less.

They came to the far side of the bridge and back to the land and the horses stepped upon it eagerly and they continued on. Brack looked again and could no longer see the man. Thinking about how all this country lay in some sort of silence and wondering what brought it to that. How maybe when a road died all that was left were the dead and the dead did not speak even as they traversed the forgotten pathways of the earth like some grim cartographers seeking always not to cut out for themselves new maps but to force the world itself into agreeance with the old.

It would be a day's climb to the top of the next mountain and Brack pulled the horse up as the ground began to rise again beneath them. Turning to look. The day now in mid afternoon and still with much light but they would not reach the summit and he was thinking perhaps they should camp now and climb it entire in the morning when Juoth said:

"We have to bury her."

The boy got off the horse so fast he nearly fell and in his hand suddenly a knife and Brack called out but had hardly spoken when Juoth turned and leapt from the saddle, pushing with the leg still in the stirrup, and came down on the boy. Lashing out as he hit and the knife glinting and turning in the air and skittering then in the dirt and the boy's cry as both fell to that hardpacked earth and Juoth with his own blade in his gloved hand and pressed to the boy's throat.

"You have something to say?" Juoth said.

The boy worked his jaw and did not speak and his skin as white now as his sister's. Juoth held him for a moment more and the boy closed his eyes and only then did the islander get off of him and let him stand.

"You ever come at me with a knife again and it'll be the last thing you do," he said. "Not all men are like the one you killed in the river."

The boy raised his chin and in his eyes danced fear and pride and determination and he said: "You're not burying her."

"I'm not?"

"You're not."

Juoth scowled and turned to the blanket with the dead girl's body in it and he pointed at it with the knife. "You smell it, boy? Don't tell me you don't smell it."

The boy was silent.

"You know what we have to do."

Brack leaned forward on the saddle and looked up at the rise and thought of her face the way he remembered it and closed his eyes for a long time and then thought also of Kayhi's face and both knew what he was and hated himself for it and opened his eyes again. "We won't bury her," he said.

Juoth looked at him. "We have to."

"I said we'd take them to the city and we'll take them to the city."

"She won't make it that far."

"She'll make it," the boy said.

They stood all three looking at one another and then Juoth grunted and shook his head and mounted his horse. Not looking at the boy again or stopping him when he bent to get his knife. Putting his heels into the horse and sitting far forward and away from the body and starting the climb. Brack watched him go and held out his hand and after a moment the boy gave him the second knife and climbed back up and then they followed.

IV

It was late that night or early morning sitting in the darkness without a fire and the boy standing a ways off and looking toward the lights of the city far down in the plains that Juoth came over and sat in the pale moonlight and looked at Brack.

"I'm sorry," Brack said. "But I told him."

"I know what you told him."

"It's only days now."

"If the weather holds."

"It'll be all right."

Juoth took his knife out and began to move it between his fingers and looked at the boy and back again. Off in the night the calling of some bird Brack hadn't heard in he did not know how long and he knew it really was the plains again. Thinking of other times coming through them both alone and with companies and once with an unquenchable fire at their backs that they could only outrun and pushing the horses for days in the heavy smoke before they found a river and crossed it and there collapsed in exhaustion.

"I know why you don't want to carry her," Brack said. "But there are other things to worry about."

"Maybe we make the boy carry her."

"It's more than that."

Juoth tipped his head, his voice dropping. Looking again toward the boy and back. "With him?"

"It's what he told me," Brack said. "The whole story about him and his sister. It was all a lie."

"All of it?"

"All of it."

"How do you know?"

"I've been in these mountains a long time and there aren't that many towns I haven't heard of and I haven't heard of any he named. Haven't heard of a plague cutting through the mountains. Or people burning their towns and running. None of it. It's all just built so we can't go back and check it. Towns we've never been to where now everyone's dead and his family too and the whole thing. He and that girl and the man they killed the only ones who can back that story up and two thirds of them dead as well."

"You think it's too convenient."

"In my experience if you think it is, it is."

Juoth held up the knife and began to stand. "Then let's just be done with him here. You know he's a liar and we know he killed that man and maybe he killed his damn sister, too. Either way we leave him and we ride on and that's the end of it."

Brack shook his head. "You saw his eyes."

"That doesn't make a difference."

"Everything makes a difference."

"So what, we bring him? Knowing all that we know, we bring him."

Brack nodded. Thinking of the kid lunging and how fast his knife was gone and Juoth on top of him. A boy and not a warrior. Perhaps able to kill another man when the situation presented itself but only if that man was just like him and also older. He was like the men in the village taking up their picks and axes to fight a dragon and none knowing that they carried nothing but kindling to a furnace for none knew what it was to fight a dragon or how quickly he would devour and destroy.

"I don't think he'll try it again and it won't matter if he does," Brack said. "We'll just do what we said and we'll bring him and leave him in the city where someone else can watch him. Then it ends."

"Does it."

"It does."

"You always stick to your word like this?"

"You knew my grandfather," Brack said. Grinning slightly in the half light. "And you already called me a damn mule."

"Then I guess I don't have anyone to blame but myself."

"I guess you don't."

The boy stood looking out for a long time and then went back to where he'd laid the body of his sister and Brack watched him the whole time and when at last a cloud came swiftly over the moon they were all three asleep and around them the world moving in its shadows and depths and turning forever as the night spun on.

Chapter Fifteen

I

She was being hunted and she could feel it crawling beneath her skin, her very bones alive.

Turning off one street and down another and then yet another. The heavy dust of this place rising and breathing it and tasting it there on her tongue. Each street smaller than the last and the buildings closing in and in the fronts of those buildings men and women opening shops or windows and watching her pass in her filth and always running. Feeling as if behind her the castle itself gave chase and swelled and threatened to consume her and she could not put enough distance between them.

In time she could not breathe and she stopped broken and terrified in a shadowed corner at the end of a street. Marking first her exit over a short stone wall, should she need it, and then crouching and breathing and watching the end of the street. Nothing of note there but still watching each one who passed and waiting for him to throw off his workers' cloak and put down the hood and grin in that twisted way and draw his sword. But they were just workers passing and she watched them and slowly her breathing evened and she could think again.

She was lost and thought that may be best for how could

she be found if she herself did not know where she was? She looked up and there were two tall buildings beside her with open windows and wooden shutters and wash hanging in the breeze and she could not see the castle. The buildings shorter on the other side and running away toward the docks. Now in this waiting she could smell the water again and she stood and began making her way toward it.

Walking this time. Forcing herself to keep pace. For everyone saw a woman fleeing with wide eyes and bare feet and no one at all saw a woman in old rags walking like the others about her and only one who knew her could put her face with anything else.

This such a stark difference from the bath and the dress and the court. The cool marble floor, the sconces smoking softly and all that smoke like a river to the vents. The glasses of wine without end and platters of food uneaten.

She reached a line with clothes hanging and went past and looked and came back and left again and cursed herself and went and took one of the shirts off of the line. Covered the shackles where they still hung with the few links of chain about her wrists. The skin there raw and broken and bleeding. She wrapped the shirt around one wrist and tied it and then clasped her hands in front of her so it covered both and again made herself walk slowly and only half succeeded.

When she passed a woman walking alone with a basket she nodded to her and stepped slightly in front of her. The woman looking up and blinking as one not accustomed to this or perhaps dwelling in some other thought.

"I'm looking for a tavern," she said. "The Golden Head."

The woman just looked at her for a moment, then shook her head. "I don't know it."

"Thank you." Trying to leave. Already lingering too long.

"But it's not here."

"What?"

The woman looked at her and down to the shirt at her wrists and back to her eyes. Pursed her lips. "Nothing around here called that."

Arisine watched her go and twice the woman looked back at her and her eyes darting and then she stepped into a small shop and began speaking. About the day's work or the harvest or a prisoner queen in the streets. Arisine hurried on and took the next two turns without reason and looked over her shoulder the whole time and did not see the woman again and never would. But she felt her there behind her for a long time.

It was two hours walking in the rising heat before she found it. One man knew the street and then another knew how far and she walked it all and stood far down the street near a cart of furs and looked at it. Keeping the furs between her and the road and watching always the street in front of her and once three spearmen rode by and everyone moved out of the street and she turned and busied herself with the furs as if they were hers and listened to the horses and they went on without changing down the street and were gone. Only after long-burning minutes did she step back out and look again at the tavern.

A small dark building, all of rock on one wall and the others timber. A wooden door at the street and windows with the shutters closed. The road in front heavily traveled. The docks quite close now and most of those going in and out sailors from the ships and some traders and once an old man was thrown out and lay in the street looking about as if he did not know where he was.

She watched it all for a long time and hoped to see him come and go in and knew she wouldn't and finally a man came for the cart and tipped his head to look at her as he walked up and she knew it was time. Stepping away from the furs and walking down the street and almost going past it and then cursing herself again and turning and going in. The heavy oak door swinging before her and the creak of the old hinges and then the warm and heavy air inside and the smell of ale.

II

He was a long time coming in and she had no money and they were watching her from the bar but she did not know what to do and sat looking about as if waiting for someone. No lie in that and yet still feeling as if they were going to come over at any time and stand her up and take a length of chain and bind together the shackles and begin walking her back to the castle.

But they did not and at last he came in and stood in the door blinking and then looked at her and looked away and went to the bar and sat. The barman came over and nodded and slid down two mugs of ale and he in turn pushed a stack of coins across the bar and picked up the mugs and turned and walked over and sat at the booth facing her. Setting the mugs down on the table and the condensation already dripping on the outsides.

"God," he said.

"I don't know what I'd have done if you didn't come."

"God," he said again and picked up the mug and drank long and heavy and set it back down. An aging man now but still in his build some of the knight that he had been and still was in title. The wars long past and all about his face. A scar drawing down from his temple, the marks from the sun when they'd marched out two weeks from Hai'njal in the desert sand and fought along the dry and dead banks of what had been a river. The gray now moving through hair that had been dark when last she'd seen him.

He looked at her. His hands cupped on both sides of the mug. She had not touched hers.

"When?" he said.

"Today. This is the first place I came."

"All these years."

She looked at him and remembered that time. It had felt unreal as it happened and even as she knew it was happening. Meeting with him the day before they'd come to her room with swords and waited behind her as she stood looking out over the kingdom and her son had been with them and breathing so loudly in that silence. Telling this man, now the only one she trusted, that they were coming. Him swearing it wouldn't happen and it happening as she had known and nothing to be done to stop it. Too many things in motion already. The great grinding gears of the world.

Or perhaps her own pride then too much to allow her to flee. That pride at least broken and left under the earth, in that dank room with her husband's bones.

"I need to get out of the city," she said.

"We'll get you a boat."

"They'll watch the boats."

"They'll watch everything. Better a boat than the damned gate. The roads."

"No." A boat just another cage, this one of lashed wood and tar and sails. She could already see herself cowering in some hold and praying for the rocking as they pushed off from the dock but instead the sound of shouting and boots on the planks above her head and horses huffing and her son yelling something and the boots coming down the stairs and her sobbing there in that darkness as it ended.

"Then what?"

"Get me a horse."

He picked up the mug and drank again and finished it and looked at hers and she nodded and he slid it over to himself. Perhaps knowing all along how it would go and what he needed from it.

"I'm telling you," he said. "They'll find you faster on a horse. They're on the roads already."

"You've seen them?"

"No, but I know how this goes." He drank again, set it aside. "I know how it goes and I know how it ends."

"You think."

"I know." He looked back toward the door and she saw how he was now a part of this and all the things in his head and for the first time she wondered if he'd said he'd meet her when still he thought it would never happen and where loyalties went at times like these. A man always loyal to the crown, but perhaps she just mistook that as loyalty to herself from a royal guard who was and had been loyal to only the crown.

But she could do nothing for it. If he wanted her, he had her and there was nothing else.

Then he looked back at her and nodded. "Go at dusk, when they change the guard. Take the Trappers' Gate. Do you know it?"

"By the river."

"It's smaller and so is the road. But get off of it as soon as you can. Go through the vineyards and up through the forest and go as fast as you damn well can and get into the mountains. He'll only hold the net for so long and if you're through it, you may live. He'll come looking, though. He'll hunt you."

"I'll figure something out. Where can I get the horse?"

"He'll be at the gate."

She reached out then and touched his hand. The shackle coming free, rattling on the table like a dead thing. "He's going to war."

His eyes widened at that. The knight he'd been still alive within him and those words the cry of his blood he'd heard all his life. "With who?"

She shook her head. "I don't know. Anyone he can."

He cursed, took up the second mug again and finished it. Scowling now and his teeth not as white as they had been and the scar turning the skin by his eye. "We'll be slaughtered. Erihon's standing army is ten thousand companies and the

Island Kingdoms control the seas. Everyone thinks the Whispermen are ghosts, but they'll rally if needed and no one knows how strong they are. They haven't fought a war in five hundred years. Any way he turns, we'll die."

"I know," she said. "I know."

"And you've told him."

"It's past that."

"He's a damned fool."

"I know and that's what I told him."

He leaned forward with his elbows on the table in the heavy leather and his sword swinging at his side to clank against the table leg. "What'll you do?"

"I don't know yet, but I have to stop him. I have to get the word out and tell the people what he is." She shrugged, the task sounding so simple and yet enormous and impossible when she thought of the size of the land and the people within it and what they'd believe.

"You have some time," her old guard said. "He'll have to drum them up. Nationalism, patriotism. Some damned thing. You don't tell people to go to war. They'll never follow you." Scowling now as a man who knew too much and hated what he knew and knew it anyway. "You make them want to go to war and then you simply lead them to the field."

"How long?"

"Depends how he does it. Months at least. Winter will fall and he can't fight then. The soonest he'll field an army—a real army, not the standing one—will be next summer. Maybe the spring if the people are behind it and he has to march."

"It's not as long as it sounds."

"I know." He sat back then and looked at her. "How'd you know I'd still come here?"

She smiled. "I didn't know. But I know you. So I came here and I hoped. And here you are."

He laughed. "Makes me sound like an old drunk who

used to be a knight."

"Then it's an old drunk that I need."

"I hope so," he said. Standing then and nodding to her. "Don't worry about the shackles. Just get to the gate at nightfall. The horse will be there. Ride hard and where I told you. He's going to hunt but you can get beyond him and he can't hunt you and rally the people both. Make him choose and hope he chooses his war."

"He will," she said. "He's a damned fool."

III

She sat in the tavern ten minutes after he'd gone and held the mug with just the smallest trace of ale so it'd look like she was drinking and then got up and went out the back. Down the alley, across a short stone bridge, up a twisting street with on both sides the close walls of homes and the doors shut. No one walking here now and all the sound down toward the water. Her footfalls loud and hollow on the stones.

It was not hard to become lost in this place, if that was what you wanted, and she fell from sight. Taking the small street to a long and gnarled stair that ducked into darkness and came back out again and everything the same. A ladder with iron rungs set into the stone wall before her. Sitting for a time on a roof looking out at the water and the little boats coming and three soldiers riding down the street and the leftmost one scowling and kicking at a child who got too close. Crossing the rooftops and jumping down when she thought no one was looking and going through a market square. No money on her at all but the smell of the food driving her to something close enough to insanity that she never wanted to know the real thing. Garments hanging on strings outside shops, people coming and going.

Always stepping aside at the sound of horse or boot. She

had not been out like this in years and still she fell back into it easily. Always able to tell when they were coming for they thought it unnecessary to hide themselves and made no effort and she had found that often it was the one who made the effort who ended up the victor. Regardless of skill or any other advantage. This true in many pursuits and this game they played just one of them.

Working her way always toward the gate. For she had to give him time, but she knew how sharp that time was. Like the blade of a knife. Too soon and the guards would see, too late and the horse would be found. Either way she'd hang and these same people would come to see her with her legs jerking in the hot afternoon air and none would remember her now as she passed them in the street. Or perhaps they would and they'd say nothing for fear of joining her and feeling how coarse a rope was.

She came to it at last as dusk fell and she could hear the boots and talk on the wall. Always the guards from the day switched with those for the night. There wasn't much to be done, but there was enough. Lighting the torches atop the wall, checking the chains for the main gate, talking about the quiet. The system of shifts the only thing that kept them alert, but also their weakness. Not for an army or ambush, but for one trying to get out. In those few minutes, she could move through and out and perhaps, perhaps, not be seen until she was riding hard and near the forest.

There she could lose them in land she knew, land she'd seen many times. Outside the gate the road ran down along the river for a short distance and then went up into a low, thick forest. To her left the water and on her right the open fields and then the short foothills. A break with no forest or cover where she'd have to ride hard. But then the hills and the true forest and in there she could lose herself and never be found.

She crouched and looked at the low stone arch. One of the

oldest gates in the city and seldom used now for trade as it had been. A forgotten passage of weathered stone and iron doors left open now for years. Closed only in times of war. He should have closed them when he knew she was gone but he was a fool and thought he would have her either way. Or perhaps he'd ordered them closed and the guards had forgotten or the order had not come down. Or maybe a certain knight had countered the order and a frightened foot soldier hadn't stood up to him. There were many ways it could have played out, but she looked now and they stood open.

Not wanting to think it, but unable to stop herself. Perhaps he didn't even know she was gone yet. All this running in secret just time wasted when she could have been on the road and riding hard for hours.

But that was already gone. If she'd thrown it away and it killed her then she'd already done it and she was dead. Little reason for the dead to dwell on their own deaths.

She closed her eyes, listening for the guards. Wondering if the horse was truly on the other side or if she would run out and find that he'd been caught and killed and his head twisted on a spike and no horse there at all. Her son waiting with his sword drawn and bloody. But she swallowed it because she had to and then she opened her eyes and trotted for the gate.

Not fast enough to draw eyes. But fast. Feeling each footfall. Pushing on the balls of her feet in the loose dirt and the falling dark. Listening for the guards above her and hearing nothing, every step so damned loud.

She went through and the horse was there. She stared at it for a moment and then looked around for him and didn't see him. Just the brown horse standing in the mud with a worn saddle and the reins down and wrapped about a post. Looking at her with huge glass eyes. Behind it the river moved in the red sunlight and the ripples broke that tapestry of blood and carried it down and away from this city of stone and iron and war.

Chapter Sixteen

I

He woke the next morning and the city was burning. The smell of it in the air and over everything a light haze and he drug himself cursing from his bedroll. The others still sleeping and the morning barely new with the sun cracking the horizon. He threw aside the blankets and took his sword from the belt strapped to the horse as he stumbled shirtless to the top of the hill where he could see out over the plains. Sweating and freezing both over scars and grime.

It was far off and still he knew the whole city was ablaze. A smoking crater across that grass sea with the dead billowing up as ash. The flames around the base churning and licking at wood, straw, cattle and men. Burning and melting the stone itself. Above, the smoke rising in an endless dark line into the cloudless sky until it was lost in the remaining night, some vile hangman's noose about this city and choking the life out of her as those within died in the streets.

The dragon had come in the night and it was gone now. This not a fire that needed any longer to be stoked. A blaze caught full and raging on its own. About the city a ring of fire slowly spreading away as the grass caught and that outer circle of dark smoke, thin and unforgiving.

He could hear nothing for it was too far. It was like watching something burn that was not real. At this distance the movements slight and everything like a painting or a mosaic or some infernal tapestry etched and hung upon the wall to celebrate a death long over. A peaceful, motionless death. But the smoke was all about them and the horses were prancing and there was nothing in the world more real to him in that moment than Cabele burning to the ground in dragonfire.

Juoth and the boy rose alike and came to stand next to him and he said nothing and held the sword in his hand with the tip pointed not at the ground but down along the hillside and toward that far-off grave of fire and ash. Muscles taut, both arm and sword like stone, as if he were some vengeful statue looking out over a world it must and would bend to its will even if that stone had to be washed in blood for it had an unquenchable thirst and nothing in this world or the next could hold it back.

The boy said something then and Brack did not know what it was and did not look at him. Juoth was silent for he knew dragons and there was nothing to say. He stood waiting and would move upon the next order but Brack did not know what to give and finally he turned and stalked back to the horse. Grabbing it and pulling himself on.

He looked at Juoth. "Get everything and then come. You'll find me there."

"You can't fight it alone."

"No one else can fight it now."

"Brack."

A silence. Brack did not think of putting away the sword but pulled the horse around on its own twisting neck. Feeling the weight of that steel in his hand.

"It's waiting for you to ride to the city," Juoth said. Handing up his bag, his clothes, his belt.

"You think I don't know that?"

"And if it comes?"

He scowled and it was the first thing that had passed across his face since he woke and smelled the smoke.

"Then I'll kill it," he said.

II

He rode hard and he did not see that which he passed. Going fast over the rise in the dust and smoke and the horse not yet breathing hard. On down that slope and into the grass sea and the city like a smoldering beacon ahead of him in the waxing light that drew him onward. A carrot perhaps, but one he welcomed and would not shy from. He leaned down low on the horse and pushed it and the animal responded both to that and his body itself, the beating of his heart and the sound of his breath and it ran hard for him with the yet unburned grass flashing around its legs.

Seen or not, the world passed about him and the charging horse. A thin river with black stones that they crossed by fording and the hoofs beating in water only ankle deep. A copse of trees and in the center of them what had once been a dwelling and was now rotted wood and nothing. All fallen in on itself. The remnants of a road leading away and then swallowed by the plains. Farther on a scattering of small creatures with long necks and legs and thin bodies covered in fur, all standing at the sound of the horse and then running in great confusion to burrow into the dirt.

He left the old road behind, for it moved in a serpentine way through these plains. Sweeping long and wide to the east before coming back. Brack knew he would meet it again before he reached the city but he did not need it and he prayed with every hoofbeat that the horse would not find a crevice or stone to turn its foot and leave him there running like a man lost. But to take the road would have been more time and he did not have it and he could smell in the smoke the dead of the city burning.

All this a funeral pyre left for him. The sole guest invited and asked to speak over them all and commit them to some world other.

He whispered to the horse as he rode. Asking it to go faster and pleading with it and talking to it to keep calm. Saying things that had no meaning but in such a way that they pushed animal and rider in their headlong flight. Raising his own head to look at that towering pillar that guided him, smoke rolling from earth to sky, and then looking down to the endless earth that was all the same and gave no reprieve.

He could smell the smoke here but again he was smelling the keep where he had seen her last and the dead there and listening to that horse rising on its hind legs and screaming in the yard. Smelling also the fires long dead that he had seen in his life and knowing what they meant. Always the death and destruction the same and so very complete.

These memories a curse he'd always bear and no choice in it. As with many curses and certainly with the worst of them. He would not let it consume him—he could not—but he let it push him as he had all his life.

The city did not seem to change and the horse's sides became wet and lathered and his own also. Each time he looked up the world storming by in perpetual motion and still that city so far off as it burned. Smoke all he could see and the fire now just low and consuming the little that was left. He looked back only once and could tell the distance he had gone but it was the damned plains and they swallowed everything and made distance maddeningly nothing at all. He could have traveled all his life or mere minutes and the city would look the same as it died before him.

And still he kept on. There had been many a ride like this in his life and he knew that the thing was not to look at the end but to find a place between. A standing boulder in the grass that he could find a quarter of an hour later by his side. A glint of water off a pond that he could mark as it went by. A small cluster of homes and fields where men and women and children stood holding their scythes and hoes and rakes and axes and looking up at him as he went through with mouths gaping and one woman raising her hand to him as he paid her not a second glance.

In that way, the distance would pass. The gnawing feeling that he was still as far away as he had ever been would leave.

But he could not do it. He had eyes only for Cabele and the smoke and flame that she was and every time he looked up he looked at her alone and she burned to nothing while he watched.

III

They came upon the body of the horse when the sun was straight above them and the day very hot. The body covered in white foam and lying on its side in the tall grass. He got down and touched its neck and went around in front and looked at it and then looked back at the boy. The boy said something that was not a word and looked at him as if it were. The girl strapped behind him. He stood for a short time next to the horse and looked out into the plains to see if there was anything to see and then he climbed back up and all three went on again.

IV

Always in his head now this swirling storm. Once as a boy he had gone to the cliffs. This in the old days and before it all and he had stood alone on the rock that ran along the top of the cliff. Seven hundred feet below the sea breaking against that same rock. Layers and layers of it with different colors and broken lines in it and all piled and moving down to the ocean where more rock fell away under a sea dark and fast and broken with crashing waves of white ice.

A storm had come from far off and he had watched it come. The dark banks of clouds growing and swelling and the thin wisps of fog moving before them. Seeming to pull the storm forward as if drawn by the ghosts of horses. The reins snapping in the wind. All around him the temperature falling so quickly he could feel it and his skin puckered and shivering and then the clouds breaking. With neither thunder nor lightning. Just an endless outpouring, a torrent as the dark hearts of those clouds wound themselves together in a blotted sky.

He had stood there as the rain fell about him cold and bitter and looked down into that sea and felt the same way he felt now. The world around him moving and threatening to pull him under and he would not let it. He had run for a time after the horse died and then he could not and he had fallen and stood and now he walked on legs shot through with pain. The sword strapped again to his back and the city burning before him.

Those clouds now the twisting smoke. The ghosts of those it had slaughtered.

He stopped then and closed his eyes. He could feel his heart beating in a way it had not for so long and within him the boundless rage. Wanting to open his eyes and throw himself forward and scream at it to come down on him, to try itself against him. Perhaps he would die and there was no difference in it. He would rather fight it and be killed and his body torn open or burned or consumed than this endless dance.

But he stood. Arms shaking in the haze. Chest moving like a bellows. And when at last he opened his eyes the rage had solidified and sharpened and he began to walk again. Still the same distance between him and the city, but a distance he felt now that he could cross.

For it must be there, and it would wait for him, to make

him the end of this hunt. And he would be. For one of them would die and either way he would be the end.

He cursed it then in a language he had forgotten, and he walked on. There was no pain and no world and nothing but that shrouded city and the beast that must be straddling its heart, crouched on twisted claws and its eyes burning as it stared out to the plains and waited for him. For what was to be and had always been since they two had begun to move about one another. Hunter and prey indistinguishable. Only in their meeting their true roles shown for what they were.

Until then each something else to the other, until flame and steel and fate lay bare that which already existed in that hidden realm where only time moved and ages passed in all directions and history and future the same. In that place all knowledge. But they here could only find it in one direction and moved as slaves to find out what end awaited them.

V

They found him where the old road came back across the plains and ran its way through his path. Here it was thicker and paved with old stones and the mud of years between them and he was kneeling on one of those stones as if beseeching some god he did not name and holding his sword now in hand and looking at the city.

Juoth dismounted and went to him. It was late afternoon now and they had ridden the whole day. He knelt beside him and Brack at first said nothing and would not look away and only at last did he turn.

"It's too far," he said.

"I know,"Juoth said. He did not look at the city but felt that it could burn forever and it would never go out. The smoke still billowing upward.

He'd thought the whole time that they would come across

people who had fled. Mothers and children and merchants and farmers. Archers and soldiers and perhaps knights who had stood to fight and then seen the thing wheeling in the sky and lost their nerve and turned and fled. For against some things a man could stand and against others he would do nothing but save the one life he had. A dragon was eternally one of those others.

At least it was for most men.

Brack tried to stand and could not and Juoth held the water up for him and helped him drink. He needed more than they had, and food as well, but mostly he needed rest. But he drank and it was something and then he could stand. The boy got down off the horse and took the body of his sister down after him. Juoth looked at him closely and he looked all right. He laid the blankets out and began to gather wood for the fire. In the plains the sun a long time going down but they would camp where they must.

Looking back he could see the line where they'd come down. Only now a distance of any size, any consequence. Halving the distance between the mountains and the city, as the farmer had said. All around them the dry grass and now before them the stones of the old road and if he laid down he could look along it and it went straight all the way to the gates of the city.

Or where there had been gates. What stood there now he could not imagine to be more than ash.

It took some time to get the fire going and when he did at last it was dusk everywhere and the smoke had made it come early. Sinking everything into an unnatural dark. He had once before seen a city burn like this and it had not been from a dragon but the smoke was the same. The way it was everywhere. Men had left that countryside because of it and never returned.

The campfire guttering in the splintered wood. They had

with them more of the dried meat and he took it out and handed it to each and they all ate. The boy sitting with the girl's wrapped body at his side as if she were a bedroll. When he handed the boy his food their fingers met and the boy's were very cold. Colder than they should have been even at night and without a fire.

"There's a ripping," the boy said.

He looked at him and then looked away and cursed and looked back.

"In the world. And air full of eyes. Have you seen the eyes?"

He did not answer and wouldn't. Putting his hand on the knife at his side and looking at the licking flames. Across the fire Brack slept already and he could see his chest rising and falling and his lips moving. Not an easy sleep. His grandfather had slept the same way and Juoth knew what it looked like and that he would not remember his dreams when he woke.

"Have you seen the eyes?" the boy said again. Almost pleading now. Leaning forward with the rest of the meat uneaten in his hand and reaching for him. Fingers open and nodding his head as if to bring about the response he sought by mere suggestion. "The air is full of them."

"Go to sleep," Juoth said.

The boy took this as affirmation and nodded and smiled and it was a horrible thing. His eyes were vacant and his smile didn't reach them and it was as if the boy didn't exist behind them. He dropped his dried meat and it fell in the dirt and he did not pick it up.

Juoth laid down himself and the boy watched him as if learning and then laid also on the ground. No blanket or pillow. His arms straight at his sides, next to the body of his dead sister. Both in this same pose and their heads fallen at an unnatural angle toward the ground. Juoth closed his eyes. Held them for a breath and then opened them. The boy was still looking at him in the night and smiling that fixed and broad smile that did not reach the rest of his face but only stretched the skin.

Then, while he watched, the boy slowly raised both of his own hands. Raising them straight-armed at first and only at last bending the elbows. Moving slowly and not making a sound and all the while looking not at what he did but at Juoth.

"Have you seen the eyes?" the boy said. "The air is full of them."

And then he reached and plunged his fingers into each socket, two of them together and straight like they were made of steel. Not making a sound the whole time, not to scream or cry out. The wide smile never faltering. He pushed his fingers into the insides of the sockets and there was a wet ripping, sucking sound and blood all in the air and down his hands and face and then he clenched his thumbs and ripped his eyes off at the stalks.

Juoth yelled and tried to rise and fell and then got up. The boy had one eye in each fist and he'd crushed them and his face was a horror of blood and it was pouring into the dirt. He was still smiling and his face as white as pooled candlewax and he was opening and closing his fists. The stalks of his eyes hanging down his cheeks. He was saying something but it wasn't a word.

Juoth grabbed the boy and rolled him over and knew there was nothing to do. The blood already slowing as it only did when there was very little left. He could hear Brack getting up across the fire and the sound of the sword coming out of its sheath and the world buckled beneath his legs. He fell to one knee and caught himself and there was the boy's blood now on his hands and pants and he looked at Brack across the small fire and then back.

The movement of rolling the boy had pulled the blanket from the body of his sister. Her with that thin hair and indistinguishable age, the dead body they'd carried through river and mountain and plain to get to a city now full only of other bodies. Perhaps not even those remaining in the pyre it had become. Bringing the dead to the dead.

He reached with his gloved hand to put the blanket back over her head. He did not know why and it wasn't something done because there was a reason. Except perhaps that the gasping boy at his feet with the ravaged face and his own eyes crushed in his hands was little more than a corpse, and this girl with her thin and blooddrained face was the same. And maybe, maybe he could bear it if it was only one, but he could not see two at the same time and so he reached to cover her again as instinct and self preservation.

And as he did so, the dead girl opened her eyes.

The Dragon Hunt

Chapter Seventeen

I

She slept that night in a tree. Lying in the darkness and a
web of branches with the stars bright above her and moving in
the air in flittering little jaunts the fireflies with bats swooping
among them. She had not been able to hide the horse but had
tied it to a tree a half a mile distant and could do nothing but
hope that the wolves did not find it and if they did she would
walk.

She would know if the wolves found it without having to
go back. It would not be the first time she had heard a horse
scream in the night and known what it meant. Once along the
Caariligan where the river poured down through the stone fields
the wolves had gotten to the edge of the camp and taken one
down and she'd thought for the first moments of sheer terror as
she jolted awake that it was a person screaming in the camp.

By the time they'd run the wolves off the horse had been
dead and the blood running down in rivulets along the rock
toward the river.

She took a rope from the saddlebag and tied herself to the
tree. The place she chose was very high and the bows wide and
wound together and she did not think she would fall but she tied
herself all the same. Lashing it about her waist and knotting it

and then wrapping it around both branches—should one break
—and tying it again. It may not prevent the fall but she thought
it would hold at least enough to save her if she did.

The forest was very quiet and she lay looking back toward
the city.

The flight from those walls had turned out to be nothing
at all. The whole way her heart hammering in her chest. Pulling
back on the horse lest it run and riding calmly from the gate as
if she were no more than some merchant's wife or a merchant
herself. Her wares sold and the money in the saddlebag and
heading down the road through the Trappers' Gate. She did not
turn her head in case the guards were looking and she would
never know if she'd slipped out while they'd changed shifts or if
they'd watched her and not known it was her or if something
else entirely, some other good fortune she could never have
planned, covered her escape.

When she reached the trees she had held her pace for five
minutes and then bent and put her feet into the horse. Riding
hard all evening up along the river plain and into the fields and
vineyards heavy with grapes and when she hit the true forest
beyond, the Huralon, she'd left the road as she'd been told and
slowed the horse and picked her way through the woods itself.

It was a very old forest and thick and in it gnarled trees as
old as the city and some behemoths amongst them rising like
the towers of the gods. So wide around it would take fifty men
with arms linked to circle them, the rough bark like the sheer
face of a cliff. No branches to be seen on this lower level and
all very straight and rising like spears thrust from the earth. She
had stood the horse at the base of one and looked up and it went
through the canopy and was gone and she could not see the top.

There were those who could climb them, with ropes and
picks, the way they climbed mountains. She had seen once
when she was a girl a man who climbed to a hundred feet and
then fell screaming and turning in the air, then a lithe girl so

adept she climbed after the man and tripled his height and then went beyond and they lost her in the fog and mist and branches and never saw her come down.

She'd ridden in that dark and tangled forest as the night grew deep around her. It had been dusk when she left and she only had the light for a short time and even then it was gray. The boulders looking like beasts hulking there in the dark. Every branch or limb a rider on a horse, coming through the forest toward her. And then even that was gone and she rode through a thick valley in the meager moonlight that fell through the branches, everything in shadow. Pausing to listen to what moved out there and trying not to think of what it was and cursing him for not getting her a sword.

In the end it was that which caused her to stop. It was not the wolves she was afraid of in this forest, but there were worse things than wolves and many things that could kill her, and so she'd come up out of that valley and ridden a half hour more through a sweeping and level area where the trees at last spread out just slightly and she'd found the one to which she tied the horse and then walked to the one she now lay in, looking at that night sky above and far to the east one of those oldest trees rising pale and endless until it was gone.

The forest moving about her. Insects clicking to each other, the high-pitched calls of the bats. Somewhere far off one of the wolves howling, faint and shrill. Another answering.

It went in waves like this, sometimes quiet and then sometimes rising in a chorus about her. It was not the noises that worried her, but the silence. For everything was prey to some creatures and when everything fell quiet, what silent and snarling beast stalked along the forest floor, winding between the trees and staring from the shadows, driving all else to hiding?

She saw nothing, but that did not mean that nothing was there. In each stifling silence perhaps the slow breathing of something that waited and watched. If it saw where she lay lashed to the tree she did not know. Or if it only smelled her in the forest, smelled the warmth of her blood and heard the beat of her heart.

Each time that silence gave way to the sounds of the night, it was like a blanket lifting. And again she would breathe and check the knots and listen and wait with everything in her for the morning sun on that distant horizon.

II

She woke and he was sitting against the foot of another tree, looking up at her and picking at his fingernails with his knife. The sun had risen already and was bright and orange in small patches as it came down through the trees. Chasing away all that was the night and making her wonder for just a moment if everything she knew lurked and lived in that night was real after all, or if she'd imagined everything and passed the night in safety with only her mind creating about her the illusion of death.

But she knew not to give in to those thoughts, for those who did were those who were dead.

He looked up when she moved to untie the knots and shook his head and kept picking at his fingernails. "For someone who's wanted by half the kingdom, you're certainly finding a lot of time to sleep."

She didn't answer, but pulled the rope through the last of the knots and looped it through her belt and dropped to the ground. Hanging for a moment from the high limb of the tree to shorten the distance and then letting go and falling into moss and underbrush. He didn't move or look at her the whole time and then stood when she fell.

"Thank you for the horse," she said.

"Looks like you lost him."

"I didn't lose him."

"Then I'm blind in my old age."

She nodded her head back the way she'd come. Noting as she did that he did not have a horse either. When she'd known him before he'd walked tirelessly in full plate and she wouldn't have been surprised if he could walk to her in the simple leather and chain armor he wore now, but his comment about his age was only half in jest. The way most things had a heart of truth in them and would never even be said if they didn't.

"I tied him to a tree. Didn't want to give away where I was."

He looked down at himself and then at the tree. "Well done."

She scowled. "If they had you I wouldn't have bothered."

He held out a hand as she started back for the horse, and she stopped and looked at him. He shook his head. "You've lost him," he said.

She looked at him a long moment and felt something in her move and heard again that silence in the night. It had not even screamed. That scared her more than if she'd lain in that tree listening as it was torn to pieces. Because then it at least would have died the way things were supposed to die.

"I'm sorry," she said.

He shook his head. "I knew when I sent you here."

"At least they won't follow."

"Not without a company."

"What have you seen?"

He looked off into that deep forest and adjusted his belt. The sword long and ancient at his side, the same he'd carried all his life. In what felt to her a previous life. "They're all over the road. Gated the city last night and didn't open it. One of the royal guards told me he's out riding and looking for you himself. But I don't think that's true."

"He wouldn't do it."

"He may not care."

"Not care?"

"That you're gone."

"Why?"

He shrugged. "How will you stop him?"

"I don't know."

"And that's why he doesn't care."

She stepped forward then, putting a hand against his chest, pushing him back against the tree. Feeling in her a surge of anger and violence like she hadn't felt for a long time. The air perhaps, or something else. Speaking through gritted teeth. "You don't think I can do it?"

He raised both hands at his sides. "I didn't say that."

"Then what is it you said?"

"I'm just saying he might not think you're a threat. If he wants war, he can get it with you or without you. He'll send men after you, but he's not going to ride out himself. He has enough power now. They'll follow him."

She stepped back from him. This her oldest and perhaps only friend. For how else had this world changed and shifted as she lay underground? The dead rising from the fields would have felt the same, cast suddenly into some new life and finding everything around them different, the very stones beneath which they'd been buried broken and gone.

"I can't let him," she said.

"Then what will we do?"

She had been turning it in her head for a long time and she knew one thing she could do and hated it and yet knew nothing else. Every turn just bringing it into a fuller view.

"If he wants a war, we'll show him he can't win."

He grunted. "You and I? Buy some bows and march on the gates, maybe? Never mind that you killed our horse."

"No," she said. "It's what you said before. He'll be slaughtered. I'll just show him it before it happens. We'll go to

194

the Island Kingdoms, to Erihon. To Mannkaran in the mountains. To Callhud and Jaskerat and The Peak." She swallowed. "To the Whispermen."

He did not speak for a long time and when he did she could barely hear him. "You're insane," he said. "What did they do to you down there?"

"It's the only way and you know it. If he wants war, he won't listen to words. But he'll listen to force. We'll gather all the armies and march them down into the valley. Blockade the river by Stoneguard. Show them how pointless it is. Show him that he doesn't want war."

"You'll bring them down on your own people. It'll be a bloodbath."

"I'll bring them down on him. No one has to die."

"But they will. You think he'll just throw it away and let you climb back on the throne? You think it will be that easy?"

"He's a fool. He's not suicidal."

He leaned forward and there was something in his eyes born of years and wars and battles and the type of knowledge that only those who survive such things can have. For most die and those who don't simply die the next time and rare is the man who has waded through so much death and come out himself alive and washed in blood and a man like that knows things other men can never know, and it was that which lived in his eyes.

"There is nothing," he said, "that is more dangerous than a caged king who does not care if others die."

III

They walked that day through the forest in the lingering light that filtered through the canopy, falling deep into this shadow world in long beams and moving through them dust and insects and birds. The flittering of animals who would in the night be as hidden as they could, buried in trees and burrows and underground. All holding their breath. Giving these two travelers a wide berth but always about now as the world turned.

There was no path but he found a trail used by deer and others and they took it along for the distance that it went where they already wanted to go. She did not know where they were but did know the general direction in which they traveled. Behind them the castle and far to their right the fields and plains and after that the rising sawtooth of the mountains breaking the world's crust. Beyond even that the towering stone behemoths of the true mountains where black stones rose for miles and dwarfed all below and these monstrous peaks with sheer cliff faces thousands of feet high and glaciers miles upon miles long that no man could cross and snow deeper than the city walls. Snow enough in some places to swallow all that was her kingdom as if it had never existed.

But so far removed were they here in this forest and the heat of midday, walking on this path of dirt and trampled grass where deer nervously stepped with their tails flicking and their black glass eyes wide. Coming to a river that they crossed on stones, then later a deep canyon where they walked along until a fallen tree bridged it. Him going across first and then nodding and her running those four steps in sheer terror. So few steps but below a fall of a hundred feet and the sounds of the water running.

They did not talk as they walked and this was how it always had been between them and she felt herself fall years back in her own life. To other trips and campaigns and worlds that they'd traveled. Some in danger and some in luxury. Another life, one she had almost forgotten she'd lived.

A life that had ended, she realized then, walking through a wide field of moss with a lone tree standing in the middle, a heavy trunk so far around it looked like a guard tower and great swaying branches holding an immense canopy. She had been thrown into that dungeon with her husband as the boy took the throne and she had fought to live even as he had died. Fought bitterly and with everything she had. Finding then the resiliency that she had within her to continue her life at all costs, to hold nothing back and to demand with every breath simply to live. Some streak in her of iron will.

And yet she had not lived, not as she was. The warrior she had been and the queen she had become, both dead. That life ended. Now walking with a man from that life she felt the difference keenly and knew how dead it was. Buried in the earth under the castle.

Her body alive, but living now a second life. A life that she did not know what it was and would have to find out for herself. A world she did not know.

Perhaps she had died before, she thought. Perhaps pieces of her died every time she moved from one point to another and perhaps it was that way for everyone. Life really no more than the whittling and shaping of a body, a soul. And with that whittling all excess lost. Those parts dead and gone and something new revealed beneath that moved until it too was cut and transformed into something else. This pattern for time eternal, until death claimed it.

IV

They made camp that night on the edge of the forest. It was cold as the night came on but they did not make a fire because of the light and they looked out from the treeline over a wide plain with roads running in it and far off the lights of a small city. A lantern bobbing in the night as someone worked his way slowly along down toward the river. Fireflies in the tall grass. Once the dark and running form of a wolf, low and silent, sweeping across the world to some end unknown.

Before them the foothills rising. These heavily forested in a different type of tree. No longer the towering oaks and tangled branches. Instead everything of short cedar and spruce, the paths between them carpeted with red needles. Here and there the white of a birch. The soil too thin in this rising land of rock and stone to support anything larger. A place where in winter the snow clung to every bow in heavy coats but here before the winter the soft scent of the trees on the air and the warm soil and somewhere far off a fire burning.

He had some dried meat with him and fruit and he took these out and set them on his bag and looked at them and took up some and handed it to her. Both of them sitting next to a long tree recently fallen, the trunk not yet decayed. Maybe a tree grown too close to where the soil thinned out, she thought, trying to break the boundaries of the deep forest and only finding as it grew too tall for support that it had asked for the impossible as the wind swirled and rose.

She sat rubbing her scabbed wrists where he'd helped her take off the shackles and closed her eyes, thinking of those chains buried in the mud as she'd pushed them down with her boot, then opened her eyes again and took a bite and it was better than she'd imagined. So long she'd been down there and this meager food a feast and all the world changed. What could all be in it she did not know and she did not think anyone did. A meaninglessness in that and also the great and intrinsic heart of the world.

He ate in silence for a moment and when he spoke in the dark he did not look at her.

"What do you want me to do?"

She stopped eating and looked at him and still he did not turn. She could see the whites of his eyes in the coming moonlight. "I thought you said I was foolish. Insane."

"You thought right."

"And now?"

"I still think it."

"You still think it."

He looked at her then and his face was calm, relaxed. A man who had seen so much that nothing he saw now struck him as anything that could not be believed or defeated. The world emptied for him of its secrets. Or so he thought.

"I'll do what you want," he said. "I don't have to like it."

"Tell me what you think."

"That we should do?"

"Yes."

He took another bite, chewed. Thought. Turning it in his mind so much that it was on his face. Then he said: "If he wants a war, he's the only one. They always are. Those in charge waging war with others' lives. He'll make them want it, but they don't now. If we remove him, the war ends." He shrugged. "It's not like other wars, where there's something at stake and no choice. Someone invades and you protect your home. It's just a war for him and what he wants. As long as he's the only one who truly wants it, he's the key."

It was treason to say and she looked at him and wondered how many others had said the same about her at times and if all rulers had to live knowing such things were spoken about them. Or if somewhere there was a ruler everyone wanted to live. And what that land was like.

"Just us," she said.

"It wouldn't be easy."

"It couldn't be done."

"Anything can be done," he said.

She looked out into the night. The lantern moving down the road was gone now. Either extinguished or inside the city walls. She listened for the wolf to see if he would call at the moon but he was silent.

"It's too much of a risk," she said. "Too easy to fail."

"How?"

"Any of a thousand ways. A guard sees us and we're captured. We can't get to him. Archers shoot us from the walls. We get in and he's not in the city. The guards kill us in the attack. You know the ways."

"Then we plan for it."

"But you can't plan for everything. A loose board on a stairway creaks and a guard looks and it's all over before it begins." She shook her head. "I can't risk that. I can't do something that will fail."

"Anything can fail."

"You just said anything can be done."

He laughed. "It can. Anything can be done and anything can fail."

She bit down on the meat and it was good but tough. Tearing it sideways with her teeth. Feeling it stretch and then rip. The salt of it. The sinews. Chewing it there in the dark, her jaw working. Finally swallowing and feeling it still in her jaw.

"It needs to be more than me," she said. "More than you. So that if we are killed, it can happen without us. It has to be an army. It's the only way to know we can force him to stand down. To do it alone risks the lives of everyone."

"Marching an army on your own city does something else?"

She looked at him and her eyes were bright and she blinked and looked again. "I have to hope it does," she said. "I have to hope it does."

V

He left the next day with the parchment in a bag at his side. Walking out to the road and not looking back and turning to the city. She watched him go, standing by that great fallen tree that had overstepped its own world and in doing brought about its own end. Only after it had grown to a great height and looked to all the world as if it could never fall. Now a broken thing sheltering those who ran from death and perhaps to it at the same time.

She'd signed the paper and they'd know it. She did not know if they'd believe it or if they'd act as she'd asked them in the letter. If any of them would. But they'd know it and they'd talk and it was all she could do. For she could only cover so much ground and now they could double it and that was something. She did not know how swiftly it all had to be brought to an end and she'd learned that in times like that it was best to assume it was already too late and to act that way and then you could never be wrong.

Even if it was too late and all was already lost.

When he'd disappeared down the road and she could see him no longer she gathered up what little she had and looked again and then turned and went up through the cedar and spruce and into the low mountains on that bed of needles, dried and dead and brittle, where the wolf had run in silence.

The Dragon Hunt

Jonathan Schlosser

Chapter Eighteen

I

Juoth sat looking at her and she at him. Or at least she looked at something within him. A vacant stare that focused on nothing. Eyes open and blinking slowly and her whole face around them lax. The color still not fully returned. As if in her her heart was but a feather and could move only so and the blood sluggish and hardened in her veins. Thinning now as she warmed. Her light hair hanging down about her shoulders and the thin dress. Lips pale white.

Other than the blinking she did not move. Had not even sat of her own accord but was only now propped up against the pile of blankets and bedrolls because he had set her that way. Unable to look at that dead face with blinking eyes as she lay on her back with her limbs loose.

Her chest rising, falling. A meager tide in perhaps some world other with a moon too small. The thinnest sound of her breathing only when he was close and it was very quiet. If the fire rose at all in the wind he did not hear her and did not know if she breathed.

It was the morning after her awakening and behind them stood the mound of loose dirt piled upon her brother. He had beat out his last with his eyes in his hands, clenching and opening and clenching those fingers. Not saying a word but his jaw working and one hand reaching for her. Tracing across her cheek a thin streak of blood. And when he died Juoth had finally been able to stand and move him away from the fire.

And then he had sat all night staring at this girl. Brack had looked at her a short time and said nothing and gone back to sleep. Risen before dawn and put on his sword and looked at the horse and the city. Juoth had nodded to him.

"Find me," he'd said.

"I will," Juoth had said. Looking not at him but at the girl. "I will."

And Brack had left. The rising of the dead perhaps not of consequence to him or at least a thing he could stomach. Juoth had waited for him to say something about it but he had not and had ridden on toward the city, toward that one thing that devoured his entire world. The smoke still rising there as if it would never cease. Perhaps the earth itself burning in endless torment. The dragon's fire a rage that could never be quenched even when all tinder was gone for it burned the very soil and could turn the whole world to ash if given the time to do so.

A charred world of the dead; a glass sky in which dragons were legion, wheeling on the hot wind of this corpse of a planet.

The eyes were in the air, he thought.

He had not slept himself and had worked all night digging the grave. The endeavor giving him just that much distance from her and all she was and if he was lucky drowning his screaming thoughts in the soil itself and he worked at it until he felt he could not dig anymore and it was not as deep as he wanted but he did not know if that depth existed as a thing that could be reached and so he settled for rolling the mutilated body in and throwing on top of it three boulders. The work of moving them end over end making his legs and chest burn but he knew he'd never sleep another night in his life if he didn't and so he threw them in and heard the bones breaking and then covered it all with dirt. Mounding it under that cold moon until he was a broken man and then sitting again to look at her.

Thinking should he be digging another grave or should he have cast them into the same. So that someday they would be dug up and thought to be lovers and perhaps tales would be written and no one would know the horror that they had truly been.

But he had not.

He spoke to her then and she said nothing. Greeting her in the tongue of the islands and the one here. Trying a word from the mountains he had heard and did not know what it meant.

Slowly she blinked and sat with that stillness about her. He thought perhaps she was holding herself up but then he thought she was still propped like some doll against the bedrolls.

He could kill her, he thought. Any time he liked. He could kill her with his sword and bury her and no one would know for those within any distance of this place shorter than a day's ride had been killed already and what was one more dead among the many? Brack would perhaps ask and he would tell him some story. It would be no more than saying she'd collapsed and died after all.

Died again.

He stood then and looked at the city. They had half the burden now but no horse and it would be a long distance. If they were to do it in a day they would have to start early and walk late and even then they may just be to those burned farms and fields outside of the walls when night fell. But they would not make it that far if they did not start now.

He went to her and stood close and walked around behind to see if she was holding herself up and cursed and spit. Looking once more at the mountains and thinking he had no part with this grandson or anyone else and then he cursed again and reached down and took the girl under the arms.

There was no weight to her and he stood her up and put his arm around her back. She did not move to support herself but her legs seemed to hold slightly and he thought maybe she could walk. He bent to pick up the bedroll and his face brushed that torn and bloodied dress and only then did he realize that the smell of rot was gone.

II

They walked like two chained in some ancient misery. Perhaps having been cursed by a witch or a god with its dying breath to toil under the sun as one animal forever, the trials of life before them for some past slight they were unable to remember. Walking these two in grass and dirt toward that pillar of smoke and the smell of it in the air always.

He'd left everything he did not carry on his person. The packs and the other bedrolls and all else. Carrying now only his sword and knife and a pouch with money he could not spend in this dead city. He had carried for a time the girl's bedroll under his opposite arm but it had grown too difficult and he'd dropped it after less than an hour. Not looking back as it disappeared into the barren wasteland.

They walked like this until the sun was up and it was noon and only then did he realize that she was walking also. Not with any strength, but it was more than mere support. She was holding what little weight she had and walking with small and slow steps. Sometimes her toes dragging in the dirt when he walked faster than she could move but trying regardless.

Her face still white and nothing in her eyes. A vacancy there as if all within her had been lost. The skin cool to the touch but perhaps warming.

He slowed and looked at her and she did not turn her head or acknowledge him in any way and carefully he took his arm out from around her back and under her arms and he stepped away. Arms out in front of him, waiting for what would come.

She stood for the shortest time, swaying there on her feet like a solider who had marched a week without sleep or a drunk with more bottles than he could remember. But she stood and she blinked again quickly and for a brief moment he thought her eyes moved, flickering and landing on his own, and then it was gone and she was falling and he caught her. Held her back up and put his arm around her and looked at her for a moment.

Thinking again about the sound of the bones breaking as the rocks fell and if that grave should have held two bodies. If perhaps it should have been him alone walking and going back toward the mountains and to hell with the rest.

But he was a man who knew his debts, even if he cursed himself for that knowledge. As often he did.

They kept on, this unlikely pair in all their contrast, and the city grew before them. It was a slow growing so that if he watched it come he felt no closer. But if he looked instead at his feet and the road before them and held that long enough, when he looked again to the city the walls were closer and the smoke darker. And he felt they may make that wall in time.

He had not been looking for the dragon because he knew he would be dead if he saw it. Brack with his crossbow and his bloodline could fight it even in the air. At a disadvantage, but he could fight. Here with a sword and a dead girl and a knife, he could not fight. The moment he saw those black canvas wings breaking the sky and heard its screech in the air, it would be too late. He could then do nothing but wait until it was upon them in bone and teeth and fire, or he could draw that knife and slit his own throat and die in the stone road or the dirt they walked beside it.

So he did not look. He had known a long time that death came for all men and he knew it now and if it came, that was just what it was.

They arrived after a time at a sort of trough dug in the ground and muddy water running dark and thick through it. Not wide but stretching away from the road and into a field beside it. Looking out over the field he could see a stone shack a long way off. This trough a channel for water, perhaps leading from some spring he could not see and irrigating the land. In the field what had been wheat or corn. All burned now so it was just black ash and this ash in the water. In that shack a body or two or three all blackened and their eyes boiled. He'd seen it before and would again, but he nodded to himself.

For they were closer now. Always around the cities would the towns grow up and then give way to the farms as they stretched into the country. This the edge of those farms, the outside edge of that wheel of life and this spoke they two traversed.

They kept on and the road improved. The stones wider and better in places and not as likely to trip him up with this girl on his arm and so he moved away from the dirt and into the road again. Walking from one stone to the next and keeping his eyes down. The girl taking her short steps in silence and sometimes catching on the edges of the stones, but walking now as he had never seen her do before.

When he paused, he could hear her breathing even without leaning close. The smell of her just of dirt and grime and blood, but not decay.

They passed in a haphazard order more farms on either side. Most of the fields burned as the fires had spread from the city, but patches standing. Withered corn and dry wheat and low fields of soy. A timber barn near the road just scorched beams, but next to it a small stable seemingly untouched.

He left her standing in the road then and went to the stable and swung open the front door. The smell of hay and horses. But it was empty and the back wall caved in on itself where he hadn't been able to see it from the road. Reins and ropes still hanging near the stalls. He cursed and walked back out to the road and looked at her where she'd stood the whole time and then put his arm back around her and they moved on.

He thought as they walked of the dragon and how it had laid waste to everything they'd touched or known. In some fashion or another, everyone they'd met had died. All about them burned. He could not tell the cause from the effect. Perhaps everything was dead for they hunted this dragon and following a beast like that meant walking through endless fields of destruction. Or perhaps it was killing all about them for spite alone or, as Brack believed, to draw them on and kill them.

But if that was all it was, some predator hunting its hunter, they could have been dead many times over. And still they were alive.

And this girl somehow both. A thing alive and with them in this life, but also dead, yet one more life claimed along this trail that fell before them with a city composed entirely of the dead all that awaited them at its long-sought end.

III

It was growing dark when they came to the streets of the small town that spread out around the walls of Cabele. Some would also call it Cabele but it was not. Just a town of peasants and farmers and beggars on the outside of the city. The stone walls still standing tall beyond it, the turrets and spires of the buildings within. Cabele was nothing compared to the true cities of the world but it had been grand and enormous to those who lived there and would see nothing else in their lives. A bastion of safety and power, now reduced to rubble.

He could see the fallen wall as they went down the main street, with small stone and timber homes on either side. This road running straight through the town and to what had been that city's gate. Everything on both sides now collapsed and burned and ruined.

A white sheet waving in the hot wind, one half still pinned to the line, the other half burned off and ragged. A home that had burned from the inside out, the roof collapsed into the house itself as the beams snapped and buckled. A cart in the street and abandoned, facing the city, as if the man who pulled it had been going to the gate to sell his wares and had watched that gate come down.

The dragon had perched there on the city wall, above the iron gate. Juoth could see the slashes in the rock from its talons and the crumbled stone parapets. All about charred the darkest black in both directions, and the whole wall fallen to the right of the gate. The stones cascading out into the street and burying homes and blocking the road like an avalanche or a living glacier not composed of snow and ice but of rock and iron.

A tower had stood near the corner but it was now sheered off, jutting brokenly into the sky. The others still standing, with many burned. Those towers where the archers had stood and tried in sheer terror to bring it down and it had cooked them alive as the arrows fell from its scales.

They kept on down the road, toward that wall. The city silent, a place where nothing moved but the ash swirling in the air and the skittering rats as they feasted on the bodies.

For there were bodies everywhere. In the homes and streets and alleys. In a town hall with the doors torn off and the inside torched. The headless body of an archer lying twisted and so far from the fortifications, thrown from the wall. His arrows scattered about the street where what was left of him had hit the ground and rolled. The blood now hard and darkened around him.

Juoth had wondered why there had not been more of them on the road, and now he knew how quickly the dragon had fallen on this place. Some had tried to flee and made it no further than this town. No doubt in the mad rush others had stormed for the walls and the archers, thinking they could live in the city. Instead giving the dragon all it wanted. Cowering together to burn as one.

Maybe some had lived. The dragon had come for the city, and maybe some had run from the outskirts of the town, running through the fields, and escaped the eternal wrath of these oldest gods. With a tale they could tell for the rest of their lives. But not many. Most had died here as it came for them, lighting a torch like a lantern to draw ships to the shore. Their bodies just fuel for what it wanted.

The walls loomed and they began to pick their way through the rubble. The girl could not do it and it was slow work as he helped her through. Lifting her light body up in both arms to set her past some of the larger stones. Stopping many times to look at the way through and the rockfall maze before them and to find a path. At the end, they would have to climb a pile of stones as tall as a house to summit what was left of the wall and he did not know how they would do it.

For the gate itself, twisted and battered as it was, had been locked from the inside. When those walls still stood. Whoever locked it a damned fool for a dragon could fly and had no use for walls or gates as he beat his way through the air and the smoke, but it was locked all the same. He could see the iron bar through the gate and all about on both sides the piles of bodies.

On the outside those who had been screaming to get in as they burned. Then, as the dragon perched on the wall and turned his fire to the inside, those already in had run back to this gate of the dead, trying to flee and knowing how little their city meant when it mattered most. All on both sides seeking what the other had and all dying as the dragon howled on the wind.

They reached the bottom of the mount of broken stones and he looked for the first time at the sky. The smoke still rose around them, but it was not as thick as it had looked from the road. It was just so much that was smoldering, but the fires were dying out. He looked up at those stones and turned to her.

"Can you climb?"

He could not mistake it this time; she looked at him. The two of them with their eyes locked and at long last something in those eyes. Not a fire but a spark. A bit of life or knowledge. Her face still, but not in the flat and lifeless way it had been. A stillness and calmness.

She did not speak and gave no indication she knew what he'd said. But he was only holding her by one shoulder and she was standing steadily on her own and she was looking at him.

He looked back at her and slowly his hand fell to the knife on his belt. Fingers wrapping around the black bone handle, so familiar. Drawing it and feeling the island steel move against the leather as it came free. A knife that had taken more lives than he could count and would claim another with this abomination before him. This thing that could not and should not be.

And then he looked back at the city wall, and Brack was standing there atop the rubble. His face covered in dirt and ash and mud. One hand out to hold himself up against the broken wall. His sword unsheathed and in his hand, the blade glinting in the light of some unseen fire beyond the wall.

"She's not here," he said.

Chapter Nineteen

I

She came to the hill above the town and looked down on it in the early morning light. Higher here as the hills began to swell toward the mountains and the air crisp. The town laid out in the valley and a river that twisted through the land. The timber homes all on the cliffs and hill faces as they wound through the forest and followed the river. A dozen hills or so, all connected and laid out and visible to her from this stone outcropping with the cedar trees at her back. She could smell the smoke from their fires and see it rising toward her in the air.

It had been just two days walking once she found the road and followed it, not staying on that road but tracing its course fifty yards off in the forest. Slower there, but it meant she was always hidden and nothing could come up behind or before her without her knowledge and she had seen no soldiers or horses. At times tempted to go back to the road, but she'd lived this long by ignoring those temptations and she'd stayed in the forest.

Now, the road before her fell down through the trees and into the town and she could see it. Logs laid into the track at the steepest places and all else dirt and stones exposed. People moving down there in the dawn. Men walking with axes to the forest and others in the terraced fields and still others at a far-off mill on the river that was itself hundreds of yards below the town and very small with the water wheel turning.

She looked at it for a long time and then she went down the road to it. A few men passing her in the other direction. A woman with a mule and a cart and a small child in the cart with dirt on his face who smiled at her as she passed and she smiled back and then wished she had not and kept on.

She didn't come to the edge of it for there were not edges to towns like these. No lines and flat areas where the town could run to some barrier either natural or of its own creation. Instead she just came around one bend and there was a home and behind it a stable with another mule and then around the next bend two more. Then a small shop for a blacksmith and him standing in the yard with a hammer in one hand and scowling at the ground for no reason she could ascertain. Then she went down a steep drop on those half-buried logs that had seen travelers unknown and around another bend and then there were homes and shops on both sides and the road widening out and the sound of water and visible down at the end of this street the river rolling by in the early morning light.

A cart came up behind her and passed and this one was empty and she looked back and down each street. Here it forked and ran off behind her and everything nestled close to the river where the ground was flat. But down on either side she could see the land dropping or turning into the other hills and the rest of the town laid out like this. The whole village a long and serpentine thing moving with the river and the hills. It would take longer to walk one end to the other than most towns she'd ever set foot in, but there would only be a tenth of the people scattered thusly in the forest.

She used to wonder in towns like this what made a man stop. And who he was, the first through here. Who sat his horse in a formerly empty place where it would be hard to live and said this would be the place and began to build his home. And others with him. Though farming here meant terracing the land and water meant backbreaking work walking it up the hills and the homes had to be built with stilts on the front or the hill dug out behind to make them level.

But she had seen it all over the world. In stone and ice and desert and jungle and water itself. Man would live where he wished and he would live everywhere. Hard as it was and the world brutal and unforgiving, he would live. There was no place yet she had found this not to be true and she did not think she would.

She walked down the road and felt them looking at her and went into the first place she could. Knowing they did not know her but they knew she was someone else. In places like this everyone was known and she could not stay. For they would remember her when the soldiers came and it would always be like this until she was in a city where she could be lost and only then would she be safe.

The building she'd chosen was an inn of sorts. On the bottom a wide open room with long tables and off on the far side a door and stairs and above the rooms. A fire burning in the stone hearth on the end of the room and another near the back. The smell of smoke but more so the smell of food. Some sort of bread and coffee and meat and eggs. A few who had stayed at the inn sitting at the tables and talking and others walking in the front to take their food in bags and leave with it for what the day held. In the morning and midday this a place for food and at night she could imagine ale and beer and whiskey and music and voices.

She went over to the far fire and sat near it at a wooden table with her back to it and the wall. Looking at the door and the far end where the owner came out of the kitchen and handed the bags to those coming in or went to the tables to refill the glasses. Two other men sitting near her and one nodding at her as she sat and then turning back to talk of something she could not hear.

The innkeeper nodded to her also and went back to the kitchen and she watched the door and then he came out again and walked over to her. Standing before her in plain brown clothes with something on them that suggested he was both cook and innkeep and maybe many other things besides. A large man going bald on the top of his head and looking at her pleasantly without smiling as a man, perhaps the only one in this town, who saw many new faces and spoke to many he didn't know and never really would for the string of them was endless and proceeded in only one direction.

"Just to eat or you need a room?"

"A room as well."

He nodded. "We have coffee and eggs and ham."

"That'll be fine."

"How long?"

"For the room?"

"For the room."

"I guess that depends. I need to get to Erihon."

"You want to get from here to Erihon?"

"Or as close as I can."

He sighed and looked out the window toward the river and behind him two more men came in and stood by the bar and he didn't look at them but she could see that he knew they were there. He looked back at her. "I don't know but I'll ask. How soon do you need to go?"

"Soon."

"Yesterday then."

She smiled.

"I'll tell you when I hear but I can tell you now you won't get all the way there from here. Might be someone's coming through can take you to Kraeg or up to the Arristone. And you can find someone else there. You don't want to buy a horse?"

He'd given her money before leaving with the parchment with her name on it, but not that much money. She shook her head. "I'd rather not."

"All right. Well, I'll tell you."

"Thank you."

"Of course."

He turned and went back and the men waiting nodded to him and he went into the kitchen to get what it was he had for them and she looked also out at the river and waited for her food. That waterway a thin black thing here by the town, with rocks and moss in it and a drifted log caught and turned and the wood very bright with the water.

She'd known she'd not get to Erihon but Kraeg was farther than she'd hoped. From there she could take any number of merchant ships across the Gray Sea and to harbor towns like Raggorie or Calipse or the Whitecrest, the only watchtower the Erihon had built two thousand years ago when they fought the Whispermen and which they still manned. Now the tower more a lighthouse than a fortress, but at least one company on the grounds at all times. Protecting at once the traders' road and the inland portion of the sea.

The Arristone would work as well, but she had no desire to travel on the River of Blood unless she had no other choice. Many would laugh at her for that but it was who she was and she knew that would not change.

Let them laugh.

He came back with the food and the coffee and set them down and nodded when she thanked him and then walked back to the kitchen. She ate and the food was very hot and good and she had to tell herself to eat slowly and could not and finally just gave in and ate it all even though he was watching her do it and she didn't know what he'd make of it. He came back once to fill the coffee and she drank both. It was stronger than she would have liked—she who had been raised on milk and sugar that you drank in the courts or on a terrace as you looked out at the countryside, lounging on pillows in the warm sun hours after those who drank the meaner black variety had already consumed theirs in the darkness for the heat and wakefulness alone and then trod in that dank first light to toil as they would —but it was hot and good and she'd had it like this many times on the campaigns and that was enough to make her fond of it.

When she had eaten she paid for the food and room both and he came back and gave her the key and nodded toward the stairs. She thanked him again and finished the coffee. The main room was still just as empty as it had been but many people had come and gone and no one who had seen her come in was still there. Or at least she thought not. But she kept looking again and again to be sure and knowing it had been too long since she'd played these games. In the end the real risk was of course the one she couldn't avoid and he was carrying her plates back to the kitchen so she stood up and went to the stairs and went up.

The room was small and looked out at the river. The walls and ceiling and floor all of planks sanded and oiled. A lantern sitting on the bedside table and light coming in from the window. The sound of the river moving over tree and stone. A small basin with water in it and no mirror. She went to the water and washed her face and arms and dried them and stood looking out at the river.

She felt that at any moment she would die. She had felt this way every time on the campaigns and at first it was horrifying and eventually it fell to the background and became as much a part of the world as light and sound and all else.

Riding through some dark escarpment once she'd felt it again returning in full and drawn her horse up and heard the yells as they came over the far cliff, a swarming mass of them with their faces painted and behind them the captains on the kralons, great beasts that they rode with claws sharper than any sword since the fall of the Ringed City and some of them mutated with two heads and the armored plates down their spines split up each neck.

But it was always around her. She felt it when they camped on a snowcovered field beneath a starswept sky with the air cold and silent. She felt it when they stood inside the city gates and clasped hands with men she knew and trusted and the whole of the army surrounded them and offered protection from everything the world had to kill them. At least now with the dragons gone. She felt it always in this life she lived and she felt it now.

What she did not know was whether her time underground had stripped her of what she needed to live despite it. Bleeding it away a little at a time so that now she would crumble and cower and die when it grew stronger, rather than wheeling her horse and drawing her sword and riding with it raised over her head for the hills where they thundered down on her like the reckoning of some long-forgotten god of war.

II

She woke and she knew they were already inside. She could not identify that which told her, but still she knew. Perhaps she'd woken to the sound of the horses in the road, or perhaps it had been boots in the hall or on the stairs. Maybe a voice that sounded as if it were from the city and not this quiet mountain town. She lay in the darkness listening and the moonlight fell slanting across from the window onto the far wall and she heard nothing more.

She'd slept in her clothes and with the dagger he'd given her lying on her chest and she stood. The bed still neatly made beneath her. Just the imprint in the wool blankets were she'd lain. She pulled one corner to smooth it and went to the window and looked out.

The river moved darkly in the starlight and she could not see anyone. Had there been enough of them they would have put a man down along the bank or at least on the back of the building to watch the windows, but they had not. That told her either that there weren't many or that they were too confident that they'd be on her before she could run.

She slowly lifted the window and froze when for a moment it screeched and stuck and she thought it wouldn't move any more. In that endless moment she heard steps and knew it this time and they were coming down the hall. Not quickly. Perhaps another guest simply walking out to relieve himself or leaving some woman's room to slink away in shadows rather than wake with her. But she didn't think so and she pushed the window again and it barked and slid up.

All below still quiet. Far off a wolf again howling at that full moon and the sound everywhere of the insects in the thick vegetation along the river. A wild and tangled place broken further on by docks and the mill. But no soldiers in their armor or anything else.

Going back to the door she checked to make sure it was latched and then grabbed the post of the small bed and dragged it across the room. Nothing to wedge it against, but it would buy her a second if she needed one. The footsteps stopped at the noise and then came on quickly. At least two of them.

She returned to the window and looked out again and the first man hit the door. He tried it without striking and the lock held and she heard him curse and then the snap as he slammed his shoulder against it. The lock still holding, another curse, and sounds in the hall as others woke up.

It was twenty feet to the ground and nothing between her and it but she looked up and the beams holding the short overhang were rough and open. A beam every two feet running down the roof. She put the knife in her belt and reached out and grabbed the nearest beam and pulled herself into the air. That feeling of everything changing in the world as the support fell away beneath her. Legs swinging forward and a stretching in her arms.

But she'd climbed that damned ladder of bricks and stones to get out of the prison and this distance was nothing to her and she swung out to the edge of the roof. Lanterns coming on in the windows running down the length of the building. Inside the sound of both men kicking at the door and then the thunderous sound as one shouldered it. The crack of the slide lock breaking free and the clatter as it fell to the floorboards.

She couldn't remember the slope of the roof or if it was flat and she swore silently. The bed grinding on the floor behind her. Then she knew she had no choice and she had to hope it was flat or die here and she reached out with one hand and grabbed the edge.

It wasn't flat, but it was a slight slope, and there was a metal brace running along the outside edge. A place for them to stand in the winter when they climbed up and removed the snow. Just a thin strip but enough to get her fingers around. She swung forward with that dark river lurching below her and grabbed the edge with both hands and turned in the air to face the inn – for one moment holding on with just one hand and her heart in her chest and her fingers grinding as they spun – and heard the bed slam into the wall as they shoved the door open.

Two men, both in black cloaks and riding boots. Not soldiers at all, but mercenaries. Little more than outlaws for the crown hunting outlaws against it. Both with short swords in hand and one with a crossbow strapped to his back. Her eyes met the taller one's and he didn't blink but started to shout and his jaw was square and thick and his teeth rotten and then she summoned all the strength she had and lunged up onto the roof. Pulling her body up to her chest and dragging it along the rough wood shingles and her arms screaming. Then throwing herself forward to get one elbow up and swinging her legs after it.

He got a hand on her boot, but only for a heartbeat. Then she kicked it away and swung the rest of her body up and sideways and rolled onto the roof.

Below her the inn a cacophony of screaming and yells and she could hear the cook yelling over all else for everyone to be quiet and she wondered how many of them there were in the hall. The hunters alone were silent and she didn't doubt that they were already pushing their way through the hall and for the stairs.

She pulled the knife from her belt and watched the edge of the roof and waited for his fingers to come over so that she could cut them from his body but he hadn't lived this long in his profession by being stupid and they never came. She forced herself to wait five seconds longer and then rolled to her feet and looked out.

The roof rose in front of her and gave her cover from the street, but it also pinned her against the riverbank. If he went down there with the crossbow and could shoot worth a damn he could take her off the roof and collect her body from wherever it landed. But no one could see her yet. To her left another building the same height as this one. She could not remember what it was, but the roof was the same. After that a shorter building with a flat roof and then nothing where a road went down to a dock.

She stood up and ran, boots cracking on the shingles, and threw herself over the gap with that drop below, stretching for the second roof and feeling all the air go out of her and perhaps the world and there was no sound. It seemed even her heartbeat hammering in her ears had stopped. In that moment something stirring within her that was memory but that was also something more and deeper.

III

A dark shape twisting in wrath. A light over the far mountains and all below them darkness. Here at this mountain pass her and the others standing and her with a sword in her hand and eyes on the sky and it was then that the very mountain shifted like some foundation deep below of pillars and marble had at long last and in neglected decay began to crumble and this world they knew, built as it was upon the worlds of the dead, was starting to fall into that space with the memory of bones and dust and she lost her balance there as the ground lurched and for one moment could see deep down the long cliff face of sheer stone and that endless drop before her. And then someone had the neck of her chainmail and hauled her back to the path and her sword falling end over end, silver washed in that breaking light, and for hours afterward she had that feeling inside her chest of having nothing below her that man was never meant to feel and instinctively feared above all else.

IV

She hit the other roof hard and fell and rolled and pushed herself back up. She knew she was bleeding but she didn't feel any pain yet and that's how it always was. Once she'd killed three men in a church as they were trying to come in through the barred doors and only after everything was done and they were piling the bodies in the street had she noticed the gash running the length of her arm.

They were in the road now and many others as well and lights on in the buildings. She put her head down and ran hard across the roof and tried to gauge the distance to the lower one and almost did and landed hard on it. Pain flaring through her ankle. She didn't know if they'd seen the way she ran or if they were still looking at the roof, but she knew they'd heard that and she rolled down to the edge and jumped. Below her the rocky falling shoreline running down to the river and there the dock and the road going to it.

She landed in the shrubs and rocks and when she got up her forearm was numb and she stumbled down toward the river and then he was on her. She heard him before she felt him and she tried to stop and he hit her in the small of the back with his shoulder. Driving them both to the ground. She felt his hand coming up and she grabbed it both with the hand she could feel and the one she could not and she brought her head down to it and bit into the flesh at the base of his thumb. The taste of blood and salt and sweat and the man screaming. The knife falling from his hand.

Twisting over she threw him aside and pushed herself away, scrabbling in the dirt and gravel. He rolled and came up hunched and holding his hand. She looked for the knife and did not see it and looked back. In that moment all still and quiet and a decision before her that must be made instantly and the whole world turning on it. Or sitting perhaps on that driven axis and waiting to see which way it would turn.

The river flowing blackly behind her and the forested bank beyond. The man on his knees with his bloody hand and him not looking for the knife but just reaching to his belt to draw his sword.

The world waiting.

She threw herself at him. Rising and stumbling and then pushing twice hard in the sliding gravel with her feet. Just those two chopping steps for force and lowering her shoulder.

She hit him hard in the jaw as he looked up, the sword free and in his hand. The bone splintering under her shoulder and the cracking as his teeth came together and a great guttural sound from him that was neither scream nor cry but something deeper and more real than either. The pain flaring and all the air going out of him and the noise involuntary in his torment.

They both went over in the dirt and she rolled to her feet with her shoulder screaming its own and his eyes were nothing but white. Both legs bent under him and the sword in the dirt at his side. A loose-wrapped black hilt and rusted blade.

She picked it up and turned and ran back up the alley to the street. There were people on the porches and she heard the horse and knew he was coming and what that meant. The crossbow must already be in his hands and if there was any distance when he saw her it would be no fight at all and so she must erase that distance now before she could see it and so she ran. Her body a machine thrust into this primal combat that would pay later but that now responded as it must and wrenched on.

Leaping up to a wooden porch running the length of the building. The wood hollow and loud under her feet. People watching her and others the road where he was coming. She listened for the horse and adjusted her gait just slightly, her eyes on the corner. He was rounding it tightly and fast and she stepped up onto the bench at the end of the porch and then pushed hard with one foot off the railing and threw herself into the air as the horse came around the corner.

She hit him in the side with her full body and he did not make a sound. At the last moment starting to turn toward her with the bow but it was too late and she knew it. They went over in a tangle of limbs and the horse stumbling back and she ran that rusted sword up to his neck as they fell. Not feeling it bite and pushing and then they hit the ground with her on top and that was what it took. Her body slamming into the blunted back edge of that blade and it pivoting through the side of his neck and both of them awash in blood.

She stood after a moment, trembling and covered in the hot blood. Her fingers tingling and not feeling like her own. All about the townspeople staring at her and everything very quiet.

Without a word she walked over to the man lying unconscious with his eyes rolled back and she put the sword through his neck until it stuck into that packed dirt of the road below. The blood boiling again and a thundering sound in her head.

She did not look at the people watching her and she turned and walked in that roaring silence to the river.

Chapter Twenty

I

They walked through the desolation and the dead. This city of absolute ruin. The white and gray stones of the walls torn and blackened. The bodies between them lying in all states, some half burned, others rent as if by a great sword too large for any but a god to wield. In other places just pieces of the dead as they'd been torn limb from limb and all those parts scattered.

The dragon had descended on this place and brought down that thin veil between this world and hell and for perhaps an hour hell had reigned.

They had fought, Brack knew, for there were soldiers and a scattering of weapons. Archers with broken bows. Arrows littering the ground, a sword with the blade snapped cleanly in the middle, the handle of an ax with the head torn off. Some of them had stood and fought and others had run and then turned to fight as it fell upon them and still others had just run and now lay dead with the marks of those claws in their backs.

In the end they were all the same and they were all dead. For that was how a dragon left a place when it came in fury on the wing and desired to kill. He'd seen ranks of men told for days they could kill it and aligned perfectly and armed with blades said to be made specifically for dragonflesh and he'd seen them all swept aside in the beast's first pass. He'd seen men rise up in desperation with nothing else but stones and field tools in their hands and he'd seen them torn apart.

It did not make a difference. It never did and it certainly had not here.

A main cobblestone road ran through the city from one wall to the other and it was that road that they took. The gate at the far end made of iron, lying off its hinges. Canted to the side and with enough room to let them pass under the wall. A deceptive distance that they could see as they walked but which would take them an hour to reach.

"How do you know?" Juoth said. His voice cracked and loud in this forsaken place.

"Look," Brack said.

Juoth was quiet a moment. "You can know you haven't found her. But you can't know she's not here."

Brack looked at him grimly, then nodded. "It's not hope, if that's what you think. I'm not that much of a fool. To say she's not here simply because she's dead and I can't face it. If she were I'd be looking for her body."

"I didn't mean that."

"You did mean it and you were right to." Brack pointed ahead, over the wall. "But look there."

Beyond the wall there stood a black tower of smoke, thick and condensed like a pillar. Swirling straight up into the sky and looking as if it could pierce the clouds. A writhing, living thing. Or very nearly.

Juoth stopped, and the girl beside him. Brack did not and when Juoth spoke his voice was faint. "Where is it?"

Brack stopped then and turned. Looking first at Juoth and then locking eyes with the girl. Something in them he had not seen before, a flickering as she watched him. This mute girl with fair hair who had been dead in that river.

"Darish-Noth," he said softly. "The dragon is at Darish-Noth. And that's how I know she's not here. Because he's tormenting me with her. He wouldn't just kill her and leave her like this." He pointed with his sword at the looming tower of smoke. "That's for me. Telling me where he is and where she is and what will happen to her. Just like this entire city."

The girl began walking forward first, still silent. Stepping in bare feet among the rubble and shards. Juoth watched for a moment and then followed her, trotting quickly and passing her. Stopping right by Brack and hissing:

"Then you think it's a trap."

Brack smiled. "Not precisely. But yes. After a fashion."

"And you're going to go anyway?"

Brack was quiet. Then he nodded. The girl had come up and stood looking at him and he met her eyes and had to look away for what was in them.

"Yes," he said. "I'm tired of being hunted. If it wants to hunt and it wants to use my sister to taunt and bait me, then so be it. I'll go and it will find out exactly what type of prey it has drawn out."

They went on and the pillar of smoke seemed to grow before them. Brack did not watch the sky but knew the dragon must sense them. Perhaps had known they were in the field while they slept. And it waited for them, content in this knowledge.

It was a foolish way to kill, he thought. For there had been many other times when the kills would have been easier and faster. Going back to the keep in the burning yards and billowing clouds of steam as snow and ice a hundred years old melted. Or in the road as they went up from the farmer's house. Or it could have faced him in the ice field, could have come to that quartered horse as an equal combatant and brought on what end would be.

A thousand more besides.

But he had always felt that men longed to be dragons for what dragons were and what they could be, this beast the realization of all that men craved. And in that also a spiteful arrogance, found likewise in so many men. As it had chosen to kill those around him and to burn cities and to drag him on toward Kayhi so that it could kill her in front of him.

Perhaps in this a deep-seated knowledge of the response such a thing would elicit, forcing him into sleeplessness and rage and waiting for him to make a mistake because of it. For a weary hunter seeing his life torn apart in front of him would not hunt the way he needed to hunt to kill a dragon. Instead clumsy and reckless. He'd seen others die this way and would see more do so. As all emotions and thoughts fell aside but anger and pain and very quickly those things became the hunter's undoing.

But he did not think so. He thought this was something else entirely, a vile torment being wrought for its own sake. To torture him and nothing more.

And he would not let himself think of what that must mean as he walked on toward that second pillar of smoke and the beast hulking at its base, breathing into it the heat of both life and destruction and waiting with black wings to shred the air and fall on him in fang and fire, a raging molten heart beating in its chest and driving it to this final stand.

II

They camped that night in the middle of the plain and still the dragon waited. Something had shifted within him and Brack felt no compulsion to run or push himself on. He knew now what this was. If it was going to kill her before he got there then she was dead already. But it would wait for this was the game that it played and there was no timeline within it. Their meeting would arrive when it did and be resolved how it would and they were both now marching to that end.

The camp was simple and they sat on the ground about their fire. The bedrolls long lost. The girl looking at them in endless silence but something within her still changing. Juoth watching in the firelight the distant city. The pillar of smoke now lost to the night but the fire burning bright at its base. The dragon fueling it and perhaps crouching in that same night and looking out long across the plain to their own small fire flickering in the stillness.

There was a peacefulness to it and he'd felt it before battle and other times besides. Always the next day drowned in blood and chaos. But this was as simple as anything could be.

For when a man thought he would die in the morning only then was his mind free of all that which usually enslaved it, all thoughts of what life held or what he must do to build toward some imagined end that he had determined he wanted or been told he wanted and all of life then a struggle to obtain it. Wondering all the time if the obtainment would be bitter when it was not what he thought it would be.

But with death standing in the doorframe all of that fell away and he was no longer blind nor bound and an immense weight was lifted. He'd seen men smile on the eve of battle who had never smiled in their lives and the next day they were run through or hacked into pieces and he felt they'd known that night before what would happen and that was why they smiled.

He looked at the girl. She was holding her hair over one shoulder in her hands and turning it with her fingers and looking at it curiously as if close to remembering something. Some way of tying it, perhaps.

"What's your name?" he said.

She looked at him and she blinked and said nothing. He met her eyes at first and felt there was the faintest trace of a smile or some bemusement on her lips and then he looked away. When he looked back she was folding her hair again and twisting it about her fingers.

"I thought you'd take seeing her differently," Juoth said.

Brack smiled softly and moved a log on the fire. Sparks rising in the night air. "Think I'd run screaming? Try to put an arrow in her?"

"Maybe that's too far. But you know what I mean." He motioned to the side at her with his head like some paralytic. "This girl was dead."

"I know she was."

"And now she's not."

"And now she's not."

Juoth scowled. "That's just what it is where you come from?"

"You told me you don't believe in magic. Said there's no such thing."

"I know what I said." The scowl deepening, then fading into something like resignation. "But that's not it. You think I'm a fool?"

"I know you're not a fool."

"That so."

"And that's why you believe in it. You saw the boy, now this girl. You know I'm not a liar and I told you that dragon died two hundred years ago. Yet it's also alive."

Juoth was silent.

"I'll tell you what I think if you want to hear it."

"I'll hear it."

"You don't want to believe in it," Brack said. "So you try not to. You're not alone in that. All men do it. I met a man didn't want to believe in the plague and told me it wasn't real and it wasn't coming on the ships. But I saw the way he watched the harbor. Even met some who told me there was no such thing as dragons, despite the dragonskulls decorating the walls of the Ringed City. It always comes back to power."

"In what way?"

"A reduction. A man is nothing in the face of a plague, a

dragon." He met Juoth's eyes. "Of magic. There is nothing we want more than that control and having a say in our lives and making them what we want them to be. Wars have been fought over it too many times to number. But against some things there is no solution and it's then that men refuse to believe. Because believing in something that takes that power and control away, and against which one cannot stand, well, that's enough to break a man."

"You think I don't want to be broken."

"If you do, you'll be the first person I've met who did. No one does. Me, you, her."

"So I'm the liar, then. Is that all this is?"

"I think you said what you wanted to believe." He leaned in, keeping his face calm. "But you always believed what was real. No matter what you said. Because you're not a fool."

Juoth sat back and Brack watched him. For a while nothing on his face but many things working in his eyes. The shadows of those things within. Then finally he smiled and said:

"You're a son of a bitch, you know that? Never met a man who told me something, then I told him he was lying, then he told me I was lying about the lying and why I was doing it. Never met a man who'd do that in my life."

Brack said nothing but grinned also as he turned again the log in the fire. They sat then in the silence for a time and it started to burn down and he didn't put anything else on it. The dragon was close enough that there would be no wolves. They would sleep and then rise and finally they would do what they'd been brought here to do. Whether it was what he thought they'd come to do or what the dragon thought they were there to do – to die – they would know soon enough.

III

He could see its shape in the twisting ruin of that spired city before the others, his eyes bred for this so that he and the dragon could watch each other across the distance when other men would walk unknowingly to their deaths. It sat on the shattered pinnacle of a short tower, the stones clutched in those talons that cut it as if made from diamond, the other towers rising around it like some thin and mangled forest of stone. Its black wings folded against its back. Before it rising with each breath a simmering glow and embers sweeping upward. He felt that he could see the scar around its neck where the head had once been cut from the body but he did not know if he saw it or if he only knew it was there. Either one the same in the end.

Juoth was watching him watch it. Glancing cautiously and his hand on the hilt of his sword, trying to look at Brack when he would not be caught and failing. He couldn't see it but he could see Brack's eyes and that was enough.

The girl walked with them in silence. Her gait easier now, he thought, but still a shell stripped of what had been within. Perhaps being filled from some unknown well inside herself or perhaps not.

Perhaps he had carried this dead girl to the field merely for her to die again. This time in flame and writhing agony. Would she scream if it came to that, or would she die mute with her mouth agape as the flesh melted from her bones? Was it that torment that would bring her back fully, if only for a moment, so that it could be stripped away again? He knew much of the world and fate and cruelty, but he did not know that.

Juoth walked closer to him and turned his eyes to the city. "What if it comes now?"

"It won't."

"It could kill us in the field."

"I'm telling you it won't."

"We're too exposed."

He looked over. "Do you think that matters? You just

walked through a city burned to the ground. Not two stones left standing. Everyone dead and scattered."

Juoth was silent.

"But it won't," Brack said. "Because it wants me to see her as it kills her."

"Your sister."

"It could have killed us a hundred times if it just wanted to kill us. This is the point. This is what it wants, and it won't strip itself of that by killing us in the field an hour from the city."

"Do you have a plan?"

"Always with the plans."

"So you don't."

Brack was quiet. He had been turning one in his head and he did not know if it would work but he did not know what else he had. "Not a lot of use for plans when you hunt dragons. They always last for about two breaths and then the dragon does something to ruin it and if your plan was all you had, you die."

"Better two breaths than none at all."

"Would you just be quiet for once?"

"You think I'm wrong?"

"Just for one damned minute."

The bodies were scattered at first. Blackened bones and bent armor and missing limbs. Two or three lying together, one by itself. Part of a body that you couldn't tell which part. A sheath of arrows dropped and scattered in flight. The dead ranks slowly swelling all around them until it was men piled on men and women and horses and carts and everything burned. The wagons splintered and destroyed and the horses gutted and many of the men killed with talon or teeth before the fire, but all burned eventually and lying in the mud.

In the earth long furrows where it had come down with its claws. Sweeping to the side and dragging them. Another curving line where its tail had swung and torn the soil and risen and then crashed down and trenched out an area the size of a horse. This cavity now filled with blood and bone. The ground about littered with swords and axes and spears and all that men carried so often to their own deaths.

The kings of old had believed you took what you were buried with into the next life and they built huge tombs filled with gold and jewels and young girls entombed to die with them. If there was an afterlife and you took what you had with you when you died, he thought, it was a whole world filled with broken swords and shattered armor and scorched earth.

It all began to thin out after a time and then they left the dead in their wake. The second city of the plain rising up before them. This one a city of dark stone and sweeping walls and spires slender and soaring. Flags had once flapped on the tops of those towers but the dragon had torn them down. The iron gates lay twisted before the walls. Around the top of that wall and below the battlements an endless line of proud and intricately carved men at arms and gargoyles with their twisted bodies and horses rallied for war. All in darker stone even than the walls and these ancient carvings still intact though they had not preserved those inside.

She's the only one, he thought. She's the only one in there.

He stopped then with the city three hundred yards before them and slowly the dragon rose and showed itself. Stretching with exaggerated sloth and arching its back, the black tail moving serpentine in the air below the tower, curling about like something else entire and alive in that air. A ball on the end cracked and harder than stone. The scales were black and the underbelly as well and its face slender and flaring out near the forehead. Those eye sockets set and burning now with the hatred it carried within it, the light flickering off the horned forehead, the spikes running up over the crown of that head and down its back.

That dead circle clear now about the neck. Free of scale

and spike, just twisted and angry flesh, hideous and mutated. The dragon for all its horror and vileness holding a strange sort of beauty, but that scar a wretched and ugly reminder of what it truly was.

"Let me go alone," Brack said. "Stay with her." Not taking his eyes of off the beast as it opened the great canopy of its wings into the air.

"Tell me something."

"This isn't the time."

"Why is it you?" Juoth said. "Why is it you that it wants? Your family that it's killing?"

Brack drew in a breath and he could taste the smoke and sulfur and he knew it well and felt all the world was in that breath. Holding it burning in his lungs. For there was nothing else and had been nothing else and in between just times waiting until this again was the world. All that lay before him and all that he was.

"It's not just killing my family," he said at last. "It's killing my children. One and then the next until there are none left." A burning in his eyes that was not the smoke, a twist of his lip. "Kayhi is the only one I can save and if I can't then there's nothing else for me. And it knows that."

It was deathly silent. A high wind whipping above the plain and in the spires and pulling at the edges of the dragon's wings. It felt as if there was heat lightning in the air and all about and every hair on his body standing on edge.

"My great grandfather didn't slay that dragon two hundred years ago." He reached back over his shoulder and drew his sword in one smooth motion, the blade ringing on metal and flashing in the air. Never taking his eyes from the beast now standing and waiting for him to come. That twisted and mangled scar about its neck where the head had been severed. "I did."

The Dragon Hunt

Chapter Twenty-One

I

She stood on the cliff edge and all below her a forest of deep green and a river cutting through it and everything so far away there was no way to descend. This cliff of sheer rock falling back to the forest. Below her an eagle gliding beside the shelves of gray stone. She thought she could hear the river a long way off but it could have been something else. Beneath her feet the tangled roots of a tree standing against this drop with those roots ancient and penetrating into cracks in the stone, into thin dirt and moss. An improbable place as it arched itself out over the nothingness but a tree older than her and she did not know if it would grow this way for all time or if it was only standing until that inevitable day when the roots gave one after another like old ropes lashing a ship in a storm and the whole thing fell with a terrible slowness to tumble end over end until it was lost from view.

It had been two days in the forest and she was very hungry. She'd followed the river from the town and no one had pursued her with the dead bodies in the street but she knew she'd underestimated him. The first time running she'd felt stupidly invincible after not seeing her pursuit and spending one night in the forest and it'd taken him almost no time at all to track her down. Without luck on her side she would already be dead or chained again in the pit.

Too long, she thought. It had been too long since she'd done this. She'd forgotten what a king was. Even a waste of a king had the power of the kingdom at his fingertips and commanded men far better than him and in that a sort of omnipotence.

She did not know where she was. The plan had been Erihon but plans were made to be cast aside and so it was. She had thought for the first day that this was the way to go and now knew that it was not and needed just to find anything at all. A town or a crossing or anything. Without which she would starve in this wilderness and then they would never find her.

She smiled. How long would he live if that happened, looking always over his shoulder? Seeing her in the shadows, waiting for her to rise against him. Knowing he hadn't caught her and fearing always that each meal was poisoned, each messenger an assassin, each banner raised against him her final arrival with an army at her back.

When really her bones rotted and turned green with mildew as the forest ate her body. All returning to what it had been.

A ghost truly in her haunting.

She crouched and looked out over that land and she thought far off she saw smoke, but she couldn't be sure. Perhaps a town or perhaps nothing but a fire, raging until it burned itself out. But it was below the cliff and she knew she needed to forget that and turn and follow it but even then she did not know where to turn. What lay before her. Walking as a blind woman with neither dog nor stick and hoping in that darkness to stumble upon that which would save her.

For she didn't want to be a ghost. She didn't want to haunt him in some abstract fashion that drove him mad. She wanted that madness to come from what the world really was for him, with her pacing and rising from those shadows. She wanted it vested in the truth. At that last moment when his fear tore him apart she wanted it to become real as she came down on that city and dragged him into the streets before all so that they'd know what happened to those who stole the throne.

Your boy, something deep within her whispered. *He's still your boy.*

She closed her eyes and the roots beneath her feet felt like her husband's bones, scattered in that pit where his labored breath had stopped and the silence had been horrible and complete and she'd known she was screaming but could not hear herself.

No, she did not want to be a ghost. For it was far better to haunt him like a demon, a twisted black shape in the night, running its talons along the stones of the hallway as it walked to the door and hunched outside, a curved black blade in hand, ready to right the scales of the world. For those scales were weighted with nothing but death and only death could put them even again.

Your boy, that voice said.

Faint and drifting and unreal.

Your boy.

She could hear it but she could feel that she was losing it. Like something once known but now not hard enough for what the world had become and slowly within her everything cracking and breaking and perhaps all that was real and true eventually lost to these ravaging fires that tore like a storm at her soul and consumed all that was and against which nothing could stand. Perhaps the foundations of men and women and the very world alike and all destined in the end for the same madness.

II

She followed all day and the next the top of the cliff. Always with the fall below her to remind her what she was. She caught a rabbit in a snare and ate it and tore roots from the earth. Eating leaves that she could not remember if they were poisonous or not but did not think so. Just one at first and then two hours later when she was still alive the rest.

The fire still burned in the woods and never changed and she knew it wasn't one fire, but many. The smoke of chimneys and a town and a mill and what all else they'd built there in the forest. She could not descend this long cliff but she could follow it and she looked always for the way down. It was a small hope but she needed something and she clung to it.

It was on the third day that she knew she was being followed. They were careful but she had been stalked many times and she could sense it above all else. A deep coldness within her. She had been asleep and she woke suddenly and she could hear them. She thought there were three but it could have been more. She was huddled in the hollow of a tree and they could not find her and she listened to them walking in the light rain and trying to be dead silent so that they'd be on her before she heard them.

She did not breathe and it was an eternity. They passed her and worked their way on, but soon she heard them slowing and understood what they were. More than just soldiers walking in the woods on blind hope. They had lost the trail and knew what the absence meant and they began to circle back.

They did not find her that night. She moved her position and was careful not to leave a trail and lay in the branches of a sprawling tree looking down at where she had been in the hollow. She thought once that a dark shape moved through between her and that place but she could not be sure. It was only there for a moment in shadow and then gone. A rainslicked cloak. A flash as lightning played in the clouds, features harsh and cold. Then nothing.

She left that morning before the sun and went down a thin trail along the face of the cliff. Climbing down until the rock rose ten meters over her head. The stone walkway just as wide as both of her feet together. Clinging to the edge with dirt and small stones skittering and falling and disappearing into the darkness. Below that horrible emptiness. But she could see ahead of her a small open area that protruded out into the air like some natural balcony and she thought it was the edge of a cave.

Perhaps this trail not as natural as it appeared, but carved by those ancient and long dead. Or perhaps those dead ones had just found it and used it. Like so much of the world it was impossible to know. But she did not think she was the first to traverse it and she knew she had to leave the forest. Here the stone hid the signs of her passage in a way dirt and soil never could.

Reaching the bottom of the trail she stepped on the wide ledge and felt the world move around her. Suddenly one misstep would not send her gasping and clutching into nothingness. She settled herself back against the wall where she would not be seen from above and breathed and looked it over.

A yawning cave mouth. The old remains of a fire on the surface of the ledge, scarring black onto this gray stone. Markings on the walls of the inside of the cave, just lines and figures. Crude and telling in that crudeness. She saw no other way out, not up or down. The trail that may have been carved ended here and nothing fell away below it except the smooth stone and the trees and the river in miniature below.

She wondered what those trees would look like as they rushed up to meet her, if the speed of her fall would seem to increase or if the nearby wall screaming past would swallow that illusion. But then she saw that dark and mutated shape again, felt the crushing wrench of a heart refusing to beat in a chest with the air ripped out, and she stepped back into the cave.

It was a place to live, she thought. They would not come down the same path or it would be too easy for her to knock them from the cliff face and send them crashing into that far-off forest. But it was also a place she couldn't live, for it was an empty stone cave with nothing for food, for water. They could camp at the top with their swords standing in the dirt and wait for her to come back up and she would either starve here or go up to them.

The back of the cave was shrouded in shadow. She stood at the entrance letting her eyes adjust and a thousand thoughts moved within her. Perhaps a whole system of caves, which she could navigate one and then the next, crawling through the tight little entrances and worming her way in utter darkness until she stepped back into the sun in some distant place, lost and tired and free. Perhaps a tunnel carved by whoever had carved the walkway down, trenching in this earth to create a second escape. Perhaps that path along the face of the cliff was the second escape itself and those long-dead had used some other passage she had yet to find.

She'd filed her way from iron bondage, climbed a wall of brick and stone, slept in a forest that ate the living, killed those who pursued her. Those things flashing before her eyes as she blinked and the shadows slowly dissolved. Perhaps this was just one more step to take before she could return to that field with the army at her back and some banner flying in the air and the smell of horses and men and the warm earth and the call of horns on the wind.

She stepped forward to find that redemption and he was sitting in the back of the cave. He had a slender short sword out and across his knees. His leather cloak wet and pooled around him. He'd pushed the hood back from short-cropped blond hair and he had no beard and he looked like a child but he was here. She did not know him but she knew a thousand like him and she started to step back out of the cave.

"Don't," he said. "Koetter is at the top. It's over."

She stopped and stood looking at him. She'd worked with assassins before and she knew what this man was from his eyes alone and had she seen them torn from his body she still would have known. There was another way and he'd seen her working her way down and taken it. Maybe in some manner she hadn't noticed he'd forced her here, herding her like a dog herding sheep, but silent and from the shadows. All to give himself this edge, this advantage in this place where there was nothing she could do.

"Sit down," he said.

"How did you know?"

"Sit down." He did not change the way he said it but something changed in the way he held the sword and she sat carefully on a rock at the front of the cave. He watched her the whole time. He did not appear to be tense but she knew how fast he would be on his feet and she would not see him or the sword until it had gone into her and come out again and she was standing wide-eyed with her heart in two pieces and still trying to beat beneath skin and bone.

"Did they tell you?" she asked.

He smiled softly and it was a horrible thing. "Those two fools in the town? No. There are a thousand of them looking for you and they are all the same."

"Then how did you find me?"

The smile broadened a bit. "There's only one of me."

She looked at him. "You don't have to do this."

"Of course I do. I'm being paid incredibly for this."

"I have money."

"You have nothing. You're a dead queen."

"I will have money."

"I'd be a fool also to take a deal like that. The hope of a promise or actual gold." He tipped his head to the side and there was something feline and dangerous in it. "What do you think I am?"

"I know what you are."

"Then why offer me that?"

Because there is nothing else to try, she thought. It felt all around her like the world was growing smaller and compressing and some great force outside bearing down and crushing it all in slowly and with unstoppable power. The confines of the air itself clutching about her chest. She blinked and it was not this cave anymore but the pit and the iron shackles and the bones in the mildew and dirt and then she blinked and it was the cave and she could not see out of the corners of her eyes.

"How are we going to do this?"

"Listen," she said. Her voice did not sound like her own. "He's not a king. He stole what he has. You don't have to follow him."

He did not move his head but he laughed and it was a dead sound and sharp and no humor in it.

"You think I care about kings?" he said. "I don't give a damn about kings. What king hasn't stolen what he has? You're all the same and the world is the same and it always has been and always will be. You and your damned honor and it's all just a front for power and money. Nothing more. Kings live and die and when they die other kings replace them until they too die. I don't care which king it is who pays me. All I care is that the king of the moment is the one with the money and he pays and when someone comes and severs his head from his shoulders and dips it in tar and puts it on a stake over the front gate, only then will I go find out who he is and how much money he has."

She tried to speak and could not. He was nearly lost to shadow. She wanted to close her eyes and the air was so thin and she didn't close them because she knew she'd see the pit and hear those chains clanking against the wall and she held them open as this unsteady ground moved below her. Some shifting of the earth's core deep within it, the broken pillars of the world.

There was one thing left and she knew it as surely as she'd known anything. Standing unsteadily to her feet. He did not move or she didn't think he did. But she knew only one way to make this darkness recede. Gasping now and sweat pouring down her face. She closed her eyes for just a moment and saw those bones in that grasping darkness and then she screamed, a bitter and shrieking sound tearing at her throat, something primal and furious and all that she had in her, and she ran at him with the knife raised in front of her and looking for that flashing sword.

She had been right about one thing: She did not see him move. There was only the faintest sound of the cloak and a grinding of stone and then his fist caught her hard in the temple one time. All that dark was replaced for just the barest moment with a flashing light, and then it was dark again and she was falling and spiraling through it and she could still hear herself screaming as the world broke.

III

She woke at last and everything was pain and she closed her eyes again and lay still. Feeling the rope around her wrists, tying her hands. The stone beneath her. The cold sound of the water dripping on the face of the rainswept cliff. When at last she opened her eyes she was lying where she'd fallen on the floor of the cave. The world sideways. His boots in front of her on the cave floor, him sitting where he'd been as if nothing at all had happened.

"This will be what you make it," he said.

In her mind she could feel a sort of humming sound, deep and vibrating in her skull. It was not a noise but something more. As if perhaps her skull itself were moving, like a bell that had been struck. The pain flaring all down the side of her jaw where he'd hit her. She closed her eyes and opened them again and that's when she knew it wasn't from being hit. It was something else within her that was stirring and she did not know what and she wanted to scream in a way that ripped apart her insides but she could not.

He was still speaking. "If you want to play this game, we'll play it. If you want to be silent while I take you back to the city, it will go a lot better. But don't put any of it on me. It's all on you and it has been this whole time."

She was not closing her eyes now but she felt like she was. She could see the swirling black and in her stomach there was that feeling of falling, of headlong downward flight. A lack of control. The whole world rushing around her and past and perhaps some world other for it never ended. The darkness moving and alive, a thing of fire and wings. First there and then gone and then somewhere else and always present. Writhing and tearing at the air.

Another voice. "I don't think she's awake."

"Her eyes are open."

"I know, but look at them." The sound of boots, one of them stepping closer. "She's not there."

The humming was swelling and growing and it was everywhere in this misshapen world of shadow and mist and the unknown. The molecules of the air itself thrumming with it. Pulsing and turning. She opened her mouth and then closed it again and it felt like the sound was in her body and perhaps she was producing it. Her tongue numb with it.

"What did she say?"

"I don't know."

Silence.

And then suddenly it all returned and everything was very clear and she felt herself sitting up. All about the sharp edges of the world, vibrant and brilliant and each edge glowing with some light of its own. In all the background that brooding darkness. The humming was gone and there was a dead silence and it felt like a lake of ice, the whole of the world about to shatter with the first plummeting stone and she felt if she looked up some burning horror would be falling on her to destroy that lake and everything would be shards with edges like razors and it would rip her apart, body and blood and all she was, cutting her to pieces. All of them shredded under this hailstorm, a torrent of wind, pelted with broken glass.

She could feel herself speaking and she could not hear the words. Her jaw working up and down and the cold stone floor below her, but she could not see the cave properly for the sheer brightness of it and everything else and she could not close her eyes.

And then there was a snapping sound like lightning falling at her feet, that cracking strike where the whole world was fire and so very bright and the acrid burning of the air and for just a second before it all went dark she could hear herself and she was screaming and she was saying over and over *the ice, the ice, it's under the ice and it's so thin, it's under the ice.*

The Dragon Hunt

Chapter Twenty-Two

I

He was bred for this and he felt in him the rising fire as he always did, walking across that plain toward the ruin of the city where the black dragon perched on the shattered tower, curled and serpentine and vile with those claws twisted into the stone, the eyes burning as it watched him. He felt it in his chest and in the sword before him and he gave himself to it.

There was nothing else but the dragon and not even himself. For a man worried about himself would die and the only one who could kill a dragon was the one who thought of nothing else but the slaughter. Who lived in this world of bone and blood and ash and carnage and who deep within himself loved it exactly as the dragon loved it. The two one and the same in that, their passion for this world of horror and death. For nothing else but the same depravity could rid this world of the creatures that haunted it, and if he must be so to end it, then he would.

And within that burning core of his body, of spine and heart, were he and the dragon both ripped open by the gods themselves, those gods would find no difference at all. When they met it would be as brothers to the same fire and the same destruction and they'd let all else fall as it may.

The dragon rose from the tower and he could hear its wings hammer the air and he did not look away from it as he began to run. Faster, his feet pounding the dirt and ash beneath his boots. He did not feel the sword in his hand for it was just the very metal of his body and his heartbeat as he ran was as even as if he slept. His breath measured in this smoke-tinged air.

It climbed before him and pivoted in the sky. The talons dark on the ends of the wings. Watching him as he came, one side of its face turned away. Holding there in the air as easily as it stood on the ground for it was a creature of every realm but the sea and moved effortlessly wherever it chose and then it threw its head back on that long neck and shrieked once, loud and ripping the air, and flicked its wings up to dive at him.

And then he saw her. In that brief moment as the beast turned in the air and came for him, he saw her standing impossibly small on the top of that tower. The very peak sheered off and smoke rising all around her and the drop endless below as she stood on what had once been the floor. Tall and straight and unafraid, her black hair curling behind her in the wind. Watching him as he ran and seeing these two sides of her fate rush toward each other to wage a war that would never end.

For one heartbeat, there was nothing. All the world holding still and silent. Air and smoke and the dragon itself.

And then it was between them, this shrieking beast falling toward him like a star torn from the heavens and teeth flashing in the firelight of the city it had killed. He blinked and he could see again the dead around him, on both sides. The bodies charred and mangled. Piled in the road and the yards. More no doubt beyond that tall stone wall before him as he neared the city, a wall made for men that could have withstood an army ten thousand strong and had meant nothing to this creature of the air. Archers and spearmen torn from the walls and thrown into screaming headlong flight, not knowing even as they fell whether they were whole or if their legs were gone to fuel this terror and the furnace within it that burned on blood.

It came down at him and he watched its face and thought for just a moment of how it had hung in the air. As it had pivoted and watched him before driving itself at him. And as it reared its head back to burn his body, to fuse him into the ground itself until there was nothing left, he threw himself to the side. Twisting, falling in the dirt and mud. The flashing of metal and a short stone wall. Pressing against it and the grit in his teeth.

And then the tide of fire flowed through, rolling and burning and the heat everywhere. Like a churning forest fire condensed into liquid, tearing into the ground and washing over the stones.

But it missed. The dragon thundered by, pulling its wings back to slow itself and then beating them hard, twice, as it rose and turned and screamed again that unquenchable anger into the air. To break perhaps the very sky.

Lying behind the wall that would never save him, Brack smiled. Pushing himself to his feet, pulling the bow and arrow from the body of the dead archer. This man not burned but missing his arm and the right half of his chest, the metal of his breastplate and his very flesh cut exactly the same, jagged edges and a deep red hollow inside.

He'd been bitten and thrown from the wall. His heart gone, turning in the air. Brack did not know if he'd lived long enough without that heart to feel the fall, the wind, the rushing ground. Or if he'd been a corpse already and merely raining into the dead below, his blood a red mist behind him.

But even in death he had held his bow, an arrow clenched in his fist. The next to be drawn, held as he'd been taught when he had to loose two as quickly as he could. Against this creature he'd not had the time, but the weapons had fallen with him, unbroken.

The bow simple and hewn with a taught string. Nothing like the power or reach of the crossbow that he should have carried but in his haste had not. But it would be enough against this half-blind creature that turned in darkness and fury, swinging around with only one burning eye left in its head. The other torn out generations ago on another field, ruptured and lanced as Brack had run forward to drive the sword into the open place under its wing.

Each time he'd seen it at a distance, the fire still burning in that socket, the illusion of life where nothing lived. The dragon a revenant, but incomplete. The scar about its neck where he'd cut the head off, the flesh crudely fused. But the eye, that ruined eye, still nothing but a gaping, smoking hole in the side of the beast's skull.

II

It circled again to come back at him but it took the turn wide and high, beating its wings against the air. Cutting far out around and calling once loud and like a hawk and then sweeping around behind the tower where Kayhi stood tall and straight and alive. He could see her face and her eyes wide and she was staring at him and only him, not following it as it circled, and he loved her more then than he ever had and he did not think of the dead but just of her. The last and youngest and the one he could save.

It swung behind her and closed and flashed the side of the tower in flame. Almost nothing, just enough to scorch the stone and leave it black and smoking. Never a danger to her.

But he watched it, for this wasn't what a dragon would do. The whole time he'd felt it. That something in this was wrong and wretched and he hadn't known what it was. From the moment it fled him at the keep, having torched the tower. It could have killed him then and had not. And again when it burned his son while he watched, leaving nothing but an old man's blackened bones in the melting snow of that desecrated village. Then too it could have killed him but had run again, leaving a clear trail of destruction that he could wade in with blood up to his ankles, living in the land of the dead.

He'd known then that it was going for Kayhi, but this had not been a race for it was never one he could win. Had it just wanted her dead it would have been here in hours and not bothered with Cabele at all and left him a corpse, dead and rotted when he arrived days later.

And now it could kill her again, if it wanted, but it forever toyed with him. Even to this end. In that there was spite and dragons knew spite and fed off of it just as men did. But men were fools and dragons were not. Never were they fools. If it meant to kill her she would be dead now and he could not stop it, but it did not mean to kill her, only to give the illusion. Putting her there on the tower, soaking it in flames too far away to do her any harm.

He stepped out into the street again as it came down. He knew it would try to kill him but he no longer understood what it was and that terrified him more in some ways than if it had just been a dragon and nothing else.

It dropped down again on those black wings and he leapt to the top of the short wall. Sliding his sword home over his shoulder and raising the bow, arrow already nocked and drawing as he brought it up. Feeling the flex of the wood beneath his fingers. It trusted its armor and did not move off of the line but bore down, bringing its claws up underneath. Each longer than his sword and just as sharp and it could cut him to ribbons or impale him as it had done with many others. Just a gasping second and wrenching pain in his gut and spine.

But he also trusted himself and he raised the bow and sighted down the length of the arrow. Feeling it and letting the bow become part of himself. The death it dealt an extension of his will. Wanting to scream as every nerve stood on edge, but staying silent and still. Dropping the arrow slightly, holding it, finding that remaining eye.

With the slightest movement, letting the arrow loose.

The snapping sound of it leaving the bow was nearly lost in the creature's scream and the wind of its wings, but he heard it anyway. His ears trained to hear everything of the hunt, even as he threw himself again to the side, this time off of the wall, falling and rolling on his shoulder toward that dead blind space to the beast's left. Knowing it would be just the slightest bit slower tracking him that way and also knowing he only needed those fractions of an inch, of a second, to live.

It came through like a tempest, a great thundering roar, and he could see the firelight on the claws as they raked the air. Could hear the beams of a house crack under the downdraft alone, the roof falling in with an uproar of dust. He turned as he rolled, instinctively ducking and pulling his arm down as it lashed out frantically with its wing and the clawed end, flailing at him but just too late. He could smell the leather of the wing as it went over his face, could have touched it if he'd just reached out.

He knew it even as he turned. The arrow had missed. Had he hit his mark, the beast would have been screaming and falling and rolling in the dirt and ash, but it was not. It was screaming in fury at the missed kill, but rising already and turning to circle again and descend for a third pass, just as it had two hundred years ago.

He saw the shaft, just for a heartbeat as it arched its neck, looking for him and trying to find him as it turned. The arrow had struck in the throat, embedded in that scar where there were no more scales, where he'd sheered them away as he'd hacked the head from the dead body. In that other life. Perhaps the bow was off, shooting low; perhaps the beast had moved its head at the last moment, trying to focus and read the depth with only one eye. He did not know but the shot had been low and it rose with the arrow like a needle, lost and insignificant, buried in the throat but far too small to be anything but an annoyance to a monster of fire and night.

He hit the ground hard and was up again and drawing the sword without thinking. Throwing the bow aside. There were no other archers near him and if he ran for one it would take him in the road with the rolling fire and that would be the end. He had to stand now with the sword and the sword alone.

It had been done, and he'd trained for it. How to move under it and bring the sword into the underbelly, looking for a weakness in that armor. How to lunge for the killing zone beneath the wing. If it was foolish enough to come with teeth bared and try to take him that way, he could go for the scar itself, tear the throat out and leap on it when it fell.

He looked back at Kayhi, so far above him, and he felt something in him change. He'd been a reckless fool to run in without the crossbow, without a plan, leaving his only ally guarding a dead girl on the edge of the killing field. But he'd been late at the keep and watched his children roasted alive in the tower; he'd been careful and smart at the town and watched his son and countless others burn on the horizon.

So this time he'd been reckless. And now he was going to die for it.

He raised the sword in front of him, felt the weight of it. That flawless steel forged to an edge that never dulled. A sword that had tasted blood a thousand times and thirsted for more as he watched the dragon sweeping around to dive again, a hurling black star in the open expanse of the sky.

He would die, but he wouldn't die alone.

III

The dragon washed the tower again in flame and then hung for a moment in the air, watching him, the smoke rising around it and fire glinting off those black scales like pitch burning on the water. It did not try to remove the arrow and he did not know if it felt it. But it watched him all the same, the sails of those wings moving slowly and rhythmically to hold its place, and then it began to rise. Gaining altitude and distance but never turning its back on him.

And suddenly he knew what it meant to do. How it would drop on him in anger and weight and crush him to the earth, bones breaking and splintering. Rendering that sword useless for even if he pushed the blade through that space beneath the wing and into its heart he would still be killed beneath it. For in many ways men and dragons were the same except in this: A man was fragile. Even a hunter. In this an inherent weakness thus spawning the myths of a race of giants as men sought through invention to cure their one fatal flaw, imagining a man as tall as a tower who could rule uncontested.

He began to run. Before him the dirt-paved road, the wall of the city too far to reach on foot. On either side the houses that could not save him and a running trail of the dead. Barns and fields and carts abandoned briefly before that death came.

Ahead a single structure to which men often fled in these times, a hulking church with stone walls and a high rising roofline, dwarfed by the wall beyond but still three stories of stone and timber. The flag that had once flown from the pinnacle burned off and smoke pouring out as the dragon had filled it with fire like a stove, but the walls standing, the roof intact.

The dragon shrieked again above him and began to dive. He did not look but he could hear it, that high-pitched whistling as it fell like the moon itself had been torn from the sky and thrown to earth, some cataclysm coming on furled wings. He ran and in the street were the bodies of the dead and he could not see their faces. The great oak doors of the church standing open and burned and still thin smoke rolling from inside.

As he went up the wide steps he looked one last time and the dragon had stretched out its wings, its jaws gaping, and then he was in the church. Sprinting still and running down the scorched aisle and the banners on the wall to one god or another burned and curled and blackened skeletons fused to the pews. They'd come here to pray and there were bodies piled at the front and a sea of wax that had been candles poured down the stone steps. The dead piled and their skin like burned parchment and their faces like wax themselves, melted and ruined, and for a moment he could imagine this room as the dragon crouched with open jaws in the doorway and filled the whole of this place with liquid fire. Pews and pulpit still burning and the embers glowing red and against the far wall the blackened outline of the priest where he'd stood with arms outstretched and been entirely consumed in the single last pumping of his heart.

He ran for the far end and the burned wooden doors and the stone rooms beyond. To put anything he could between him and this horror falling and ripping the world apart. Running with his sword before him and stretching for those ten slender stone steps at the end of the room. The pews filled with the dead rushing by on each side and the sound of some gasping screams, one of these wretched souls still alive in his melted and burned body and entangled with the rest, but he could not see which.

And then the dragon came through the ceiling.

The heavy beams splintered and there was a tearing sound as if the air itself were coming apart at some invisible seams. The stone shingles cascading down and shattering around him, exploding as they rained to the floor. Running through dust and shrapnel and everywhere the sound of the dragon screaming as it plummeted to the ground. The far wall ripping from its foundations and falling in with a shattering of stained glass and the thunder as the stone blocks buried the floor and the pews and the dead.

Brack dove forward and lost his sword and picked it up again. Scrambling up the last three steps and turning back to look.

The roof entirely torn off, the smoky light pouring in. The dragon drawing itself up and beginning to stand in the piled wreckage, looking unnatural and depraved, some malevolent being hellbent on the destruction of the world, all scales and wings and teeth, cast out by gods and men alike and now rising to tear both from their place in the world and establish its own rule over all there was.

It began to turn its head to look at him and he could see the jagged hole where the eye had been, nothing but a black scar and wet, viscous redness inside. A ruin of a face on what had been a beast once beautiful in its own fashion. Now the look of some mad king or an animal caged and driven with hunger and fury.

Brack leapt down the stairs, running for it as it drew itself back up. Legs burning with each step, crashing through the wreckage and smoke. Running toward it and also to the side, keeping that ruined eye in line with him as it searched desperately for its prey. Pushing its wings out but unable to turn as quickly as it needed with the remaining walls of the church around it. Even with one fallen, this space confining and limiting.

Only for a moment. The shortest of moments in which all of life was truly lived.

Brack came up under the rising wing with both hands on the hilt of the sword and he thought he could feel for a heartbeat the tall grass against his legs. As he lived his life a second time, this endless cycle. The dragon began to turn its head and did not see him but somehow it knew, perhaps also reliving that gashing death in the field of blood and gold. Drawing in its legs, tensing to leap back into the air, that space it owned and always had, to launch itself from the pull of the world. To defy gravity and the earth itself and this man who would strip away its life and once again tear out its heart.

As the wings beat down for that savage escape, Brack slammed hard into the beast's scaled side, running headlong in desperation, and drove the sword once again into the space between its wing and its body, pushing the blade in to the hilt as the black blood poured down over his arms.

And then it was gone, throwing itself into the air, ripping the sword from his hands and leaving him drenched and shaking in the ruin of the church.

IV

He stepped through the rubble that was left of the wall, climbing those thrown and piled stones, and stood atop the heaviest of them to watch the dragon rampant in the air. Wheeling and rending that air as it screamed in fury, the very houses shaking with it. A sound so horrible it was as if it had never been meant to be heard by man, as if these beasts were supposed to have lived their time and died and then man his and never the two at once. And perhaps that the root of all the violence and killing between the two lines, as these creatures that were both meant to rule found each other battling tirelessly for the same world.

He could not see the sword but the dragon was pitched to one side. That wing not moving properly, not getting the full extension. It could fly but there was a burning torment in each beat of the wing, in every meter climbed. There embedded this blade like a thorn to a man, but white hot and ripping apart the beast's entrails.

Then it came around again, pain or not, torment or

triumph. The black jaws hanging, those rows of teeth as fine as needles. The horns atop its head and twisted. The long tail curving behind it almost like some ghastly deformity, slack with the pain.

That eye deep-set and burning, never leaving him.

Brack looked to Kayhi as the dragon swung around behind the tower, meaning to pass it one last time on its way to kill him. So that she could feel that updraft as the wings beat, could smell this foul creature with a body like a rotting corpse. Could feel the heat from the furnace in its chest. Kayhi, small and lost in that shattered stone tower, standing straight as ever, her head now turning with it.

So that he in his shaking fury could see it all laid out before him.

He knew then that he would die and he knelt and took the knife out of his boot. Six inches of steel meant for cutting out a buck's heart and tearing off the hide. A tool and nothing more. A wooden handle with gold bands, the blade beaten silver. He spun it once in his hand to get the weight of it and drew himself up. No cover now with the church destroyed. One more stand and perhaps he could find some way to sink the knife in the creature's eye as it killed him.

He looked at her once more, this last child, as the dragon raged toward the tower.

Her footsteps were fast, choppy, calculated. Two steps with power as the dragon neared, and then she threw herself into the air. The beast still behind the tower, her body small and dark and falling with her hair whipping upward in the wind. A plunging wraith almost lost in that vast gray backdrop of smoke and stone and the dead city, hurdling toward the ground.

And then it was beneath her, never having seen her jump, blocked by the tower and its eye always on him. Brack could not feel his heart and it had stopped in his chest. Wanting to scream and run and bound somehow in unseen iron. Watching his daughter fall, arms and legs outstretched, her dark dress billowing in the air.

She landed on the dragon's neck. Above its shoulders, her feet and arms wrapping it as she struck, the impact hard and silent at this distance. A speck swallowed by the black beast, consumed by it. To anyone else invisible, but he could see the way she grasped it, strong and graceful, taking the blow to her chest that must have stripped the air from her lungs, not letting her momentum throw her aimlessly around that scaled neck but letting it carry her downward, one hand gripping a single horn on the dragon's head, the other reaching forward.

Grabbing the arrow from that torn flesh, the scar about its neck. Ripping it free in a spurt of blood.

The dragon screeched, began to pull up, swinging its heavy legs beneath and beating its wings to slow its descent. Twisting its head toward this parasite on its neck. But Kayhi just swung with the movement, arrow in hand. Light and agile and muscles like cords from countless days with him and their swords in the courtyard.

The dragon came down toward the earth in a twisting firestorm of air and dust and smoke, the frantic beating of its wings billowing everything around it. The buildings shuddering and stones pelting Brack's face, chest, arms. Black blood pouring now from both its neck and its side, some of it burning, some heavy like pitch or the blood of the long dead.

Just as it came up to land, Kayhi swung forward on that horn, ten meters above the earth and nothing but that hand keeping her aloft, throwing her body forward. Her other arm pulling back and then flashing forward like lightning, the huntress in flight with her golden spear, and she buried the arrow in the only eye the dragon had left.

V

They hit the ground and it seemed to tear it open at the deepest cracks, the fault lines, those plates wrenched apart and the inner workings revealed for what they were. Brack was thrown from the rubble of the church and everything came down around them, houses and barns and silos. Cracking stone and timber like the end of the world, the billow of dust and smoke drenching the sky.

He rolled and came back to his feet and ran. Could see nothing now but dragon's shape, dark and clouded, writhing behind that wall of dust. A tangle of wings and claws and teeth. The great tail lashing forward and then gone and then coming back to strike the ground with a snap of its own.

It was screaming and it was like no sound he'd heard from a dragon before. Nothing in it of anger or horror or mere pain, but of pure agony. The way a man screams on the field when he is caught up in the cavalry and he does not know the bottom half of his body is gone until he looks down and sees his own entrails in the mud and he does not scream long but there is a deep and real and violent way that he screams with blood in his mouth. And that was how the dragon screamed now, with the strength of a thousand dying men.

He ran into the dust and found it. First the tail swinging past as he ducked. Then a raking claw on the end of a broken wing. It smelled him and lashed out in all directions in fury and pain and still he ran. Something striking him hard in the side and the sound of his own ribs breaking lost in that scream, but he pushed himself back to his feet and stumbled the last steps and then he was at its side. Falling heavily against those hot scales, breathing this air like fire itself.

Grabbing the hilt he tore the blood-soaked sword free. With any other sword the blade would have been a splintered ruin but this steel was fine and unmarked, though covered in blood and the end glowing red hot.

He could not see her but he ran wild and gasping for the

beast's head. He could hear its teeth gnashing in the air. He leapt up over the front legs and took two light steps running along its back, then jumped down beside that long serpent's neck. The scales the size of breastplates, growing smaller as they ran up toward the head.

It twisted out of the gloom and dust and then he could see it. That ruined face. Blood pouring down along the scales. Gaping holes of torn flesh where the eyes had been, smoke rising gently from them. Furious within this raging storm.

And then he felt the inward rush of air around him, the dragon drawing one final breath into that furnace. For it may not see him but it could smell him as always and as he could smell it, these two combatants intertwined over two lifetimes and in some ways always chasing each other. Ages past and still waiting for a final death. It would cover him and itself here in flame, turn him to nothing but bone and ash with its dying breath.

For that brief second, Brack thought of each of them. His children in the keep where they'd found a brief peace on the icebound edge of the world. His son now an old man as they sat drinking tea before the fire in his cabin. Kayhi as he kissed her forehead, as she dove from the broken tower.

He drew the sword back and screamed and his scream and the dragon's were the same and then he lashed out with the redhot blade, chopping it downward with everything in his body and soul. Swinging it with two hands over his head like an ax, a crude and vicious weapon, free of all elegance and skill, its only end violence and death.

The blade bit into that open bleeding scar, slicing down through tissue and bone. Cutting even in that one swing between the vertebrae of the spine, splintering the bone. Slicing arteries and veins and ripping the beast's windpipe in two.

And for the second time in Brack's life, the dragon's head fell from its body. Falling slowly forward and the jaw still working up and down and behind it pouring a river of blood and fire. The scream suddenly and completely gone and in its wake just choking blood in its windpipe and lungs. The headless body for a moment unaware and still trying to blow out that last breath.

The head landed heavily in the dirt and he could feel it shuddering the world one final time. Grinding sand and stone beneath it. The skull taller than a man standing. Rolling in that dirt and the face tipping toward him with those hollow eye sockets and the jaw moving once more, the teeth painted red and glistening.

And then it was still. All was still. The very world frozen as this beast was torn once again from its fabric. This undead abomination returned to what it was.

As the dust and smoke fell in this aching silence about the hunter, standing still himself with sword in hand, he turned to look for his daughter.

Chapter Twenty-Three

I

She could smell the fire as they came up over the hill and could not yet see the smoke against that slate morning sky but knew from far off. Something deep within the bones of man, that scent of fire on the wind. In days before time this perhaps the greatest threat and always moving before it.

The distant beat of wings in the air; sheltering in caves.

They crested the hill and stood and the horse bent eating and they were gathered before the wall of the city. How many she did not know. More standing atop that wall and leering. Soldiers leaning on their elbows in chainmail with their steel helms next to them on the wall. The poor of the city in the mud and the dirt. The others on the high ground where the hill rose gently to the orchard with its white-blossomed trees. The firewood lashed and piled and the stake rising from it and the girl in her white dress bound to it with chain.

Standing firm now, hair in the wind, the dress billowing back past the stake. The fire still far below her and rising and the smoke taken in that wind and blown from her face so she could look out on the people of this city and the last place she would ever see.

She'd watched them at the stake before and they were all

different. Some stoic and silent and making not a sound until the very end when they all did. Others trying from the very first to breathe in the smoke, desperate gasping breaths. Still others screaming from the moment they were lashed and crying to be cut free and wretched before the smoke or flame got to them and only worse when it did.

With this girl she could not tell. Too far away, her small white form against the stone wall. She could have been any of them.

He drew up next to her and looked at her and looked at the city and turned and spat. "You know who that is."

She looked a long moment and blinked and turned her head and looked again. "I know," she said.

"He says she helped you."

"She didn't know anything."

The mercenary laughed. "Oh, I know. I'm not this rabble. Never think that."

The queen sat very still and felt something cold and small sinking endlessly into her. A deep winter twisting and withered.

"Why?" she said. Barely able to hear herself.

"Why? You wonder why a king kills people?" Tipping his head to the side. "You've been around this long enough to know that."

"But why her?"

"Same reason as anyone else."

It was growing now and she knew she would kill him and she didn't need to say it. She didn't know if he knew it as well. She had met some who would but she thought in him, with all this skill and knowledge that he had, even as someone who walked in the same world she did, was this brooding arrogance that he could not shake and would never want to and that would only be stripped from him at the very end and by then it would be too late.

"Fear," she said.

"It's the only thing that matters."

"That can't be."

He rested his hands on the saddlehorn. This a man secure in his own lack of servitude, but also at his heart still a servant and the silver for it riding on his belt. But a different kind of man, and showing it in the way he held himself.

"Of course it can," he said. "A man is what he is because he fears being something else. A king is a king because everyone fears what he can do. Whenever they stop fearing him that's when someone else rises up and then the king becomes a tarred head on a stake and someone else becomes king and then they fear him instead." Looking at her there in the open air. "You didn't fear him enough and now look at you."

She kept watching the twisting fire and it was too far away. They could see very little and even at a dead run in this country she'd never make it before the girl was dead. She thought of all those times this slight girl had come in and taken her to the bath, helped her with her clothes. Simply doing what she was told in life and all she'd ever known and doing it as well as she could. And now torn out to come to this end.

"He still didn't need to kill her," she said. "He has me."

He smiled again. "Yes, but he also has to make sure everyone else knows what happens to people like you. There are things that happen when power and fear come together and this is one of those things. He'll use it just like any king. Make them believe what he wants about her and turn her into some vicious evil and everyone will praise him for rooting it out and fear him at the same time and when he raises those banners they'll fall behind him even though he sends them to their own death because they'll know that death is the only thing that awaits. Might as well find it on a field with a sword in your hand."

"But he wanted them to love me," she said. "That's all he had to hold his power. To keep his own generals from a coup.

The people had to love me."

"Not now. Didn't you hear?" Looking at her and grinning. "Turns out you're the one who killed the king. Wanted the throne for yourself. When he found out, he tried to arrest you and you ran. The people are already in a frenzy. Their beloved queen, a murderer. A regicide. Some of them are burning your likeness even now, no doubt."

It felt as if all the world were in that moment dissolving about her. Everything unreal and so thin. Especially the air as it all came apart.

"He already told them the king died in battle." Those bones in the dark. Endlessly those old bones.

"They don't care," he said simply. "In time, they'll forget."

"Forget their own idea of history."

"Just a different lie."

"But still the history they knew." It couldn't be, couldn't be, couldn't be. Closing her eyes and then opening them again. All she loved before her and yet lost.

The mercenary shrugged. "He writes their history."

They rode down then and she thought she could hear the servant girl screaming at the stake. She knew it was just the wind and that they were too far away, the trees edging up and blocking their view as they descended on the old dirt road, the dust rising in the air around them, but she could not help but think it was the girl. She closed her eyes and could see her with the flames moving up her legs and in her hair and so she opened her eyes again and looked out at the country around her.

A calm and green land, full of forests and fields and blue rivers falling noisily through stones. An open land and prosperous. Something her family had worked at for a long time, to make it a place where kings and shepherds alike could enjoy what it offered and relax in safety and never look to the roads in fear. Never hear the rumbling thunder of thousands of horses and marching men, never hear the tearing shriek of a warhorn in the air.

And now, as the servant girl screamed in the fire, she felt it was all coming to an end.

II

They did not go to the city. They came down to the outskirts and took an old farming road out west and into a small forest. A stretch of trees that had once been logged and then allowed to grow again and still here and there the immense old trees that had survived that first cutting, a hundred years older than anything around them. Perhaps two hundred. Their gnarled trunks black and towering above the rest, their huge sweeping canopies. Nothing like the deep forest she had been in, but still those old trees in all the young, green growth like stewards of some age long past.

Here the road narrowed and they went up and down two hills and out into a field of grass and moss and sand. The city far off to the east now and this a place she had never been. The trees breaking for the field and heavy still on all sides, secluding this place from the world.

In the middle of the field stood an old house. Not the size of a keep but large and made of stone. Ivy running up the sides and still thick and green for the season, though it would become thin and withered and barren in the winter, as the snow descended and swept this whole field in white. Heavy wooden shutters over the windows and a wood shake roof. A single tower rising like some brooding watchman from the far corner, the roof sharply peaked next to it, an enormous chimney on the opposite side. A black iron flagpole standing off the top of the tower, but no flag flying from it.

Before the house stood a dry fountain. The shape of a naked wood nymph with her hands raised, where water had once sprayed and fallen into the wide bowl. That bowl the same stone as the house. It was marred with age and discoloration and parched dry as it must have been for years at this abandoned place, and he was sitting on the edge of the fountain picking at his fingernails with his knife.

He did not look up as they rode across the field and stopped before him. Both climbing down, her more slowly and the mercenary with a soft grace. His hand not on his sword, she saw, but close. Trying to act casual about it and also looking at the two guards who stood near the fountain. Another by the heavy oak doors at the front of the house, standing on the second of three stone steps leading up.

"You were true to your word," he said. "That was very fast."

The mercenary bowed his head slightly but did not ever take his eyes from the prince. "She was not hard to find."

"And not too much trouble?"

"Not at all."

Then he finally looked up, holding the knife poised in the air over his outstretched fingers. Looking her up and down in a way she did not care for. His hair longer now and falling down the side of his face. Something in his eyes both calculating and wild.

"Good," he said.

"Shall I go?"

He went back to his fingers. "No, no. Stay for now. We won't be long." He smiled slightly as he dug in with the knife. "I didn't bring your money, but I have it. We'll ride into the city."

The mercenary did not respond.

She looked at the three guards, and they were not men she knew. She wondered how many of those were left, how many he had replaced. She knew many of the generals were gone. The leadership changed to those he knew followed him and him alone. Some of the old ones relieved of their posts and others sent into battles they could not win, killed on the field perhaps with the knowledge that they'd been sent to die and perhaps not. But dead all the same.

"Who did you talk to?" The prince spoke softly, still working with the knife.

She didn't answer.

The movement stopped, but he didn't raise his eyes. "Who did you meet with?"

"No one," she said.

"We both know that's a lie."

"It's not." She looked back the way they'd come. The trail that had once been a road barely visible in this forgotten forest. "I just ran. I stayed at an inn and asked about passage over the border. No one would take me."

"Tell them who you are?"

"Of course not."

"Of course not."

She scowled. "Ask him. No one was with me."

The prince looked up. Tapping the flat of the blade against the tops of his fingers. "Well?"

"That's true enough," the mercenary said. "We watched her in the village. Two others were after her, when she was at the inn. She fought them, ran into the forest. From there it was easy to track her. Found her in a cave along the cliffs. No one with her."

"So you don't think she's lying."

"I never said that."

"No."

"All I know is she was alone when I found her. We didn't see anyone with her in the village."

"What about the night before?"

He shook his head. "Didn't hear anything then. A runner came when she was spotted near the town and I went."

She scowled. Wondering who had seen her, who had

called it in to him. How long he'd been watching her while she wasted her time with the others and then stumbled headlong into the wilderness, with no plan and no direction. All that work climbing out and digging those steps and just days later she was back where she had begun as if nothing had changed.

He looked back at her. "You see? I have eyes everywhere. We will find out who you talked to."

"There's nothing to find out."

"Then who killed the guards at the Trappers' Gate?"

A piece turning. The stones of some mosaic that devoured the world. Now comprising the world itself and all of them bent to its will. These unknowing pieces. She felt that it all must have danced on her face and she closed her eyes and when she opened them again there was a darkness at the corners.

He stood slowly, put the knife back on his belt. The soft sound of the metal whispering against the leather. Then he walked over to her, turned his head away. So close she could smell him, could hear his breathing. He motioned to the guard near the door, beckoning him over, then turned his head with his hair hanging in his face, his twisted lips almost against her cheek.

"Don't lie to me," he said. "You aren't any good at it."

III

The guards took her into the house, the old wooden doors groaning as they pushed them open. Inside everything cast in shadow and dust. White cloths hanging over the abandoned furniture. A long dining room with a table and chairs, all covered, leading out to a sitting room with a massive stone fireplace on her right. The stone chimney she'd seen outside rising up and through the roof. On the far wall the doors into the kitchen. Shelves along that wall with cups and plates covered in cobwebs, a candelabra standing with the wax candles half melted and drooping.

He led the way and they went left, through a door into a smaller sitting room. All around on the walls a stained painting on paper, a scene of a knight fighting a red dragon. Standing with the dragon towering over him, a lance in its side, the knight's horse lying behind him and only a sword in his hand. Behind him the city was on fire and people fled, but he alone stayed. She looked to see the crest on his shield to find out which legend it was, but could not make it out in the shadows before they were through the room and another door.

A dark and twisting staircase beyond. His footsteps hollow in the shadows. The wooden stairs against cold stone walls, circling around her. Going slowly up the tower on the western side of the house, with light falling in from the old slot windows. The kind designed for archers, though she was sure this house had never been held against a siege. The torch sconces on the wall, also covered in spiderwebs and unused for a long time.

The stairs went around twice and then opened into the room at the top of the tower. Perhaps ten feet in every direction, perfectly circular. The ceiling overhead of wood with exposed beams running up to the peak. The windows here much larger but the shutters closed and light just filtering in through the cracks.

There was nothing else in the room. More of the neglected torch sconces, the dirt and grime of the years, but nothing more. No chairs, beds, dressers. She thought at one time there must have been, for this felt like a lord's home and this was not a defensive tower. Just another bedroom, perhaps a status symbol. But it was empty now and she did not know if the people who had lived here were dead or had simply left, but no one had slept in the room for years, perhaps generations.

He opened his arms, spun in a slow circle. Smiling but not kindly. Then he walked over to a window and slammed one of the shutters open, striking it hard with the flat of his hand. It cracked loudly against the stone outside and the light fell into the room. She felt a clutching in her stomach as she saw that there were bars on the windows. He pulled his hand back in through them, grabbed one and turned to her, putting a show into tugging on it.

"Stronger here," he said. "Don't think I didn't check."

"Please," she said.

"What? You don't like it? This was a beautiful house once." Then he laughed and let go of the bar, walking toward her and stopping with his arms folded over his chest. "But don't worry, you won't be here long. They're coming to pick you up. I just need to make sure they know where you are. Can't have you running around the forest again."

The feeling in her chest tightened even more. Every time she blinked she could see her husband's bones, molding in the damp next to her where she sat chained to the wall. Her eyes burning.

"Just one thing," he said. Stepping closer. Something in his look that was real, that was not just a game. She hated that she could read that in him, but she could.

"Please," she said again.

"What did you use to do it? When you got out?"

It was so dry in the room. That heavy smell of disuse. The wind ripped through the tops of the trees outside and she thought she felt the tower sway with them. She stumbled, but he didn't.

"Tell me," he said.

She thought of the man in the dark. On the other side of the pit, emerging from that darkness to smile and help her climb. *Have you heard, he said.*

"A spoon," she said. "I used a spoon."

He looked at her a long moment. Not even blinking.

The mountains fall, he said. They always fall.

"A spoon."

"Yes."

They always fall.

He stepped back quietly, walked over to the shutter he'd opened. Reached carefully through the bars and pulled it closed again. A slight tapping as it met the stone.

"It was just me," she said. "It was all just me."

"You and a spoon."

"Yes."

He sighed. "It doesn't matter if you lie anymore. You're here now and that's the end of it. You can tell me what happened or you can lie and you're going to the same end either way." He walked to the door, the guard stepping out before him. Turned back with his hand on the frame to look at her.

The world was cracking, she thought. Seeing the servant girl screaming in the flames. It consumed her, that white dress blowing in the wind and smoke. For all she thought she was doing to save them, to stop the madness and the looming war, maybe she was just killing them. Just as surely, but doing it one at a time. Killing them all and not getting any closer to saving this land her father had built.

"He didn't know," she choked out at last. The tower swaying with every gust now. She felt she was going to fall and sat down on the stone floor. It was cold and hard and she could still feel it moving but at least she wouldn't fall as far. That dress billowing in the fire. "Just tell me you won't hurt him. Do whatever you want with me, but tell me you won't hurt him."

He cocked his head to the side just slightly. "Who?"

"I don't know his name," she said.

"The person you met with?"

They always fall.

"No," she said. "In my cell. The old man in my cell. He didn't know." The flames roaring up the stake as she closed her eyes, the girl no more than a blackened skeleton bound in chain, her arms thin and withered and her hair gone, her head wreathed in flame but still screaming. Somehow still screaming.

He looked at her in some way she had never before seen and in his eyes moving the lights of confusion and humor and a terrible and scorching hate, a boiling beneath the skin, something in him that could not be quelled. Opening his mouth and then closing it again and shaking his head.

"The man in your cell?" he said. That twisted scowl of a grin coming back to his lips one last time. "What man? There was no one in your cell. You'd been alone in there for two years."

Chapter Twenty-Four

I

She was on fire. He ran to her and the ends of her hair were burning as she lay in the smoke and dust and he threw himself on top of her. Smothering it with his body. The pain in his ribs. Even with the dead dragon and the destroyed city, still smelling that burning hair. Then pulling himself off and rolling her over.

Her eyes wide open. He thought for that one moment that she was dead, this last of his children. She could have been killed a thousand ways in that fall and he thought she was dead and pale and a horrible fury broke in his chest and then she blinked. Once, then again. Opened her mouth with blood on her lips and closed it again and just the faintest sound of her breathing.

He picked her up and carried her, stepping past the severed head of the beast. Its great body lying still and crumpled next to it and those eye sockets like ripped holes in the air leading to the darkest night in some other lost world, everything torn away now and the fire inside dead and even the black blood slowing. A dead thing as he'd seen it before and now dead again.

Juoth stood with the dust and smoke swirling around him

in the field. He hadn't stayed where Brack told him but he also wasn't a hunter and he hadn't reached them before it died. The girl behind him in the shroud of smoke. They appeared out of that air like some beings of the dusk with the city behind. He walked past them with Kayhi in his arms and they said not a word and fell in and followed.

He could feel her breathing now, but it was shallow, shuddering. He reached down as he walked and brushed her dark hair back out of her face and the blood from her lips, but the hair fell back and the blood returned. And he knew that something deep within her was broken.

This city not yet dead. He went in wordlessly through the main gate where it hung open. People prying themselves from the battered world within. Stepping out of rubble, climbing out of holes. Falling back from him, peasants and soldiers and lords alike. Most staggering past with a stunned, exhausted gait, covered head to toe in dust and ash, walking past without seeing him toward that still beast in the field. To see this thing that had fallen on them from the wild, in the blackness a screaming nightmare, a bloodsoaked horror. Now a slaughtered husk of a being, the flesh still warm.

The furnace still smoking in its chest.

No one came within ten feet of them, the crowd moving as he walked through. Not looking at any of them. Down the wide gray brick road that ran through the heart of this place. On all sides the switchback steps rising to the top of the wall where archers and spearmen had made their stand and died. Ahead the temples and towers and these great buildings rising out of a sea of stone. Everything here made of brick and stone and very old, built in the days when men knew dragons were in the air and knew also how timber burned below them.

He walked toward the temple, for it was the only hope. He didn't know what god it was meant for but he had been in a hundred cities and more and he knew there was nothing else. If no one there could save her then she was already dead and there was nothing to be done for it but going back to the dragon and tearing it into so many pieces no one would ever find them all.

Reaching down again to wipe away the blood. Watching it bubble slightly between her lips. Wiping it again.

The doors of the temple were closed as he walked up, heavy black iron doors with stars and serpents forged into them. Twenty feet tall and not nearing the top of the temple itself, where it rose into a flat plateau and then four spires, all identical. Two women coming up from the side, around the corner, and stopping when they saw him. Falling back and into this desolate crowd. Looking over their shoulders as they went.

He did not say a word, but the door began to swing open with the faint sound of chains. Each door ten feet across and opening into the temple, a sliver of pure darkness appearing between them. Then, dancing on the iron itself, the flicker of torchlight.

A man stepped into the gap when it was two feet wide, and the doors stopped. The man was old, his hair stark white, but he had no beard. His face like wrinkled leather left in the sun and his eyes so dark in contrast to all else about him. Wearing a simple white robe and holding in his hand a small silver dagger.

He looked at Brack, his eyes strong and alert and never leaving Brack's face, not for the crowd or for a glimpse of the dragon beyond the wall. Then he turned slightly aside and held out the arm with the dagger into the dark heart of the temple.

"Bring her," he said.

II

They went inside and the temple was a maze of black steps leading up and down and iron rails, all cast in that orange torchlight. A long thin passage running forward, perfectly straight, and far down an open space with a raised dais. But the priest motioned to the side, to a long staircase without a railing, and began ascending.

Brack followed. Behind him, the doors started to close again, though he could not see the chains or what it was that moved them. He could just hear the sound of those chains somewhere within the walls.

They went up the stairs until they were high enough that a fall would kill any of them but Brack, all trailing in a line with the dead girl between them and Juoth at the end. Glancing back over his shoulder at the doors, looking just once over the edge of the staircase.

When they reached the top it was not the end, but just the bottom of a spiral staircase, made of iron. Sheer vertical. Rising up fifteen feet through nothing at all, just blackness and air, and then going through a round opening in the stone ceiling. The priest began going up and they followed.

As they went through, the stone surrounded them on all sides, but with space between it and the staircase. More torches hung on the walls, far enough out of arm's reach that he didn't know how they lit them or changed them, but they were new and burning all the same. The feeling of it disorienting as they went around more times than he could count. Rising in this upright tunnel of stone and firelight. Finally coming out at the top and stepping into an open chamber.

Here in the heart of the spire it was all white marble. The floor, the ceiling, the walls. The frames of the windows on either side; the pedestal for the bed under the nearest window. That bed draped in white sheets and furs, the pillows as pure white as snow in the mountains where men couldn't reach. Next to the bed a small hearth and a fire burning and sunlight falling in through both windows.

"Put her here, Ironhelm," the priest said. His voice holding no age at all.

"She's bleeding," he said. Suddenly feeling the ash and dirt and blood covering him as they stood in this place that looked entirely untouched.

The priest smiled. "Don't think of the sheets. Put her down."

He went across and laid her gently on the bed. Her body so small and frail now in this near death and the furs swallowing her. Her head drifting to the side, her dark hair falling in all directions. He slowly slid his arms out from under her and thought for the shortest moment of kissing her forehead when she left, the horse rearing in the fireflame as the keep burned, and then he rose.

"They'll be here," the priest said.

Brack turned. "Who?"

"The healers."

"You can't help her?"

The priest turned both of his palms upward, lowering his head. The dagger was gone and Brack did not know where to. "I am afraid I cannot. But those who can are coming."

"She might die."

"I know," the priest said. "Who is she to you?"

"My sister."

The priest looked up at him slowly and Brack did not look away but he felt something in him when he met those eyes. He had stood and looked at more men than he could remember who tried to look him in the eyes and make him fear them but most of those men were dead now and he'd never felt anything like this.

"You don't have to lie to me. I know who you are."

He swallowed. "My daughter. She's my youngest daughter."

"You know he should have killed you."

"Who?"

"The dragon."

Brack nodded. "I know. Many times."

"Then why?" The priest looked at Kayhi on the bed, her chest moving just slightly. "Why did he wait for you here?"

"Did you see it?"

The priest nodded to the windows of the spire.

"Dragons are just men," Brack said. "They're just men and they fight for revenge the same as any man and it makes them just as foolish. It wanted me to watch her die and so she killed it."

"You think that's all it was?"

"If it wasn't, I'd be dead."

The priest was quiet for a moment. "Perhaps," he said at last. "Perhaps."

Two women came in through a door in the wall. Brack had not seen the door and did not know how it could be, having seen the spires rising into empty air from outside the temple, and yet it was. A seam in the marble bricks slowly sliding aside at the far end of the bed and both of them stepping into the room. Each wearing robes the same as the priest's, but theirs as red as blood. Their hair cropped close to their heads. One with skin nearly as white as the marble and the other as dark as those towering doors below.

"You see," the priest said, nodding with a faint smile. "They're here."

The women went to Kayhi and knelt and began to work. One wiping her lips of blood and lifting her head. The other running her hands down the girl's face and neck and ribs. Holding her hand against her stomach and then her breast to feel both the breathing and the heartbeat. Then nodding to the first who took from her pocket a small vial, removed the cork stopper, and poured what appeared to be no more than water into Kayhi's mouth. Just a thin trickle, then holding her head again as she worked to swallow.

Brack turned and Juoth was not watching them but

watching him and he stepped past him and went to the far window and looked out. He could hear them working still behind him and the wretched breathing that was his daughter and he looked far out over the wall to where the dragon lay. He could not see it for the wall but could see far off the people gathering and staring. This thing that had once been near to killing them now headless and broken, and in that some gruesome attraction.

Or perhaps merely the draw of disbelief.

He felt a hand on his shoulder and turned and the women stood together in front of him. Like the priest, they did not look away or shy back from him, did not appear to think him anything more than a man. Or did not care what he was.

"We've done what we can," the woman who'd touched him said, speaking softly. "We'll know in the morning. If she dies, it will be tonight."

"Thank you," he said.

The woman looked at him for a long moment. "Stay with her," she said. "All of you." Then, turning, they went back out the way they had come, through the door in the wall of the spire. Slipping through that marble as though they had never been. He could not see what lay beyond.

When he turned from them, the priest also had left. Faintly his footsteps descending on the metal of the spiral staircase, treading that iron down into the dark.

III

He hadn't thought of her mother in a long time. The strongest memory right after leaving the keep, that place blackened with fire, sheltering in the snow-buried cave and dreaming of her that time by the river. Her face in the warm sunlight and the riverside garden around them. In that dream he had only seen her for a moment and then she was gone and he'd woken in the snow and the cold.

That night in the marble spire, he dreamt of her again. Kayhi's mother, with the same long dark hair and that thin but strong frame, the same power and fire in her eyes. A woman the girl had never known but that she had become nonetheless.

He finally saw her again but this time it was not in the garden or near the river. Nor was it in the Ringed City or the fields and vineyards beyond.

After they'd married they'd rented a house in a high mountain pass. The town so far below them they could barely make it out. The dirt path to this place walking in stones along the spine of the mountain range, the open green fields falling off on both sides. From below they looked like fields you could lie in on a summer afternoon but when you got up to them they sloped away so steeply and then fell into stark cliffs and walking all along that spine was just a step or two either way from a drop of a thousand feet.

The house was small and made all of stone and set in a place where the spine dropped into one last true field, a hundred yards of grass and flowers in either direction. Behind the house a stand of tall trees where treading in the moss and browned fallen needles they sometimes saw rams and mountain sheep with their spiraled horns and heavy coats. Inside the house a single room with a hearth and a bed and the fire always crackling warmly and the sunlight falling in through the windows.

He dreamed of her sitting in that field and the time he'd taken the wine in their stone mugs, each filled so full he thought they'd spill because this was not a place where you worried about the conventions of pouring, and he'd walked out to her. Looking at her in that yellow dress with the wind pulling it back and her hair also and her looking out over the wooded mountains, far over the town, to the distant mountains where they reached all the way up into snow and winter. But here the heat of the sun and when he sat beside her and handed her the wine she smiled and leaned and kissed him and waved a hand out at the world before her.

Look at it all, she said, both then and in the dream.

He'd smiled and said nothing and drank the wine which was cold and good. The sun on his neck. The weight that was always on his back for this day gone. Finally gone.

Where do you want to go? he'd asked her.

She leaned over and put her head on his shoulder and just looked out at it. The dark rock crags that fell away and the thick green forest and the other path far below them, twisting in the treeline. A beautiful and tranquil place, set above the real world as if this was somehow another world entire up here, another plane in which men could choose to live if they wanted. Where the things that harvested the men below could not reach them and perhaps nothing was real and perhaps it all was.

And now in the dream she said: *You'll kill her, Ironhelm. You'll kill her.*

He woke and it was dark and he was lying on his back on the marble floor. One of his furs rolled under his head, his arm against the base of the raised bed Kayhi lay on. He could see instantly in the dark as always and he looked and did not even need to for he could hear her breathing in the night. Still that harsh and strangled sound, but still breathing.

His own heart in his chest pounding and all around him that long ago mountain field fading, the stone house behind them and the soft pressure of her head on his shoulder. He closed his eyes and it was gone and he scowled in fury. At what he knew not. Perhaps just himself. For the warped and shattered memories he carried and the way his dreams now twisted them in the night.

Because that day she'd not spoken at all of a girl who would not be born for nearly a year, a small and furious girl thrust screaming into the world two months before her time and writhing and strong even so. On that day when they'd actually sat looking out at the world below them, soaring over it and everything it was, she'd said:

Nowhere. Nowhere at all.

IV

When he woke the next morning they were in the room and he did not move, watching them in their red robes as they worked over her. He did not think they knew he was awake but then without turning one of them said to him:

"She's alive."

What a world it was, he thought, where that was welcome news. He sat up slowly and stiffly and looked over to where Juoth and the dead girl were also waking and then pulled himself to his feet. He thought how quiet it was and then realized her breathing had softened and he looked at her and some of the color had come back to her face. Her eyes closed, her lips parted and free of blood. Her chest just rising and falling.

One of them turned to him then while the other helped her drink again from the vial, and she said:

"I can't tell you what the future is for her, but she won't die today. She may not die at all from this. She's very lucky. You both are."

"I know," he said.

They finished with her and he watched and felt helpless, so lost in this. The opposite of his trade. Something he knew nothing of and never would and in that some hopelessness but it was what it was. When they were done they both nodded to him but did not speak and went out the way they always did and it was silent in the spire.

Juoth came over and stood in the window and then they just sat for a long time. Something they had not done in he did not know how long. Since eating with the farmer who was now dead by the fields that were long burned. Perhaps then. Other times as well but nothing like this.

Every time after he hunted he felt empty. It was a thing that wrapped him up and consumed him and became the entire world. The stalking and baiting and lying in wait. Listening for black wings in the air or standing in the scent of smoke distant and drifting. Planning the kill and working with arrow and blade to be ready and then it was all fire and steel and the eternal screaming as a being nearly eternal itself was slaughtered. A fraction of a breath compared to the whole hunt, and then a ringing silence and nothing left for his ravenous appetite.

"Are they always like this?" Juoth said. Looking down at his gloved hand, flexing it there in the pale light.

"Like what?"

"I saw them. The way they watched us in the street. The distance they gave you."

Brack smiled sadly. "Yes," he said. "In the cities. They always are."

"Do they know what you did?"

"Of course they know what I did."

"Then there should be a damned feast. Not these cowards shuffling in the dirt."

Brack shook his head. "Most men cannot kill other men," he said. "The men who can, can't kill dragons. I'm a man who kills dragons."

"And so you terrify them."

"I don't blame them."

"You should. You damned well should."

In the rising sunlight the dust and smoke had settled beyond the wall. People were in the streets again, more people than he could believe were crawling from this rubble. Thousands living in the dark and shattered stone and now finally clawing to the daylight with the dragon dead. He knew there were more in the fields beyond, probably with their tents thrown and fires roaring and camping even now all around the cold body of the beast. As if in that they could claim some of the kill. A piece perhaps of another history that would in time be forgotten.

Juoth looked at him again. "What are you going to do with it?"

"Who says I'm going to do anything with it?"

"All this time. Don't think I think you're a fool."

"I have what I came for."

"So you're going to take this chance again? Two hundred years and you didn't learn a damn thing? Two hundred from now you want to stand in front of some other city and kill this thing again."

He was quiet, thinking. Looking at Kayhi. She did look better but she had not opened her eyes and it was those eyes he wanted to see.

"All right," he said. "I'm going to do something."

"You going to tell me what it is?"

"I'm going to have you do it is what I'm going to do."

Juoth grinned and looked off over that battered world and nodded. The skin on the side of his face healing but pale where it would scar. In that a constant reminder of that town burning to the ice, the old bones in the ash. The hair growing back thin and the color of smoke.

"You were wrong," he said. He did not look at Brack as he said it.

"I've been wrong about a great many things."

"About the dragon." An aching pause. "And your daughter."

"When?"

"What you told me. What you told the priest. It's a small room."

"I told him what I saw."

"Then your eyes aren't Tarek's eyes."

Brack felt the flinch in his own jaw and for a heartbeat sat holding it and knowing what it was and then closed his eyes and breathed and opened them again.

"It never wanted to kill her in front of you," Juoth said. "This whole time that's what you said and the whole time you were wrong. She'd be dead if you weren't. That tower like a torch. That's what you saw."

Another breath. Then: "I know."

"Well."

"It was to force me to make a mistake. I ran in alone, with a knife and a sword. Me. A hunter all these years. Like a child to the slaughter." Looking behind him. That small body on the wide bed. "And it would have worked."

"I spent years with your son," Juoth said. "And he told me one thing more times than I can count."

"Tell me."

"There's always more," he said. "When you think you've found it there's always more." Looking over at last. "There's a depth to everything in this world. It may be endless. Everything we believe is there on the top and it floats and dies but what is real is somewhere lower. In the shadows of what we see. And all that matters is what's real."

"You add that part yourself?"

"Listen to me."

Brack reached, put a hand on his shoulder. Nodded once and felt that depth all below him as it had always been and also felt that no matter how deep he swam in the murk and the dark all he did was find that it was deeper and deeper, some cavernous expanse swallowing time and fate and desire and the world itself as it moved out in all directions and everyone he'd ever known mired in it and out there somewhere swimming silently the passing shadow of a great and unknown beast, a leviathan toward which they all descended.

"I am listening," he said.

The morning burned on and after a long time he finally felt hungry. He knew he had eaten in the field but he could not remember it and he did not know what it was he'd eaten. Could not remember a single meal since he left the keep. As it always was. Knowing the tables he'd sat at and the fires he'd cooked over but nothing more.

He went to the bed and stood. Thinking of the moment of her birth and the way she'd looked at him with those eyes and the blood in her hair. Her weight the first time he held her.

And then far off in the field he heard a horn sounding. One long note, clear and ringing in the air, and then another. He could almost hear the banners flapping in the wind, the rattle of the armor and swords, the soft thud of the horses' hooves magnified to a dull thunder as they came on.

The horn paused for just a moment and then called out again.

Beside him, Kayhi opened her eyes.

Chapter Twenty-Five

I

He stood in the field with the sword heavy on his back and he could smell the blood and the dragon burning. The grass beneath his feet cracked and withered from the heat. The smoke rising thick and gray into the morning sky.

They'd quartered it before dawn, working in the moonlight. At first just him and Juoth with sword and ax. Then others coming and joining. A solider with an ax of his own. Two carpenters with hatchets. A group of men and women from the forest with a long, two-handled saw. Dragging on either end and singing as they worked, some song in a language he'd never heard, surely as crude and vile as he thought it was from the light in their eyes and the roaring laughter every time they hit the refrain. Laboriously hauling that saw through flesh and bone and the blood splattering all down the front of their clothes.

He'd dragged the head aside as they worked. Looked once again at those darkened sockets, just two pits where the eyes had been. He'd seen this same beast die twice and now as he pulled the head aside he couldn't help but feel like the jaws were going to open again. That the furnace was going to burn, even with the head torn from its body. And so he'd taken his sword and swung in long, sure strikes to cut the flesh and hide and skull itself into pieces.

And then he'd carried them over and started the fire. There were plenty of logs and beams from this battered town, and half of them had just burned. It did not take long until it was raging and he could hear the dragonflesh sizzling as they threw it on. Committing this beast that was so much fire itself to a last inferno. Turning finally to ash. One last time through the flames.

Now he stood and watched and there were more people than he could count. Perhaps all here to extract in this way some vengeance on this creature that had come for them. That had killed their families and torn apart their walls and brought on them some dark wrath they'd thought was only found elsewhere. In the hinterlands. The mountains. The wastes. He'd killed the red dragon before the Ringed City's gates just two decades ago but it was not the first time that he'd seen a lingering disbelief in this stretching world, nor would it be the last.

As with most things too terrifying for men to believe, they never really did until it was upon them. Always believing the dragons would come for someone else until they lay dying among the slaughtered masses of a burned city and only then knowing that, if given the time, the dragons would come for them all.

Once it had been quartered they'd begun flaying off pieces of flesh. Ten men carrying them and covered in blood. Children walking with splintered bones and flaps of skin. Stacking them all on the fire like kindling and logs, watching as it burned. That black blood turning to steam, and the flesh and bone rising as smoke.

When it was done there would be nothing left but charred and blackened pieces. Nothing that could ever draw breath again.

Though he still felt himself looking to the sky, waiting for the hammering of wings in the air.

She came slowly across the field, walking in her white dress among the twisting, maddened crowd. These butchers that they were. The smoke a wall behind her, the dirt and mud and bootprints a maze in all directions. A flurry of activity, and yet she looked only at him as she walked.

"Kayhi," he said as she stopped in front of him. He'd sat with her all the day before, leaving the dragon to rot and cool. Just sitting with her, then staying up half the night before tearing himself away to set to this gristly work. He didn't feel it was real there in the spire, surrounded by marble and doors he couldn't see, and he didn't feel it was real here on the field of battle. That she was real.

"How are you?" he said.

"Fine."

"I told you to stay there."

She smiled. "I know what you told me."

He looked out again to where the company of soldiers sat on the edge of the field. All from the Ringed City, and what a march it must have been. Their armor sleek and smooth, the same deep silver of his own, like the slate gray of a morning sky on the water. The furs they wore underneath, and those dark helmets. Some with rising horns or antlers or wings, others smooth and unadorned. Red capes blowing in the wind.

It was their warhorn that Kayhi had heard.

"Should we go with them?" she said.

"I don't know."

"What do you want?"

He waved a hand out before him, where the carnage continued. Two women walked by with a split leg bone between them, carried like a slain deer. Walking toward the spitting fires. "I want to burn this thing and be done with it."

"You know that's no answer."

"Some damned type of daughter you are."

"I blame my father."

"Then tell him what you think."

She shrugged, also looking at the soldiers. Those who had come unannounced, but had left for this city long before word of the dragon could have reached them. Long before the keep fell in fire and snow. More than half a year they had to have marched to get this far.

"I think," she said, "that you can pretend that this is the end all you want. You, a dragon killer, just doing what he was made to do. But you know that it's not the end. You don't kill a dragon twice and think that's all there is to it. Or you'll be killing them all twice and then all three times and then you'll be dead."

"You think it'll happen again."

"Anything that happened once can damned well happen again."

He licked his lips, chapped and covered in soot and sweat. Closing his eyes and thinking of riding down in the snow, of the dry fields and dead cattle, of the forests and the plains. All that for one dragon that he didn't know where it came from or how it was alive. And now it was dead again and he knew just the same and perhaps less.

And she was right. Everything he'd done would be done eternally if killing a dragon no longer meant tearing it out of existence. If it meant anything less than finality, he was lost.

They were all lost.

II

He went into the tent, still smelling the caribou in the dried furs, their tireless muscles in the frozen wastelands of the north, and stepped into the lamplight. His eyes not needing to adjust to this darkness, always as they were ready for any light.

The warmth thrown about on the walls, dried and taught, from two lamps on the ground.

Havrain stood looking at him with his arms folded across his chest. He wore his thin furs and the long red cape but his armor and helmet lay piled on the cot. There were no tables for the soldiers of the Ringed City cared nothing for appearance and everything for warfare; one less table was perhaps one more sword, one more crossbow. They brought only what they needed when they marched and nothing more and when the land behind them was red mud with their enemies lying slain in it, they left with just as little.

"Captain," Brack said. Raising his closed fist briefly to touch his chest. A salute he'd not done in a long time.

"Forget the titles, Ironhelm."

Brack scowled, but there was a light in his eyes. "Some army you've let this become."

"It's as much an army as it needs to be."

"That it is. And I'm glad to see it."

"You'll always be a soldier."

Brack looked across the cot. Sparse as the tent, the white furs still rolled at the foot. Lashed together with a leather strand. A pack of clothes tossed at the other end as a pillow.

"First you're late," he said. "And now you're not staying."

Havrain nodded, pressing his lips together. "Not any longer than we have to. Tonight if I have my way."

"You march all the way from the Ringed City for two nights watching a dead dragon burn, then you march back? And through this land, too. You know they could take this as an act of war in Kraestal."

The captain snorted, shaking his head. "If that coward they have on the throne wants to stand against the Ringed City, let him stand. It'll take us all of three days to raze that place to the ground. Two if we fight past dinner."

"That's asking for a mutiny."

Havrain laughed. "I suppose."

"But you're skirting it," Brack said. "Who sent you? We both know it was before the dragon was in the plains. So you're not hunting it."

"No, we're not." The man reached down with arms powerful from years in this world, adjusting a swordbelt that didn't need it. "We didn't know of the dragon until two weeks ago. We pushed on as hard as we could, but we already were and there was nothing more for it. Doesn't look like you needed us anyway."

Brack was silent for a moment, watching him. Then he scowled again and looked back at the flap to the tent. "Then you're here for me."

"We are," Havrain said. Quietly. Looking at Brack now, but not looking like a man who enjoyed it.

"Was it Wayland?"

"Wayland's dead."

"Then who runs the priesthood?"

"Carron. But it wasn't the priesthood. It was Marazene."

He tried not to let it show on his face but he felt that it must, even with this captain who was only human in the dimly lit tent. He could feel the heat from that lamp now, smell the oil burning and the hides so thick and full of years and must.

"The emperor himself," he said at last.

"Yes."

"Tell me."

"Do you want a drink?"

Brack looked at him a long moment, then nodded. "Do you have ice?"

"It has been too long since you were a soldier." Havrain went to a bag lying next to the cot and the furs, untied the pulls around the top, reached in, and pulled out a stout glass bottle that could only be from the South Sea. The cork in the top, the gold lettering. He held it up in the light so that Brack could see the warm, rich color of the bourbon inside the glass, then stood and handed it to him.

"This is a drink?"

"We don't have cups. That bottle itself is a foolish luxury."

Brack pulled the cork out and turned the bourbon in the bottle once and raised it to his lips and drank. It tasted like dragonfire. He lowered it and handed it across and the captain drank and handed it back.

"Tell me," Brack said.

"Two years ago we lost a company in the mountains. The whole thing, not a sound. Nothing recovered. Two teams spent a month each looking for them and the most we ever found was a dagger with the blade broken off. Buried in the snow. Then the winter came on and we called it off and in the spring no bones turned up. Just gone like ghosts."

"A whole company."

"We waited that spring for war and nothing came. Even after the passes were clear. The watchtowers on the spine didn't see anything. We moved a company to the old fortress to watch the underground river, but it was as silent as it's been in a thousand years. Since Earmond's army died in their burning ships. Everything was quiet, from every direction."

"And a solider hates peace."

"When my men are dead I damned well hate it." Havrain motioned for the bottle back, took it and drank again. As unflinching as he'd ever been. "We didn't know who would come but we thought someone would. Then that fall we lost another company, this one in the foothills. Doing maneuvers. A green unit but still a company of the ironclad and not prone to being killed to the man. All dead. We went out when they didn't report and found them. The heads, anyway. In a clearing of dead birches, all on stakes. The skin stripped off of them and the eyes eaten by the birds. The helmets and armor all gone, just a ring of dead men's skulls."

"A ring."

"I know."

"What was the third one?"

"You know there was a third?"

"Marazene doesn't send for me unless there's a third. If there are more it's worse than you're letting on."

Havrain nodded and Brack watched him drink again. Thinking of that snowswept country around the Ringed City. The jagged foothills of stone, the forests of cedar and birch, the spine of mountains rising up into their far off and snowdrenched fury, a white backdrop running up to the harsh blue of the ice sea.

"The third time," the captain said. "The third time, they killed Crathe. Two companies and the entire town. Nothing left alive. Had to be five hundred people dead, maybe more if there were ships in port. We don't know how many there were. They burned the whole thing to the ground. We found two ships on fire and floating, all hands dead. Men lashed to the masts and railings, chained belowdecks. All alive when they put the ships into the current and lit them up."

"So they're coming down the coast."

"We don't know. We don't even know who did it."

"And he sends for a dragon hunter."

"It wasn't a dragon," Havrain said. "I went to Crathe. I saw it. It wasn't a dragon."

"But I still am what I am."

Havrain raised an arm, fire playing now in his eyes. A bridled fury just below the skin. "You tore that thing from the sky and now it's just burning pieces of flesh and bone. That beast that destroys cities at its pleasure. Whatever is coming for the Ringed City, you can wade through it like a god. I've seen you do it." Nearly snarling now. "Marazene isn't sending for a dragon hunter, he's sending for the man who stood on the wall at Terrorth and killed five hundred men before sunset. He's sending for the man who rode alone into Keelok and rode back out not an hour later with the king's head. That's who he sent me for."

Brack was silent, closing his eyes. Smelling the caribou again and flashing quickly in his mind that house in the mountains, sitting there with the wine and the warm glow of the sun. Then thrown back to this, a march toward winter and some unknown enemy, standing in darkness and obscurity, surrounded by a ring of staked heads.

"It's an abuse," he said at last. "You know that. It's an abuse of what I am."

Havrain looked past him, the fury fading somewhat, but settling into a grim determination that was this man in every memory Brack had of him. Enlisted once and now a captain on the back of that sweat and focus and singleminded will.

Then he reached up and he touched his closed fist to his own chest. His hand just slightly shaking. "We need you," he said. "We all need you."

III

Brack stood outside the tent feeling the bourbon in his bones and skin and looked to where they still carried pieces of the dragon to the flame. Kayhi stood between him and the fire, her back to him, the smoke rising all around and above her. This girl who had really killed the dragon, the only family he had left in this world. A man who had lived the lives of ten men, and he had one daughter left alive.

You'll kill her, Ironhelm. You'll kill her.

But he hadn't. He'd come this far to save her and she'd saved them all and now he was being asked to leave her again. All the time he had and it was never enough.

He kept waiting for her to turn and see him but she did

not. Watching the burning of the dragon, its hewn body turning to ash and smoke, the great killer of the world finally drenched in a death of its own.

As he stood looking Havrain came out and stood next to him. His arms folded. The sun flashing in that red cape and off the hilt of his sword. This a sword unadorned, not the sword of a king set with jewels and forged into the rampant form of a lion or a horse or an eagle with outstretched wings. A simple tool, the sword of a man who used it to kill and then cleaned it and then used it again and who did not think of the way it looked but only of what it could do and what he could do when he held it.

"I'm not asking," he said quietly.

"I know you're not," Brack said.

He'd known since he heard the horn and knew again when he saw the company. The captain could tell him any damned thing he wanted about where they were or why they were marching, but he'd come with a company because it was an order, not a request.

They knew something of what he was in the Ringed City. Perhaps half of it. Hunters there were talented killers. Men with years of training. When one rode in the ranks on a field of battle, men looked to him. Whispered about what he could do and waited for the slaughter. A single hunter riding with an army could rally them all because they felt, deeply within themselves, that the hunters had no equals.

But, always, they thought those hunters were men.

He didn't know how old Havrain thought he was. But the things he'd spoken of had happened so recently. There were many other things Brack had done, things now passing into legend, attributed to hunters most believed to be dead. Other men living other lives. Things that made the stand on the wall of Terrorth seem like nothing at all, the blood pouring down that wall like a mere pinprick.

A company could never take him. Even in the place where they bred their hunters, almost no one knew what they truly were.

But the company meant they would try.

"Let me finish this," he said then. Still watching Kayhi with her back to him. "Let me burn this dragon. I'll come to you in the morning and we'll talk."

"We ride in the morning. We have to."

"Then we ride. But give me this first. I hunted this thing down from the mountains and it killed my cousins, my grandfather. Let me burn it." He turned and looked at the captain, his thick beard the same color as the furs he wore, a man so entrenched in who he was that he'd never sit quietly before a fire in old age, closing his eyes in the silence. He'd sit with a sword across his knees and a scowl on his lips.

Or he'd not live to old age at all, because someone equally entrenched would someday arrive and tear out his throat and then move on toward his own end.

Havrain nodded, watching the smoke as well. The fire in his eyes like flame on glass. "The morning, then."

Brack walked slowly across that field, torn up by the dragon and the horses and the men, a sea of mud and the coming winter. The ash falling back to earth and melting into that sludge and the dragon slowly becoming the very place it had destroyed. Becoming the soil and the mud and the grass itself. Perhaps eventually the stone. Thinly, very thinly, the dragon becoming everything they knew, even the place where someday children would run and laugh and play in the summer warmth. Beneath them always the dispersed and dismantled body of this creature of darkness and fire.

He got to what remained of the head, just shattered bones and bloodsoaked earth and a scattering of ripped flesh. Knelt there and reached into the mud and picked up one of those teeth. As long nearly as the hunting knife he wore on his calf. A small and meaningless tooth for a dragon, but enough to reach his heart. The larger ones already cast into the flame.

He held it up carefully in the sunlight, turning it, then softly touched it to his lips. Taking from his pocket a long leather strand. Wrapping it about the tooth, knotting it, then raising it and circling it around his neck. The leather cold and hard but the tooth warm where it fell against his breastbone.

The fingers that took that strand from him were slender and cold as well, delicately tying it so that the knot settled against his spine. He knelt there, tipping his head down and looking at the carnage around him, until he felt them slip away. The tooth hanging firmly in its place.

Then he stood and turned, and Kayhi was there, looking up at him. This girl he knew only one way to save. One way that he hated and loathed more than anything, but also the one way he could stop hearing her mother's voice.

Or, perhaps, the reason he was hearing it at all.

Some things in this world impossible to know until they were behind you and it was all too late.

You'll kill her.

"Why?" she said.

He didn't answer, just tipped his head to the side. Blinking away the memory.

"Why the tooth?" she said. "Don't tell me you're taking trophies now."

He smiled. "No, I certainly am not."

"Then why?"

"This dragon was killed before," he said softly. "You know it. The head cut off. The body buried. It should have been gone, consumed by the earth and the water alike, but it came back." He reached up, laid his fingers against the tooth. The heat moving through it. "Someone told me that anything that can happen once can happen again. At least now I'll know if I have to kill it a third time."

304

IV

He stood in the spire, that pristine marble and the furs on the bed. Juoth sitting on those furs and tying on his boots. The dead girl standing and looking out the window. Turning once to look at him and her face impassive and unreadable, those pale eyes blinking twice and then turning back to the view.

"What did you do for her?" he said.

"For your sister?" the priest asked.

Brack looked at him and he did not turn away. Holding his gaze unflinchingly, but with great knowledge in his eyes. Both of them knowing he lied even as he lied.

"Yes," Brack said. For there was comfort in lies. And he'd never met a priest who did something, no matter how small, without reason.

The priest nodded. "She wasn't badly hurt. Just knocked unconscious. They gave her some herbs, a drink. She should be fine. There wasn't any bleeding on her brain. We didn't have to drill."

"Then how did you know?"

The priest smiled.

Brack looked again at the dead girl. She was so still as she stood in that window. Almost carved of marble herself.

"That one," the priest said. "What happened to her?"

"I don't know," Brack said.

"Ah."

For the third time, that knowledge.

"Watch her," the priest said. Something changing in his voice. "To be sure she's all right."

"I will."

"You must."

Juoth rose and Brack reached a hand out to the priest. He took it carefully, and there was such strength in his grip, despite his age. The vigor of a man decades his junior. Brack had expected it and again it was a thing they both knew and he nodded and then they went out and down that spiraling iron staircase like descending some great throat in the middle of the temple and out into the courtyard. The city empty now with everyone outside still in the field. A cold wind coming up and sweeping over the walls. He almost looked up to see her and her hair caught in that wind but he did not and instead just went to the switchback stone staircase beside the gate and began to climb.

She was waiting for them at the top, standing where the wall remained heavy and intact. Thick enough for passageways beneath their feet and a wide battlement that wrapped the city. The town sprawling out in all directions around them. They went across that cold stone and Kayhi turned for a moment to watch them come and smiled and then turned back to the world before her as they fell in on all sides.

"Look at it," she said.

The dragon was nearly gone. The crimson sun rising on the horizon, the mountains far off and blood red in the light, the painted snow and ice. That same brutal light edging onto the plains where the coals and the dragon's body smoldered and hissed. A long bed of blackened bones and little flames still licking over them. This pyre where the dragon had fallen blind and screaming to the earth, the girl swinging from its neck with the arrow through its blistering eye.

He reached for her then and she leaned against him, so small and wrapped in her cloak. He closed his eyes and saw her falling and heard her scream then over the dragon's and opened his eyes again. As if to assure himself that it was dead, that this time it was dead and only the ash remained.

On the edge of it all the captain stood before the tent. His eyes not on the dragon's burning but on them where they stood atop the wall. That cold wind coming down off the mountains, swirling the blood red cloak behind him. The firelight on his breastplate and helmet. Behind him the ice of winter flashing coldly as the mountainborn light fell, smoke and death and carnage on that wind.

The Dragon Hunt

Epilogue

Beneath her feet the heavy churning of the machines deep within the mountains. An incessant vibration that felt as if it reached the ends of the earth. The ever-present smell of sulfur and fire and smoke as she walked the halls, the remaining stone passageways of this ancient ruin. A place crafted in ages now forgotten, hewn out of the stone by men
(perhaps)
so long dead that even their bones had turned to dust and the dust to stone and no more were they known or remembered. A forgotten scourge, torn out of history, shattered and destroyed and it all so long ago no one knew who had done it.

She walked in the darkness with only the dim oil lamps lighting the stone in front of her. Those ageless marks from the picks. The darkness making it feel smaller than it was, but the stone ceiling actually a dozen feet above her, the passageway at least that wide. She did not know if they had built it this way to walk six abreast or if they had been a towering, hulking people for whom this was space for a single man.

But she felt that she knew, all the same.

The passage came to a bridge and she crossed it and an endless dark below her. Far, far down a faint light. Or a trick of the eyes. She would not look and crossed the bridge slowly, feeling a cold wind moving above her. Looking up and seeing that same towering darkness above and reaching on to an untold distance.

Her sword at her side, heavy and made of rough, black-forged metal. A cruel instrument made not for looks or grace but for tearing the entrails out of a man and moving on to the next. The hilt wrapped in twisted leather. The back edge dented and chipped but the front filed to a razor's edge.

She stopped on the other side of that bridge and closed her eyes. There for a moment a complete darkness. Feeling at her back the drop and wondering if she were to take a step back and to the side if she'd open her eyes as she fell. Or if she'd just keep them closed in sleep and let herself fall and feel the wind pulling at her dark cloak as she descended into the madness below.

She did not know. She never knew.

The passage continued and she went on and up the great stone staircase where the lamps no longer burned. The cold growing with each step. A frost on the front edges of the stairs, thin and just felt slickly under her boots. When at last she stood at the top she could see her breath in the air and the thin light now filling the landing. A cold and meager light full of mist and ice.

She looked behind her, into the nothing. Found her fingers on her sword and slowly put both hands into her cloak. Wrapping it and clenching the rough fabric. Then she turned and walked out the tall arch of stone and soot and frost and stood blinking on the balcony.

Below a drop of ice and snow over black rock, falling away for a thousand feet. Just the thin stone rail between her and that soaring fall. Clouds thin and cold below her. Finally at the end the mountain sweeping out into a glacial plain as far as she could see, running off in windswept fury. The snow so hard it was just shards of ice chased in that wind, swirling across the frozen expanse. Behind her the mountains still rose, climbing into this stark wasteland to impossible heights, the highest peaks even now lost in those vicious clouds, the air gone up there and the cold so deep it would rip the breath from your lungs and leave you as stone itself to be buried and lost.

Perhaps even now, bodies up there in the snow. Fools lost in ages past, still forever, unable even to rot.

Far down the balcony before her, the swirling of his cape in the ceaseless wind. Everything about him white, from the eyes to the skin to the hair to the long fingers wrapped around the edge of the rail. His clothes and belt and even the leather around the hilt of the silver sword. But that cloak itself the deepest black she'd ever seen, the sky at night with no stars and no moon, a deep void of nothing, nothing.

He turned as she stepped out, and she did not look down. His pupils alone a red like fire and ruby, burning in that dead face. Slowly, a long red tongue emerging to wet the thin and pale lips, cracked and chapped in this frigid gale.

And yet he stood in this world, his hands uncovered. Ice in his hair and eyebrows and on his boots. Looking at her with his red eyes and not blinking at all. Not a shake or tremor. Just the slightest mist before him as he breathed, thin and shallow breaths as they passed through his filed teeth.

She did not speak as she walked toward him, and he turned back to the frozen hell of the plain. There was ice on the balcony and she walked slowly to keep her footing. Or she told herself that was why she did it. Even believed it

(perhaps)

as the frost cracked, leaving thin tracks behind her.

When she stopped at his side he did not look at her, but raised his hands from the rail, clenching them once. Those long and serpentine fingers. It almost looked as if the bones moved under pale and stretching skin but the flesh did not move with them. Almost.

Then he snarled, just the corner of his lip twisting upward.

311

One rotted and pointed tooth below, the skin creasing like it wasn't skin at all. A bloodless twisting. Above them the howling wind ceasing for a moment its torment. And in that brittle silence, he said:

"Someone has killed my dragon."

Jonathan Schlosser

The Dragon Hunt

I was going to write this about the author in third person, but then I canned it. It felt too weird and formal. I'm a real person, just sitting at my computer with a cup of coffee, wearing flannel pants and a hoodie in the teeth of a Michigan winter.

I live here with my beautiful wife Brittany and my two sons, Fitz and Fin. Fin is too young to know he lives here yet, but he does. Fitz loves to go bouldering with me and eat sour gummy bears off of the top holds.

If I'm not writing, I'm probably running. If I'm reading, I'm hopefully doing it by the fire with a glass of bourbon.

Anyway, I hope you loved the book. It was great fun to write and years in the making. If you did like it and you wish you could give me a high five, you sort of can. Please consider taking a second to leave a review. It would mean the world to me and it seriously makes a huge difference. It's the lifeblood of Amazon. And then if I meet you someday and you tell me you left a review, I promise I'll give you that high five.

But above all else, thanks for buying this book and reading it. Thanks for spending your money and, more valuable still, your time. It's all precious and I'm glad we could spend this little bit of it together.

-

Cover art by Andrei Bat.

Made in the USA
Middletown, DE
26 March 2019